WHERE
THE SUN
DON'T SHINE

J. Aaron Parish

WHERE THE SUN DON'T SHINE
by
J. Aaron Parish

2nd Edition 2018
1st Edition Trade Paperback 2013
All Rights Reserved

Dark Recesses Press
657 Craigen Road
Newburgh, Ontario
Canada K0K 2S0

Edited by Jodi Lee
Cover Art © 2013 Andrew Smith

Library & Archives Canada ISBN
978-1-988837-14-7

Publication Credits

"That Ain't a Mosey"
Triangulation: End of Time by by PARSEC Ink, July 2007;
The Zombist: Undead Western Tales by Library of the Living Dead, July 2010.

"For the Good of the Flock"
Abominations by Shroud Publishing, June 2008.

"Just Enough"
Bits of the Dead by Coscom Entertainment, July 2008.

"...Hitman"
In Bad Dreams, Vol. II: Where Death Stalks by Eneit Press, October 2009.

"First Night in Jennings Grove"
The Edge of Propinquity, December 2006.

"After, Life"
Every Day Fiction, August 2008;
The Best of Every Day Fiction 2008 by Every Day Publishing, November 2008;
Best New Zombie Tales, Vol. 1 by Books of the Dead, April 2010.

"Like Father, Like Daughter"
Courting Morpheus by Belfire Press, March 2010.

"Stone Heart, Vinyl Floors"
Harvest Hill by Graveside Tales, October 2009.

"Little Monsters"
New Bedlam, 2010.

"Final Edition"
Grants Pass by Morrigan Books, August 2010.

"Where the Sun Don't Shine"
Residential Aliens, October 2009;
Residential Aliens Issue # 5, January 2011.

"Crank Case"
A Thousand Faces, July 2008.

"A Twist of the Knife"
Flashing Swords, May 2008.

"Of Bones and Blades"
Speculative Realms: Where There's A Will, There's a Way, December 2008.

"Dreadneck"
Andromeda Spaceways Inflight Magazine Issue 33, April 2008.

"Tapewyrm"
Dragons Composed by Kerlak Enterprises, March 2009.

DEDICATION

This book is dedicated to my wife and children, who put up with my madness; to my mother, who first instilled in me a love of reading; and to Carol Parrish and Jerry S. Davis Jr., who for some strange reason encouraged my fledgling writing.

TABLE OF CONTENTS

PART III

PART I

Each Dying Ember

THAT AIN'T A MOSEY

Pete chewed anxiously on his bushy beard, brown hat turning over and over in his hands. Doc had been muttering and fussing over the prone figure for nearly an hour. With his ashen skin and slack features, Billy Ray might well have been a corpse if not for an occasional twitch and a constant, braying moan. A grimy bandage wound around his left arm just above the elbow. They had done all they could for him on the trail. If Doc couldn't help, he'd likely be dead by morning.

"So, what happened?" the doctor asked, barely pausing his inspection.

"It was a misunderstanding, that's all." Pete sighed. "We stopped near an Indian village a little ways on the other side of the Red River. Billy Ray's a good kid, but he ain't got the sense God gave a mule. He won a few tosses in a dice game, but they said he cheated and wanted their money back. That boy's too stupid to cheat. I sent them packing and made sure we were gone early next morning. Three days later, an Indian just appeared out of nowhere and shot Billy Ray with an arrow. John Boy said he was jabberin' something about stealin' and poisoning the white man for the land." Pete shook his head. "He's been like this for better than a week."

Doc, a short, round man with a fringe of white hair, carefully probed the small, bloodless gash with a scalpel.

"I've got to tell you, Pete, I'm stumped." His lips pursed as he adjusted his spectacles on his nose. "The arrow didn't do much more than graze him. His breathing is strong. The wound wasn't kept as clean as it should have been, but there doesn't seem to be any infection. All we can do right now is wait." He patted Billy Ray's chest, whose moans took on an odd, keening note. His eyes popped open.

Pete stepped back with a gasp from that wild stare. The cowboy bolted upright and sank his buck teeth deep into the doctor's shoulder near his neck. Doc screamed and tried to pull away from the mashing jaws. *He's chewing,* Pete thought wildly. He swung a mallet-sized fist and connected right between the eyes. Billy Ray dropped back to the table in a boneless heap and resumed his groans. Blood stained his mouth like a cheap whore's lipstick.

Footsteps announced the arrival of a scrawny, gap-toothed man carrying a shotgun in both hands. A trio of cowboys pushed their way in behind him, gazes flickering from their fallen comrade to the doctor's bloodstained shirt.

"You alright, Doc?" The skinny man lowered his shotgun.

"I'll live." Doc tried to pull his waistcoat off and gasped. Pete rushed over to help, nose wrinkling at the coppery tang of blood. "Just a flesh wound, Ned. I got worse bites from a coyote up near Greenville once."

Doc motioned to Ned, who set his gun down to help remove the doctor's shirt. As Ned went to wet a towel in the rain barrel out back, Pete ushered his men back out the front door.

"What just happened, boss?" John Boy asked once they set foot on the porch. Worry lines wrinkled his handsome features.

Pete just shook his head.

"You think he's gonna be OK?" Jason asked softly. His twin turned a questioning eye toward the trail boss. Joshua never did say much.

"This beats all I've ever seen, boys." Pete shrugged. "Doc says we'll just have to wait."

They waited. The twins hunkered in one corner, and John Boy worked the cylinder of his pistol. Pete folded his arms and frowned at the door. Finally, it opened and the doctor stepped out, bowler hat on his head, gingerly working his shoulder. Bandages across his neck peeked out from the collar of a fresh shirt. Ned followed with a cigarette dangling from his lips.

Doc gestured to a pen behind the building he shared with the cattle lot manager. Dozens of longhorns milled behind a wooden fence, bellowing at each other. "I take it you're watching the cattle tonight, Ned?" He nodded. "I doubt you'll hear anything out of our guest tonight, but stay out of my office all the same. If he gets rambunctious, come find me. We'll be down at the Tap." He shivered. "Let's go. It's a bit nippy tonight. A brisk walk ought to warm me up."

"Doc, it's August." Pete frowned; sweat had long since soaked his own shirt. "You sure you're OK?"

"Fine, fine. Just one of the trials of old age. I could probably catch a chill in the Lake of Fire." He shuddered again. "What do you say we go get that drink?"

Lost in thought, Pete led his horse by her reins while he followed Doc through the streets of Fort Worth. John Boy, Jason and Joshua followed in a small clump, talking quietly amongst themselves, something about a Mexican filly and whiskey.

Gunshots rang out, telling Pete they had entered the part of town known as Hell's Half Acre.

The cowboys behind them made their goodbyes and sauntered off down a side street, laughing and clapping each other on the back. Pete stepped closer to Doc, trying to loom over the old man and appear threatening enough to ward off any trouble. Apparently unconcerned, Doc led him to a building that looked more like a factory than a tavern. It stood two stories tall with a couple dozen stove pipes rising through the roof. As he tied his horse outside, Pete saw the sign read "Waco Tap." He could hear the din even before they walked inside.

"Find a table, and I'll get us some drinks," Doc yelled above the roar. Pete nodded.

He found a semi-secluded spot in the shadows and slumped in a chair. Frowning, he ran his fingers across the battered wood until Doc returned and thumped a large mug down on the tabletop. He took a long pull from his own cup before joining Pete in a nearby chair.

"You look more burdened than great Atlas. Worried about your friend?"

"Yup."

"Don't be. He'll be up and moseying about in no time. I suspect he's got some kind of nasty poison in his system that's just got to work itself out." He took another swallow.

They sat there for hours, talking and drinking until Pete got up to get yet another round. He squinted. The floor had grown fuzzy, and it seemed as if everyone had six legs. The light had gone wrong, too. Despite how much he had drunk, Doc looked pale, his skin almost gray.

Pete grabbed a new pair of mugs and threaded his way carefully back to their table, swaying with the floor to keep the beer from spilling. He almost made it when someone's extra leg tripped him up. Amber liquid splashed a pair of pretty black boots behind him.

"Whoops," he muttered.

Sudden pain in the back of his head sent him sprawling. He rose, clutching his skull as he turned. A cowboy glared at him, his clothes and hat as black as his soaked boots. His hand rested on the butt of a holstered pistol.

"Didja jus' hit me?" Pete's thoughts wobbled around but refused to coalesce. His brow lowered. "You hit me!" He lunged forward.

A loud *click* brought him up short and lifted much of the alcoholic haze from his brain. He stared down the barrel pointed at his face like a mouse waiting for the rattlesnake to strike. "Whoa, there. Let's not get carried away. How 'bout I buy you a drink?"

A finger twitched on the trigger. "A drink ain't gonna clean my boots, now is it?"

Hands raised, Pete backed up a step and stumbled just as the pistol roared and bucked. His head slammed into the floor.

Shouting brought him back around. He stood slowly, wincing at the headache building behind his temples. The shooter had disappeared. A crowd stood gathered round his table. *What on God's green earth?* Pete staggered over, shoved his way through and stopped with a cry.

Doc was dead, slumped back in his chair with arms spread wide is if for an embrace. Crimson poured from a large hole in the center of his chest. His final expression was one of surprise. Pete reached down, picked the doctor's bowler up off the floor and gently placed it back on his head.

A hammer cocked, bringing his attention around. On the other side of the table, the cowboy had raised his gun and pointed it once more at Pete. "You made me shoot Doc." He came around next to Doc's body and spoke in a low monotone. The barrel trembled. "What kind of spineless coward hides behind an old man?"

Hands reached up and dragged the gunman backward. Doc leaned forward and bit into his neck, tearing out a large hunk of flesh in the process. Blood spurting, the cowboy screamed and fired at the ceiling, his finger spasming even after the revolver emptied itself. Doc leapt on the dying figure, biting off whatever he could and swallowing without hardly bothering to chew.

Thunder boomed across the saloon. Doc flew off the corpse and landed a couple of feet away on the floor, the hole in his chest suddenly larger. The bartender reloaded his shotgun and yelled, "What was that?"

Pete's head swung toward another scream. Doc had crawled over to the crowd and was gnawing on someone's ankle. He slowly rose to his feet and staggered toward Pete who stood rooted, unable to turn away from the white-haired blood-soaked apparition shuffling his way.

Another pistol cracked. The shot caught Doc in the shoulder and spun him around. Hands outstretched, he started toward the shooter with a feral growl.

Spell broken, Pete dashed for the door, dodging men who had their guns drawn, knocking down others who didn't move fast enough. He slammed through the swinging doors, glancing back one last time to see the black-dressed cowboy rise from the floor and attack a man standing next to him.

He ran to his horse and ripped her reins loose from the hitching post. He reached into the bedroll behind his saddle and jerked his rifle free. Digging his heels into her sides, he urged the horse to a run and prayed for dawn.

Dawn brought little relief.

Pete hunkered in the courthouse, listening to the sounds of Hell unleashed on Earth. He glanced out the window. The street looked clear, but he knew how quickly that could change. He sighed and fell back to the floor. His panicked flight the night before might have well cost him his life. *And maybe my soul.* He gripped his Winchester until his hands hurt. He breathed deeply and wrinkled his nose at the smell. Nearby, Bell stamped a hoof and whickered.

"I know you don't like being in here, girl," he said softly, "but it's a sight safer than being out there."

He hadn't paid much attention to where she was leading him at first, glad to give Bell her head so long as she took him somewhere else. She ran south, straight into the heart of Hell. Whatever was happening in the Acre had started here first and spread like wildfire. Once he took the reins and tried to head out of town, it was too late. Every turn brought him face to face with wild-eyed, savage monsters eager for new flesh. None seemed capable of more than an awkward shuffling gait, but they didn't need to move quickly. These creatures didn't tire. They didn't rest despite gaping wounds that savaged their bodies. As far as he could figure, all they did was hunger.

Finally, exhausted, he had dragged himself into the courthouse and barred the door. None of the critters had found him yet.

He jerked at the crack of gunshots nearby and shrank into a corner. He paused, brow furrowed. He had seen countless moaning figures sporting gun belts, but they all ignored their pistols, as if they had forgotten how to use anything other than their hands and teeth. Pete slowly rose to a crouch and peered out the window.

John Boy walked shoulder to shoulder with Jason and Joshua, backing down the street. Every now and then, one of the twins would take careful aim and squeeze off a round. John Boy struggled with a set of bulging saddlebags. The moaning crowd pursuing them never faltered, but those that got shot fell for good. *Did they find a way to kill those things?* He jumped to his feet and ran to the door, shoving aside the table he had used as a barricade.

"Joshua! Jason! John Boy! Over here!" He fired his rifle in the air.

Their heads jerked his way. Grinning with relief, they broke into a weary run and clambered up the stairs. Jason stopped about halfway up and fired at the approaching crowd. One head snapped back and disappeared from sight.

"That's all it takes?" Pete asked.

"Yup." Jason holstered his weapon. Several more had been tucked into his belt. "A bullet in the brain, and it's all over."

The monstrosities were just a few blocks away as he ushered his men inside. Seeing Bell in the courthouse sparked weary laughter. Pete started to shut the door and paused when he saw a familiar, exhausted person staggering down the street from the other direction. He stepped back out. "Hey! Over here!"

"Pete," Joshua called. "What are you doing?"

"It's Billy Ray," he said over his shoulder. "Doc said he'd be up and moseying in no time. I guess he was right." He turned back to the street. "Billy Ray! Over here!"

"Pete," John Boy said.

"We're right here!"

"Pete!" His tone grew more urgent, and he grabbed Pete's arm.

"I ain't gonna leave him out there for those things." He shook the hand off angrily. The monsters had nearly reached the corner of the courthouse. "Billy Ray!"

"*Pete!* That ain't a mosey, and that ain't Billy Ray—at least, not any more."

Pete looked again. Cursing loudly, he slammed the door, grabbed the table and shoved it into place. Pete and the twins wrestled several heavy desks around it. John Boy kept wandering off to check the bags he had set in the corner.

Something thumped against the door. Pete jumped. Another blow fell, and another. He crawled over the barricade and placed one ear against the wood. He could hear scratching and a wavering groan that rose and fell in long undulations.

Wiping sweat from his brow, Pete sat on one of the desks and unbuttoned his shirt. Noon still stood a long way off, and the courthouse was already turning into an oven. He watched the twins take up stations by the windows while John Boy gingerly rebuckled his saddlebags for the fourth time.

"What you got there, son?"

John Boy ran a hand through his black hair. He appeared rumpled, like evening wash tossed into a corner instead of hung out to dry. Joshua and Jason looked like something run through the wringer, too, but it was more apparent with John Boy. He had always been a dandy, bathing and changing his clothes as close to every day as possible, even on the trail. Sighing, he picked up the bulging bags and carried them to Pete.

"Take a look," he said.

Pete unfastened the buckles carefully. From the way John Boy carried the thing, there might well be a live rattlesnake inside. He tossed the flap back. Inside were several thick, tan-colored sticks, each roughly a foot long with a long tail of twine. Pete scooted off the desk with a shout. The thumping on the door increased for a moment, then resumed its steady beat.

"You gonna try to blast your way out of here? You gone plum *loco* or something?"

"It ain't to get out, boss," Jason replied softly while he watched out the window.

"Then what's it for? You got enough dynamite there to blow this courthouse to kingdom come!"

"It's for the railroad. There's a train due in at noon from the east."

Stunned, Pete fell to the floor, his butt smacking the wooden planks. The biggest news from here to the Red River had been that the railroad through Fort Worth had finally been finished last month. He bounced to his feet. "Why blow it up? We can get out! Just hop a train and head for New Mexico or even California."

"No, sir," Joshua said, his gaze still locked on the street outside. "Even if we made it to the tracks, those *things* would follow us every step. I reckon we're just about the only fresh meat left in town."

"So what? You've seen how they move. They couldn't keep up with a horse, much less a train."

"We can't let that train get here." Jason had picked up the conversation. "No one knows what's goin' on here, boss. Whatever this thing is, it spreads like fire in a dry prairie. What would happen if those things got on a train bound for Lord knows where?"

"But we can't just..." He trailed off, shaking his head.

"What do you want us to do, then?" John Boy said in a harsh tone. Pete blinked; John Boy never got angry. "We can't sit here. How long before they figure out how to break a window? We've still got a lot of ammo, but they're everywhere, and we can't shoot them all. It's too late for Fort Worth. It may be too late for Texas. But, by God, we can save somethin'."

Pete's head sank, and he sagged against the wall. *I can't believe they're givin' up so easily. But what if he's right?* Jason started humming a tune. His brother quickly picked it up, and John Boy joined in after a moment. Pete remained silent, eyes shut. After a moment, he recognized the song as "In the Sweet By and By." *We shall meet on that beautiful shore.* He opened his eyes.

"I don't like it, but you're right: We ain't got a choice." He took a deep breath. "How do you want to do this?"

The three glanced at each other. "It's got to be you, boss," John Boy replied. "We'll try to give you some space out there, but you've got to do it."

"What?" he roared. "I ain't leaving y'all here—"

"You got the only horse, boss," Jason said. "You said it yourself—they can't keep up with a horse."

"Then we go together. Whoever gets a shot at it goes. One of y'all can ride Bell just as well as I can."

John Boy shook his head. "This has got to be done quick. We can't all be walking down the street, waiting for a chance to get in the saddle." He smiled. "Besides, you treat that horse better than I do my momma. I don't think she'd go out there for anyone but you."

Pete wiped his eyes with the heel of one hand. "Alright, you bastards." His voice broke. "If we got to do this, let's do it. We can head out back while they're all up here."

They nodded and gathered around Bell. John Boy tied the saddlebags on the horse. Pete grabbed her reins and led the way. They wandered through the building, checking doors and hallways for any sign of an exit. Bell's eyes rolled in the tighter passages, and she bumped her head against the ceiling several times. It was all Pete could do to keep her moving. John Boy brought up the rear, cursing loudly whenever he stepped in the more physical signs of Bell's nervousness.

The sun had climbed well on its way to midday when they finally burst through the back door and scrambled into the street. Pete spotted a few shambling figures, but they apparently hadn't been noticed yet. He mounted and booted Bell to a slow walk with the twins on either side and John Boy in the rear. Even here, they could hear groans from the other side of the courthouse.

"Shoot if you see anything headed your way," he said. They nodded. Each carried a pair of cocked pistols, with another pair in the holsters at their sides. Pete rode with the butt of his Winchester propped on his thigh.

Jason fired first. They had gone maybe three blocks before catching the attention of one of the lurching figures. She shuffled toward them with reaching arms, a plaintive moan rising from her throat. Half her face had been ripped off, exposing muscle and bloody bone. John Boy vomited noisily as the top of her head exploded.

After another half-dozen shots and four dead monsters, the wall of sound behind them grew louder. It grew like a wave until it crashed around them as a shambling crowd poured around both sides of the courthouse, moving slowly but steadily their way. John Boy fired in rapid succession, and several fell.

"Save it," Pete said. He urged Bell to a faster pace. The men jogged to keep up. John Boy struggled to reload while they moved.

It didn't take long to leave their pursuers behind. Pete and the twins took care of the few who got in their way. He shot a bullet-riddled deputy and lowered his rifle. The echoes bounced along the street, then returned, building rather than dying. He drew rein and frowned at the street. "What *is* that?"

"Boss." Joshua tugged at his pants. "We got to keep moving."

Behind them, the groaning had gotten louder. Pete twisted in the saddle in time to see a crowd shuffling into view. "Yah!" Bell broke into a trot and the men into a run.

Thunder continued to roll toward them.

Pulling back on the reins, he halted and cocked his head. His men stood, gulping air. *Where have I heard that before?* He glanced back at the moaning hunters, who had gained enough that he could make out individual features. Most, he didn't recognize, but he spied Billy Ray in the front next to a scrawny, tattered figure that might have been Ned. He turned back to the north. *Oh, Lord, no.*

"Turn back!" he yelled and wheeled his horse around. "We've got to find another way through!"

"What is it, boss?" John Boy asked.

He sat silent. The pursuit had passed the last side street behind them, and there wasn't time to make it to the next one north. *We're cut off.*

"Pete?"

He looked down at John Boy's worried face. "Stampede..."

A long, gurgling bellow interrupted him. Several more picked up the cry until it sounded like a bugle call for the armies of Hell. Longhorns ran through the street. They moved in an odd, stilted manner that somehow managed to cover a lot of ground. Most had ribbons of flesh hanging from their bones. A few looked more like running skeletons than anything.

Pistols cracked behind him. Pete turned and saw several of the shambling figures fall. "What're y'all doin'?"

"Clearing you a path, boss," Joshua replied through gritted teeth. "You got to get to the railroad. Did you forget?"

"We'll never get through that."

"We don't have to," Jason said. "Just you."

"But..."

John Boy slapped Bell on the flank. "Ride!"

The horse reared and took off. Cursing, Pete leaned low over her neck and urged her to move faster. Guns barked. Bullets droned by like monstrous bees. And the monsters fell.

He was among them in the space of a few heartbeats, angling for the nearest side street. Hands reached for him. Bell screamed, trampled several into the street and moved on. The horse's weight carried them most of the way through, but she started to slow as the hands grew more insistent. He kicked them aside, clubbed others with his rifle and fired point blank into the seething mass. They seemed uninterested in the horse. They all wanted him.

Where's my cover? Frantic, he twisted to look behind him. He could see no sign of the men. Longhorns swept through the street where they had been. The beasts would crash into him any second. He booted Bell's ribs. She lashed out with her front hooves and lunged forward. They were nearly there. He fired, worked the lever, fired again. Something grabbed the barrel and yanked the rifle out of his hand. He grabbed the reins in both hands and held on, shouting at Bell to move. A hand fell on his boot just as she broke free. He kicked, but it wouldn't let go. Behind them, the bellowing rose in pitch. It sounded like the stampede was almost on top of him. The horse surged through the last of the line. Another hand fell on his knee and nearly dragged him out of the saddle.

It was Billy Ray.

Pete balled a fist and smashed at the face even as Bell danced away from the shambling critters, scrambling up on the wooden sidewalk next to a saloon. He punched again as she pinned them against a wall. The onetime cowboy would not let go.

A few noticed their struggle and turned their way, only to be swept aside by a mountain of hooves and horns that smashed down on them.

Billy Ray climbed.

Pete stopped trying to knock him loose. He put his hands on the clammy shoulders and heaved. His mouth drew down in a grimace and cords stood out in his neck, but he could feel Billy Ray's grip slipping past his knee, then his ankle.

Billy Ray sank his teeth into his wrist.

Screaming, Pete tore his arm free and lashed out with a booted foot. His heel caught Billy Ray in the forehead and smashed him against the wall, splitting his skull with a loud *crack*. Bell backed away, and Billy Ray fell limply to the sidewalk.

Pete nudged the horse in the ribs. She took off at a gallop down the street. He kept her pointed north, but found himself unable to focus on much beyond the mass of pain in his arm. *How could anything that hurts so bad feel so cold?* He shivered and groped blindly for the saddlebags behind him. *At least the dynamite is still there.*

He forced himself upright as Bell ran past the last of the buildings. He angled her east, away from town. Sunlight winked off the new metal rails beside him.

Pete slowly leaned over until his forehead rested on Bell's neck. She slowed to a walk, then stopped. She whinnied softly. Pete snorted, shook himself and straightened. He grimaced and swallowed, trying to keep his groggy mind focused on the task at hand. *Train... coming. Must stop... train... coming.* His thoughts spiraled and fragmented. *Must... train... stop... coming...* The world turned gray, then black. He slumped forward.

The noonday sun baked the landscape, quiet except for an occasional stamp of a hoof or nervous whicker from Bell. She danced side to side as if trying to dislodge her still rider. But his fists and knees had locked in a death grip, allowing him to sway but never fall.

A sudden snort sounded, followed by a protracted groan. Pete sat upright. Bell's eyes rolled wildly, and she reared. Hands jerked on the reins as if unsure how to use them. The horse landed back on all four feet and stood still except for an occasional nervous twitch. And still the moaning continued.

Train.

Pete grunted and swatted at his head, trying to dislodge the errant thought. It wouldn't go. *Train.* The tracks nearby vibrated slightly, followed by a growing rumble from the east. *Train.* He looked around wildly, trying to make sense of a world painted in shades of red and gray. *Train.* The thought seemed important somehow, but he couldn't focus on it, couldn't focus on anything beyond the all-consuming hunger.

His gaze fell on the warm flesh underneath him. *Food?* He leaned over and placed his teeth on the beast's neck. Despite a tempting pulse beating underneath the skin, he sat back up. It seemed wrong somehow. Unappetizing. But the hunger demanded. His moan took on a plaintive note. He bent back down, jaws spread wide.

The rumbling grew louder. *Train.* He straightened, shaking his head like a dog with a rabbit. Still the thought rose, this time followed by another.

Train... coming.

Understanding dawned. His lips peeled back in a feral grin. Saliva streamed down his chin.

Food.

FOR THE GOOD OF THE FLOCK

Our Lady of Victory stood nearly empty this late in the afternoon; the only other soul they had seen so far was an elderly secretary who informed them the priest was in the Adoration Chapel. Most of the lights had been dimmed, and their footfalls echoed strangely. Anna felt goosebumps running up and down her arms. *Stop that! This is the house of God.*

She crossed herself and looked at her husband, who kept tugging at his tie and collar. She smiled; he had listened when she asked him to wear suitable clothing. Her own dress made her look something like a black beachball, but she had picked the nicest clothing she owned. First impressions were important, as her mother had always said. Anna frowned at the two boys following him. *Why couldn't they have listened for once?* Stephen wore a sweat-stained track uniform from his old school. His younger brother, Zachary, sauntered in his ripped jeans and red T-shirt, skateboard tucked under one arm. Her scowl deepened at the black ballcap perched backwards on his head. Anna flicked the bill, knocking it to the floor.

"Hey, Mom, how 'bout you just ask me to take it off next time?"

She slapped his cheek. "Don't sass me, young man."

"Yes, ma'am," he replied sullenly and retrieved the offending cap before stepping into the chapel.

The brick-walled chamber was just as gloomy as the rest of the church, with only a spotlight shining on the monstrance in the center. A handsome, dark-skinned man dressed in black sat in the front row, staring at the altar so earnestly Anna felt embarrassed to have intruded. She reached up to tug on Bill's sleeve and released the door. It slammed shut.

The man jumped at the sound and turned a glare on them that seemed equal parts murderous rage and guilty shame. Anna hissed in surprise and backed up a step. The man approached them a warm, inviting smile. Anna shook her head. *Must have been a trick of the shadows or something.*

"¡Benevidos!" He spoke softly, but his powerful voice carried easily. Anna found herself toying with a lock of her hair. "Welcome to God's house."

"Howdy!" her husband said. "We just moved here and wanted to come check out the local church. I'm Bill Weidner."

Bill's country accent sounded harsh in the still room. He seized the priest's hand in his own meaty paw. The two were of equal height, but the pastor was leaner than her bull-necked husband. A muscular frame strained against his black suit, and wings of white stood out in his black hair. *Mamma would say she could eat him with a spoon.* Anna blushed. *I don't know that I'd bother with the spoon.*

Bill introduced the rest of his family, starting with his wife. Anna heard herself giggle slightly as the priest took her hand and smiled down at her. Her cheeks felt as if they were on fire. Then he moved on, asking Zachary about his skateboard and what tricks he knew. Even the normally sour twelve-year-old was smiling and nodding by the time the priest moved on to Stephen.

Some strange emotion crawled across the pastor's features as he spoke briefly to her oldest son. He leaned in close, nostrils flaring slightly. Her burning face cooled while Stephen talked about his sophomore year and the medals he had won at school. *What is he doing?* She'd tried to ignore the media attention the Church had received in recent years just because a few bad priests couldn't keep their hands to themselves, but something in the way he looked at her son made her uncomfortable. It reminded her of the way a coyote might stare at a rabbit. She chewed on her bottom lip.

"Welcome to Paris. I am Father Guillermo de los Lobos."

"Los Lobos? That's pretty good." Bill chuckled. "Just like the band, huh?"

Anna winced, but Guillermo simply laughed. "*Sí*, but please do not ask me for '*La Bamba*.' My mother told me I sing like a baying hound." He spread his hands. "What brings you to this far corner of Texas?"

"Company transfer," Bill said. "They moved me out here from Mobile to see what I can do about manufacturing."

"*Con mucho gusto.* I am happy to have you here. Our parish sees so little young blood these days. Have you found a home yet? Moving for your job can be very hard. There is so much running around, with much to do in a little time."

"We've looked like headless chickens the last few months, but the company took pretty good care of us." Bill laughed again. "We got ourselves a nice two-story house over off Church Street. She's a real beaut. You ought to see it some time."

"I would like that very much. *Gracias.*" He looked at his watch. "Regretfully, not today. I have matters to attend to. It is good to meet you. Please to not hesitate to contact me if you need anything."

"Will do, *padre.*" Bill flapped his hands, shooing them out the door. "We'll see you Sunday."

"*Vaya con Dios.*"

Anna watched the three boys shake hands with Father de los Lobos and file out the door. He followed them out into the hallway and waved as they left. She thought she caught that hungry gleam in his eye once more as she turned away. *Surely the diocese wouldn't put someone like that in charge of a parish, not after all that's been in the news.* She shook her head and waddled after her family.

A sharp smack echoed down the hallway. Anna turned back. Father de los Lobos waved with one hand; the other held something glittering against his cheek. His smile looked slightly pained. She blinked and headed down the hall, her mind already turning to unpacking and arranging furniture.

Guillermo let his smile slip as the woman turned a corner and disappeared from sight. He dropped his rosary back into his pocket, careful not to touch it any more than he had to. His cheek and hand burned where he had slapped it against his face. The ache would linger – as well it should – but he could feel the flesh already healing.

Groaning, the priest walked the other way toward his office. *I was doing so well. Why did they have to move here with their young, tempting flesh? Lord, please help your weak servant.*

This small Northeast Texas town had seemed an ideal place to send him, home mostly to elderly, wrinkled and above all unappetizing parishioners. There had been… slips in the last couple of years, of course, but the diocese had suggested ways he might distract himself. Guillermo had started to think he might have finally broken free of the hunger. Then this new family arrived. The fat wife might make an interesting morsel, but it was that boy who grabbed his attention. He looked lean and healthy, and his scent… *I'd like to see that one run.*

He halted in the hall before his office. The priest shook himself and growled, wiping a string of drool off his chin. *No! I will not give in again!* He shoved a hand in his pocket, tightening his fist around the silver rosary until his knuckles cracked. *Our Father, who art in Heaven, hollowed be Thy name…* He ran through the prayer while searing pain cleansed his mind. Momentarily free of temptation, he opened the door and walked to his desk. The priest sat and stared at the phone. He had hoped he wouldn't have to make this call again.

Finally, he sighed and grabbed the handset. Guillermo called up an outside line and slowly dialed the number burning his mind as surely as silver. He stared at the angry cruciform indention in his palm while the line rang at the other end. *Please, Lord, let them still be there. I don't know if I have the strength to do this again.* A click and a pleasant female voice answered.

"Hello. Tyler Diocese."

Thank you, Lord. "This is Father Guillermo de los Lobos in Paris. I need to speak with the bishop, if he's in."

"Hello, Father. I think he's here. Please hold."

Music floated down the line. Doubtless they meant to be soothing, but the priest couldn't stop tapping his fingers impatiently on the desk. After what felt like an eternity in Purgatory, the line clicked and a welcome, scratchy voice spoke.

"Hello, Guillermo." Lee Hodo sounded like he might be smiling, which came as no surprise. The Bishop liked to smile. *Too bad I must ruin that for him today.*

"Hello, Excellency."

"Oh? Is this to be a formal call, then?" The voice had taken on a worried tone.

"I am afraid so. I have been having…thoughts about some of my parishioners."

"What sort of thoughts?" All traces of amusement had vanished.

"The same as before, Excellency. Evil, hungry thoughts. A new family has moved to town, and they have a very healthy *hijo*…"

"Guillermo," the Bishop said like a parent scolding a particularly naughty child. "I'm very disappointed to hear this. You were doing so well. It's been close to a year since we had one of these discussions. I had started to think we were past such setbacks." He sighed. "You understand I'm going to have to report this to Rome. I can't keep this within the diocese this time, not after your previous lapses."

"I understand, Excellency." He paused. "For what it is worth, I am quite ashamed."

"I have no doubt of that, but that will carry very little weight with the Vatican. Not many wanted to give you the chance to enter the clergy, not with all the bad publicity we've been getting. This could sway the few supporters you've had, I'm afraid."

"They could kick me out of the Church?" Guillermo's hand crept to his white collar. "What would I do then?"

"Try to remain calm. I'll do everything I can to keep that from happening. You've done a lot of good work despite your unique temptations. That should count for something." Lee sighed. "I'll make the call tomorrow. They'll probably want to move quickly on this one way or the other; I should have news for you Monday."

"What should I do until then?"

"I would recommend fasting and private time with your rosary. Pray without ceasing. You need to be strong, especially now. This is not a good time for you to weaken, you know. Think of your flock and what is best for them."

"Of course, Excellency. Thank you."

"You're a good man, Guillermo. I still hope we can save that part. Take care, my friend."

"*Vaya con Dios, mi amigo.*"

Tossing the phone into its cradle, Guillermo slumped back in his chair with lips twisted as if he had eaten something sour. *I know they watch the calendar, but did he have to be so blunt about it?* He glanced at the datebook on his desk. Sunday's block, which showed a pale circle in one corner, had been circled thrice in red. *Lead us not into temptation, Lord.* He picked the telephone back up and dialed the front desk.

"Barbara? Please call Father Cantrell in Sulphur Springs and ask him to hold Mass here Sunday."

"Why? Are you not feeling well, Father?"

"Just do it, *vieja*," he barked. Sighing, he softened his tone. "My apologies. You are right, I am not well. Just please call Father Cantrell. He'll understand."

"Of course, Father. You know, I thought you looked a little under the weather this morning. I told myself, 'Barbara, there's a man who should have stayed in bed today...'"

Her stream of words cut off as he slammed the receiver down. The plastic base cracked and the handset broke in half. *Foolish old woman. I'd tear her throat out, but I doubt it would shut her up.* Guillermo shuddered and closed his eyes; his mouth felt too small for his teeth, his skin too tight. *Let go.* He growled at the whisper coming from the back of his mind. It always spoke to him in times like this, taunting him with his father's wild voice. *He told you: It's your flock. Who cares about a few sheep? Why deprive yourself?*

No! He groped in his pocket until his burning fingers told him he had found the rosary. *I am not an animal!*

Drawing the string of beads out, he balled the rosary in his fist and clenched the searing metal. Pain cut through some of the red fog that had descended, but didn't lift it entirely. His body trembled as his soul fought the transformation threatening to overwhelm him. He opened eyes on a world that had become much sharper. His nose twitched, searching for the scent of prey nearby...

Though I walk through the Valley of the Shadow of Death, I will fear no evil...Thou...art...with...me... Guillermo shoved the rosary in his mouth.

Agony set his brain aflame. He muffled a scream against his arm and beat his fist on the desk. Antique oak cracked and splintered.

He trembled on a razor's edge, fighting to regain his balance while damnation waited for him to fall.

Finally, his quivering subsided. The priest spat the silver out with a gout of saliva and blood and collapsed on his desk, panting. He had taken a step over the precipice and somehow managed not to fall. The beast was not gone, however. He could feel it, snarling and looking for an escape from its temporary cage.

Guillermo scrambled to his feet. *I have to get out of here.* He snatched the rosary from its puddle and put it in his shirt pocket, ignoring the pain in it brought. Walking to the door, he placed one hand on the knob, paused and sniffed the air. No one was nearby. *The old woman must not have heard the noise.* Barbara liked to take her hearing aid out when she got to reading one of her romance novels. *Maybe she's asleep.* He stepped through and shut the door behind him. The priest dashed through the halls in near-silence until he burst through the main doors.

Twilight spread across the parking lot. He breathed deeply and smiled. The town stank, as did every other place in this country – was there no place free of all the cars and factories? – but it felt good to be outside, away from the cages humans built for themselves. Here he could run and hunt with nothing but the horizon hemming him in.

Shaking his head, he trotted across the asphalt for a small house set in the corner of the church's property. *"Be strong,"* the Bishop said. *I am trying, Lord, but it is hard. Please lend me Your strength.* He staggered inside, shut the door and locked the deadbolt. He switched on a lamp and threw himself on the couch. A portrait hung on the far wall, its bushy-haired subject glaring down at him, seemingly rebuking his weakness. Guillermo's lip curled in a challenging snarl.

"Why did you have to have children, Father?" His tongue still ached, and his voice came out as a rasp. "Why could you not be happy keeping this curse to yourself?"

Foolish question, he chided himself. When not terrorizing the countryside around Zacatecas, Rafael de los Lobos loved nothing more than gathering his litter and regaling them with tales of how their kind had once ruled the night. His stories always ended the same way: "The world was as it should be in those days. A man dared not step outside his door at night for fear of the wolves. Then civilization came and drove us into hiding. But what once was will be again!" Then Father would pace the floor until full dark and venture into town to get drunk on tequila or blood, whichever was most readily available. Mother had been a restraining influence, but she had been killed in Mexico City years before. Father's moods and drinking grew worse after that.

As the eldest, Guillermo bore responsibility of caring for his brothers and sisters. He did the cooking and cleaning, made repairs on their run-down house and performed odd jobs for the neighbors to bring in a few more *pesos*. He made sure the other children attended school. Whatever Father thought, they could not hunt down civilization and tear out its throat. Better they learn to live in the modern world than try to hide or die fighting it. At night, he lit a candle and struggled to learn from their textbooks.

Father spent his days as a guide for *turistas* who visited the city. On those rare nights not filled with drinking, he took his children by ones and twos to hunt whatever prey they could find. Guillermo loved those moments with his father, particularly when they had men to hunt. Cunning quarry made the kill all the more satisfying, the meat that much sweeter.

Then had come the night Father staggered in the house, declaring it was time for his "pack" to drive men from the city...

The priest shook his head. *What am I doing? The Bishop said to pray, not dwell on the past.* Yet he found it hard to banish the memories – the thrilling chase, jaws tearing flesh and crushing bone. He growled at the portrait. *Why did you do it? You had to know they would kill us all. If I hadn't gone off to find my own meat, I'd be in a silver-lined grave next to you and my brothers and sisters.* He dug the rosary from his pocket once more and watched the silver burn his flesh. *The priests took me in, even knowing what I was. They helped me cage the beast. And now I seek to repay that kindness with betrayal?* He knelt beside the couch and clasped the rosary between folded palms.

Lord, help thy servant. My spirit is truly willing, but I fear my flesh, Lord. It is not weak. He began to whimper from the pain in his hands. *My flesh is strong, and it hungers. Lead me not into temptation, but deliver me from evil, I pray. Show me what to do.* No answer came, save a building desire.

The boy's mother had been fearful. He could smell it on her, see it in the way she looked at him. She knew he wanted her son for something, that lovely boy who looked as if he could run and run...

Saliva ran down his chin and pattered onto the sofa.

Lord, I have sinned. Please take this cup from me before I drink of it. Blood ran from his hands. His nose twitched. It had been long since his last hunt. *Too long,* that voice whispered. He quashed it ruthlessly. After his last "lapse," a young blonde woman who worked at a diner downtown, Bishop Hodo had suggested that if he could not banish his desires, Guillermo should sublimate them. It was an agricultural area, why not hunt livestock? The loss of a few cows and horses was better than murder. He had found it a satisfying, if boring, substitution. He shook his head in disgust. Cows were slow and stupid. Horses could run, but they weren't much brighter. *Father would laugh at me. Where is the challenge? What thrill can there be in bringing down a side of beef?*

A passage from Hebrews rose unbidden: "It is not possible that the blood of bulls and of goats should take away sins."

He dropped the rosary. "No," he whispered. "That is no solution. I will not give in." Sweating, Guillermo dropped his head once more. He tried to focus on the rosary, say the proper prayers, but he couldn't focus. *What would you have me do, Lord? I do not know if I can fight this again. I am so weary. I am trying to call upon Your name, but I see no wings, nothing to help me rise above this. Why hast thou made me thus?*

He paused. The question was from the previous week's sermon from Romans. Perhaps the answer lay there. The priest reached a dripping hand toward an end table and opened the drawer. He pulled a Bible from inside and opened to the concordance. The passage he sought was in the ninth chapter. He flipped more pages. A trembling finger ran down the text and stopped at verse twenty: "Nay but, O man, who art thou that repliest against God? Shall the thing formed say to him that formed it, why hast thou *made me* thus?"

Get thee behind me, Satan. I will not listen. The Lord said to feed his sheep, not slaughter them! The Bishop told me to be strong. What did he say? Think of your flock and what is best for them.

Yes, but doesn't a good shepherd cull the flock to make it stronger?

He raised his head. He hadn't thought of that before. Even in his father's voice, it had the ring of truth. What did Paul say in his letter to the Corinthians? *Who feedeth a flock, and eateth not of the milk of the flock?*

Guillermo shook his head and jumped to his feet, pacing back and forth. *What should I do? It sounds wrong, and yet it feels right.* He lashed out in frustration. His arm caught the lamp and sent it crashing to the floor. Darkness enveloped the room.

No. Not complete darkness. Silver light flowed in through the windows, the glow of a nearly full moon high overhead. It sang to him. Not the irresistible pull it would become in a few days, but a strong call nonetheless.

The priest threw back his head and howled. One clawed hand reached for his collar and ripped it free. He tossed it on the couch, where landed on the silver rosary.

"No more," he growled. "I have been made thus. I will not ask why."

Stepping toward the door, Guillermo ripped it free of his hinges and tossed it in the bushes beside the porch. He howled again and grinned. *Too long.* He ran, a fluid, shifting shadow in the night.

The wolf headed toward Church Street, where his prey waited. The diocese would have questions no doubt, but that was a matter for later.

Tonight he would hunt.

He must. For the good of the flock.

JUST ENOUGH

Sneakers silent on the patio, Aaron pushed the glass door open, walked inside and closed it behind him. He crossed the office and leaned against another door, sliding to the floor with a sigh. He let one boy slip to the carpet and shifted the other, biting back a groan as his shoulder and elbow throbbed in protest. Jay snored softly. *Wish I could put him down*, he thought, then shook his head. The two-year-old would wake if he did. *Don't need him crying. Not with them so close.* Aaron gazed out the glass door, thumb working the hammer on a revolver in his waistband.

Zachary stirred at his side and peered up with bleary eyes. "Me hungy, Daddy."

"I know, buddy. We'll find something to eat later. Just be still for a bit, OK?" Aaron cocked his head. *What was that?*

The three-year-old pouted. "Want Mommy."

"Ssshhhh." There it was again, a distant but growing moan. He pulled the gun free and checked the cylinder. Two rounds. *Not enough.* He gave a humorless chuckle. When he'd snagged it and four boxes of bullets from the hotel manager's desk, it seemed a limitless supply. Now he had to get the three of them off the island with only two. *Not nearly enough.*

A herd of slack-jaws shuffled past the door, staring straight ahead. Aaron froze and clutched the boys. *Please, let them go by like last time.* He recognized some, fellow vacationers they'd sat next to at dinner a few days ago.

Another familiar figure shambled by. His breath caught.

"Mommy!" Zachary's shout shattered the silence. Several monsters halted. Aaron kept his gaze locked on the one that had been his wife. Long, stringy hair swung as her head swiveled from side to side. Aaron stood. Zachary wriggled and cried. "Me want Mommy!"

Jay jerked and wailed. Melissa's head snapped toward them. Drool dripped from her chin. She took a step forward, bumping into the glass door like a fly at a window. He heard her growl as she tried again and again.

Aaron shoved the struggling child behind him and groped for the doorknob. Zachary pushed himself free and streaked across the office.

"NO!" Aaron shouted. "Come back!"

He paid no mind, pulling the brass lever handle as Melissa bumped the glass again. The door swung inward. She grabbed the boy laughing and reaching up for her. Sobbing, Aaron wrenched the door behind him open and slammed it shut as Zachary's giggles turned to shrieks.

He wiped his eyes clear and turned to find himself in a storage closet.

The door rattled and thumped behind them. Groans arose on the other side. *Won't hold but a few seconds.*

He sank to the floor. There was no way out, not even an air conditioner vent he could shove Jay into. Aaron lifted the pistol and stroked the crying boy's head. He looked from the steel barrel to the rattling door and back.

A few seconds. Two rounds.

Just enough.

...HITMAN

Percival snatched the Quill. Burning cold burrowed into his hand. He gasped as the spines grew and dug into his flesh. A page turned. The Quill jerked down to the paper and started writing in his own, neat hand. Blood trailed the nib. Once completed, each word writhed and darkened to a shadow that seemed to float above the white paper. Percival tried to pull free, but couldn't unclamp his hand or stop the movements of his arm. Already he felt drowsy and weak. He looked down at what had been written and groaned...

Percival Taylor crushed a brown leather satchel to his thin chest with one hand. The other roamed, seemingly of its own accord. Fingers combed already immaculate black hair, then wandered down to shove wire-frame glasses back up his nose before giving his tight collar a sharp tug and straightening a red bowtie. They walked down the front of his white shirt, checking each button, wiped nonexistent dust from the arm of his chair and headed back for his hair.

"He will see you now, Dr. Taylor."

Percival jumped, fingers tightening on his bowtie and pulling it slightly askew. The pretty receptionist flashed a brilliant smile and pointed at a set of double doors to her left. Percival swallowed and rose on uncertain legs. He wrapped both arms around the satchel, as if seeking protection from what lay beyond that wide portal. He pushed the left-hand door open. *Time to see who called me here.*

It was like walking into a steakhouse. Leather covered everything, even the framed rodeo scenes. Horns and antlers figured heavily into the decorating scheme, both as wall hangings and furniture. A glass-topped wagon wheel sat in the middle of the room, surrounded by a ring of couches. A longhorn head protruded protectively from the far wall, jutting out over a large mahogany desk. Seated at the desk was a compact man with bushy brown muttonchops sprouting from underneath what looked to be at least a ten-gallon hat. He waved a hand without looking up from his paperwork.

"Be with you in a sec, doc."

Percival walked hesitantly toward the desk. He halted at the sight of a black, leather-bound book displayed in a glass box on a wooden table. Three clasps in the shape of talons held it shut. The tome was enormous, perhaps three feet on a side and at least a foot thick. Its ebony surface looked smooth except for a small silver figure embossed on the cover. He leaned forward. A robed skeleton hovered in the darkness with a large scythe over its head ready to begin the harvest. The book stood out in this office like a rodeo clown at a monastery. Tracing the edges, Percival's eyes found a soft rounded hump near the top corner. It looked like a feather. He jerked upright. He positioned his hands side by side in front of his heart, palms up in the sign of a Holy Book.

A soft cough interrupted his inspection. Blushing, he ventured to a high-backed chair in front of the desk as the cowboy stood and watched him with bright, blue eyes. *Heaven help me, he's actually wearing jeans, and is that a belt buckle or a dinner plate?*

"Howdy." He held out a beefy, calloused hand. "I'm James Robert Akerman."

"Charmed." He gave the proffered hand a single, prim shake and sat. *"James Robert" indeed.* He shifted in the chair. *I'd have thought he would prefer something like Jimmy or Jim Bob.* The satchel froze halfway to the floor. *Jim Bob Akerman?* Color drained from his face, and the bag fell from nerveless fingers. "The Cowboy Mafia?" He clapped a hand over his mouth.

"That's what the papers call us." Jim Bob shook his head ruefully and resumed his seat. "Ain't that a kick in the teeth? Still, we've kind of taken a shine to it around here." He chuckled, leaned back in his seat and propped his boots up on the desk. "Shows we're getting' some attention."

"But what would a criminal organization want with me?" He jumped at a sharp slap on the desk.

"There's no call for name calling, doc." He leveled a warning finger. "I got a lot of real nice people workin' for me, and I won't have you talking about them like that. I might've had a few run-ins with the law, but what businessman hasn't?"

"I see." Percival took a deep breath. "But my question remains: What would a... businessman... want with me? I don't have any money or connections. I'm just an English professor."

"Why'd you show up, then?"

Eyes narrowed, Percival leaned forward and hissed. "That letter you sent ensured I would come." He sat up straight and ventured a small smile. "Although if I had known you were the one threatening police action, I would have reconsidered. I doubt very much the authorities would put much stock in the word of a *businessman*."

"You'd be surprised, doc," he replied mildly. "I got all kinds of cops willing to listen to me."

"Perhaps, but you have no proof. As soon as I got your letter, I took steps to make sure all evidence was erased." He grabbed his satchel and stood. "Good day, sir."

"Sit down, doc." He punched a button on his phone. "Tiffany, send in Mr. Green, please."

"Yes, Mr. Akerman."

Jim Bob stared at him, fingers interlaced and thumbs tapping. Percival remained standing. The door opened to admit a tall, bucktoothed man with blond hair. He walked over and placed a thin, plastic case on the desk. A DVD glittered inside.

Percival frowned at the newcomer for a few moments. Then recognition dawned, and he half-sat, half-fell back into his chair. Jim Bob nodded, a small smile forming underneath his mustache.

"Thanks, Mr. Green." He waved a hand in dismissal and turned back to his guest. "That little disc there holds some pretty sick pictures taken directly from your computer."

Fear gnawed at his belly as Percival watched the technician he had hired to wipe his hard drive leave the room. "How... why..."

"Good questions, doc." He stretched and popped his knuckles. "I told you before I'm a businessman. I got interests in a bunch of different areas, but I reckon they all come down to two things: information and persuasion."

"How in the world does anything from my computer help your 'business'?"

"It gets me a favor." Boots thudded back to the floor, and Jim Bob leaned forward with his elbows on the desk. "They call this the Information Age. That means it ain't who you know, doc, it's what you know. I get people tellin' me stuff all over the place — police stations, city hall, businesses, colleges." His eyes glittered. "Your dean owes me for helping him out with a little jam last year. He passes on tidbits of information he thinks I might find interesting. When I heard one of his folks might come under investigation, I thought to myself, 'Jim Bob, there's a fella you can make use of.'"

So that's how it happened. Everyone thought Dan Rogers had just been lucky when the charges in a drunk-driving incident that left a little girl paralyzed suddenly evaporated. "You think I'm going to be some kind of informant for you just because you've got a disc with a few pictures on it?"

"There's a sight more than a few pictures on that thing, doc. I'd have never figured literature had anything to do with a bunch of naked kids. No wonder all the fruity types want to go to college." He shook his head. "I tell you, Percy, you're in a heap of trouble."

"My name is Percival." He gripped the arms of his chair tightly. "So what do you want me to do? Spy on my coworkers? Eavesdrop at the faculty picnic?"

The cowboy chuckled. "Nah. I got bigger plans for you." He pressed another button on the phone. "Sometimes information ain't enough. That's when you got to turn to persuasion." Two hulking, denim-clad brutes stalked into the room on booted feet. One carried a box, which he set on the desk. The other took a small cell phone from his shirt pocket and laid it on top. The pair took up stations on either side of Percival's chair. All traces of mirth vanished from Jim Bob's face, leaving behind the expression of a gunslinger about to draw. "You're going to take this here box to this address." He pulled a small square of paper from a shirt pocked and handed it over. Written in a barely legible scrawl was an address: *400 West Seventh Street.* "Just leave it someplace inconspicuous. Then you drive away and call the only number stored in that phone. That's all."

"What's in the box?"

"It's best you don't know."

Percival tried to stand, but the men placed their hands on his shoulders and forced him back down. "And if I don't?"

"Percy, I don't think you understand. That wasn't a request. You do it or those photos go to the cops and a few choice news outlets. Think how that'll look — local professor arrested for kiddie porn. What'll it do to your mother? I hear she's got a bad ticker. I don't know if she could survive a shock like that. And don't forget that feeble little sister you visit every weekend of so at that nursing home in Texarkana. People can get real nasty when they hear about pedophiles. It'd be a shame if someone took it out on her."

Percival wept. He stared wildly around the room. *Please, just let me wake up.* His gaze settled on the book sitting in its case. Sobs faded to hiccoughs as his hands formed a book in front of his heart.

"You're one of them Book Cult folks, ain't ya?" Jim Bob looked at him with interest.

His lips thinned. "I am a member of the Church of the Divine Library, yes."

"Well, ain't that somethin'?" He stood and walked to the case. He opened the glass front and traced the silver figure on the cover. "She's a real beauty."

He could only nod. *How did a criminal come to possess such a holy relic?* He tried to stand, but those hands kept him firmly in the chair. "You don't strike me as a religious man, Mr. Akerman. Why keep a copy of one of the books from the Divine Library here? Surely some other artifact would serve you just as well, and it'd have to be cheaper."

"And it's blasphemy for a no-good crook like me to lay his hands on it." He chuckled. "What would you say if I told you this ain't a copy?"

Percival shook his head. Of the seven Books God had scattered across the world for men to find — Earth, Wind, Fire, Water, Light, Shadow and Souls — this cowboy claimed to have one of the few to have ever been recovered? *Figures he'd pick the one that speaks of death.* "Impossible. It's been lost ever since Saint LaCroix discovered it in Europe and brought it to this country. You expect me to believe it just turned up in your office after two hundred years?"

"God works right mysteriously, if I remember my Sunday school days correctly." He walked to the wall behind his desk and tapped a frame underneath the longhorn's head. "I've seen it in action. That book made me what I am today."

Surprisingly, the frame didn't contain a picture of livestock or men shooting at each other, just a ripped piece of heavy paper carefully mounted for display. One scrawled word was visible despite the damage: 'hitman.' It had been written in an unusual dark ink. Even with light shining on the paper, it looked more like a shadow trapped under glass than writing. Percival gasped. *How many charlatans have tried and failed to duplicate that? No man can copy God's work.*

Jim Bob nodded, unclasped the Book and flipped it open. A black, thorn-laden Quill had been tied to the back side of the front cover with leather thongs. The cowboy drew a pair of heavy leather gloves from a drawer in the table and donned them. His fingers lightly brushed the Quill's spines. The ebony feather trembled slightly.

"I had this thing for years before I knew what it was. Took it from a guy I was hired to kill. He had a big, fancy house, and I grabbed everything I could carry once the job was done. Hid it in a box for the longest time. Even when I heard stories coming from your Book Cult, I couldn't hardly credit the idea. *The Book of Shadows*, to answer any question about your own death you ask it. I never believed it until I put a few drops of blood on those thorns there and asked one question: 'How?'"

"But why tear it? You couldn't have thought to mitigate your sin by that point."

"'Sin'! That's a good one, doc." He laughed and thumped a fist on the case. "It wasn't me. The thing wrote so hard it ripped the paper into shreds. I reckon that spiny pen was mad I didn't just grab it. But it told me all I needed to know."

"Wouldn't more information be helpful?" Despite himself, Percival was fascinated. "If you knew whose hitman it was, you might be able to make preparations, set your affairs in order..."

He shook his head. "I don't need to know who might be gunnin' for me. I figure everyone is. How do you think I built my business?

There's guys out there who'll cut your throat if you start elbowin' in on their territory. But if I don't trust nobody, they can't get near me before I gun them down myself." He beamed proudly. "I beat that Book at its own game."

"Nobody 'beats' the Divine Library. People have tried with other Books. They've all..."

"Failed. I know. But the way I figure it, it's cause they're thinking too hard. They try to look at it from every angle and get hit between the eyes while they're doin' it. Me, I don't worry about the angles. I just blow them all away." He pointed at the leather-clad Book. "Whatever's in that thing is a tricky little devil. You give it a little blood, and it gives you a teeny tiny little bit of information and lets you drive yourself nuts with it. You want more information, you got to give up more blood. But that thing don't strike me as the type to let go once it's got its hooks in you. I decided to play the game its way, and I won."

He signaled his men. They grabbed Percival by his forearms and dragged him to his feet. "What is the meaning of this? I can walk, you lumbering oafs. Put me down!" Ignoring his protests, the goons walked to Jim Bob, dragging Percival with them. The small group stopped at the Book of Shadows as the cowboy untied the leather straps, moving awkwardly because of his gloved hands.

"Touch that quill."

"I will not!" Percival writhed in the dual iron grips keeping him aloft. "Heaven help me, I'll deliver your package. But you cannot make me do this!"

"I ain't askin' doc."

"But... but... surely you know I can't. I'm no priest; the Books are not meant for one such as me. God forbids it!"

"Yeah, I know. I always thought that was kind of weird, but hey, I figure every man's got a right to his own religion."

Percival sagged. "So you won't make me..."

"Actually, I will. I said you got a right to your beliefs." He nodded at the two men. "I never said I cared."

They grabbed his right hand, forced all but his index finger into a fist and rammed it onto the nearest spine. He moaned at the prick in his finger. The goons released their grip, and he fell to the floor, weeping.

Pages flipped on the book until they reached a blank sheet of paper. The Quill dragged across the paper, scratched briefly and returned to its resting place. Jim Bob looked at the parchment while he secured the pen back in place. He let out a low whistle.

"Now that is a kick in the teeth." He lifted the Book with both hands and turned it. "Doc, you got to take a look at this one." Percival closed his eyes. "Aw, now, don't be that way. Ain't you curious?" He shook his head. A rustling sound came from inches in front of his face. He pictured the cowboy grinning and shaking the pages at him. "You know you want to."

Sweating, Percival moaned and chewed on his lip. What could impress a crime lord so much? *Lord, I'm weak. You know that.* He opened his eyes. A single word swam into focus. He fell back, fist pressed to his mouth muffling his whimpers.

Jim Bob laughed. "Didn't I say you was in a heap of trouble?"

It read: "GOD."

Sniffling, Percival pushed his glasses up and scrubbed at red eyes with one hand. The other clutched a brown bottle that clinked as it connected with a countertop. He jerked away from the sound, swayed and nearly toppled. His free hand caught the counter, rescuing him from gravity. The motion sent a precariously stacked pile of filthy plates and bowls crashing to the floor. He dismissed the mess with a wave of his hand.

He shuffled into a dimly lit living room. His steps pushed discarded wrappers, soiled laundry and empty bottles out of the way, clearing a weaving path through the clutter illuminated only by a television's flickering light. No sound came from the TV, and he ignored the images flashing on the screen. Throwing himself into a recliner, Percival jerked on a lever to raise the footrest and took a swig of beer. He grimaced at the taste. The Church forbade alcohol, but he couldn't find anything else to lessen the pain. *What's one more sin at this point?*

"That's uncivilized," he said, slurring. "Gotsta do it, though. Time to be a man! Yeehaw!" His voice cracked, and a fresh bout of sobs wracked his thin frame. Groping for the remote, he punched the mute button.

"...thorities still say they have no solid leads in this case." A calm, professional female voice blared through the apartment, clashing with the scenes of devastation.

Rubble filled the screen. Men and dogs sifted through the wreckage, occasionally pulling someone free of pulverized bricks and shattered glass. A few of the rescued were able to walk away. Most lay still. Little of the building remained standing. One wall appeared untouched, four stories rising above West Seventh Street with a terra cotta frieze capping the top windows. It had been buttressed while rescuers worked. Less than half of two more walls remained, and the fourth had been obliterated.

"At latest count, more than a dozen people have been injured and nearly two hundred dead or missing. John Hart has the latest at the scene. John?"

The image cut to a smartly dressed black man with a microphone standing in front of the rubble. "Thank you, Becky." He swept an arm back. "Police are stumped. They say they have little more information about this tragedy than they did when the explosion ripped through downtown Fort Worth three days ago." Percival took another drink.

"No one has claimed responsibility for this attack. The police department declined to comment except to say they are investigating several terrorist organizations."

The screen shifted back to Becky, with John boxed in a screen over her left shoulder. "Has anyone with the *Star-Telegram* made a statement, John?"

"No, Becky. So far, we've been unable to reach anyone with the newspaper, leaving us to wonder, like the rest of Fort Worth, when the *Star-Telegram* will be able to print another edition."

Percival grunted. Glass met glass and shattered. The room went dark as the TV screen imploded. Something buzzed and sizzled inside, releasing a faint whiff of smoke. He sat in the dark, weeping. Occasionally, a hand snaked down to the satchel propped against his chair to trace its content's hard angles through the leather.

The whole thing had been so easy. He left Akerman, caught a cab to the newspaper offices downtown and walked in without a single question. A dingy bathroom in the basement offered the perfect place to leave the box. Sweaty and shaking, he turned back three times before he finally made it out of the building. He stood outside and dialed the phone, half hoping he'd be claimed by the expected blast. Surprisingly, Akerman answered.

"Thanks, doc," he said and hung up.

Relief threatened to drop him into the street. Percival hailed a taxi and gone to a restaurant for a long dinner before heading home. He puttered around the apartment, straightening and cleaning. A knock startled him, but the hallway had been empty when he opened the door. A thin, brown rectangle lay on the floor. He picked it up and shut the door. Inside, he found the DVD he had last seen in Akerman's office. A scrawled note had been taped to the case.

"Great work, doc! Turn on the news."

Frowning, Percival popped the DVD into the microwave and set it for five minutes. Then he turned on the television to a scene of carnage straight from Hell.

In the days since, he had only been out to buy beer and one sleepless night for a special purchase. His hand patted the satchel again, and his face hardened. *Time to get going.* He dressed as carefully as he was able, but a glance at a mirror on his way to the door showed a haunting visage with sunken eyes, tangled hair, rough stubble and a cockeyed blue bowtie around a grimy collar. He shrugged and went downstairs.

He rode in silence in the cab, staring out the window at the fading day and clutching the satchel to his chest. Once they stopped, Percival blindly paid the fare and climbed out of the taxi. He swayed on the sidewalk, neck craned back to look at the glass-clad office building towering into the sky. The top floors glittered as its windows caught the last vestiges of daylight. A scowl etched itself into his features as he lowered his gaze and carefully staggered to the door.

It swung open.

What if he's expecting me? Percival shrugged uncomfortably. *Does it matter?* He shook his head, squared his shoulders and marched through the empty lobby to a bank of elevators. He pressed the triangle pointing upward. An immediate *ding* made him jump. An elevator to his right slid open. He stepped inside and hit the button for the top floor.

As the doors closed, he sagged against the rear mirrored wall and let the tinny strains of the "Ode to Joy" wash over him. The car stopped once, on the twelfth floor. A young woman in a pantsuit started to step inside. She saw Percival hugging his bag and backed out.

"I'll catch the next one," she stammered as the doors closed.

Just as he was starting to relax, the elevator halted at the thirty-eighth floor and the doors opened with a small chime. One arm still wrapped around the satchel, Percival flipped back the flap and reached in with his other hand and walked out.

He paused briefly at the double doors, then slammed a shoulder into the wood. The right-hand door shuddered open. He shambled through to the office beyond. His satchel bulged rhythmically as his fist clenched and unclenched inside.

Jim Bob sat at his desk, reviewing paperwork. A large revolver sat to one side, gleaming in the fluorescent lights. He looked up at Percival's entrance and grinned.

"Hey, doc! Good to see you. I thought you might show up." He gestured toward the empty office. "I had everyone leave. Figured you might be kind of upset, and I hate to cause a scene."

Percival stopped just inside the doorway, drew his hand from his satchel and let the bag flop to the floor. He tried to steady the Uzi with both hands, but the black barrel trembled and wandered around his intended target.

Jim Bob sighed. "Now, doc. Is that any way to greet a business partner?"

"I'm no partner of yours."

"What else would you call us? We have engaged in a mutual exchange of services, haven't we?"

Shaking his head, Percival muttered under his breath. He tightened his grip. "The newspaper? Why?"

"Down to business, I see." He chuckled. "They ignored my advice not to run a recent series of articles about my dealings with certain city officials. They made things difficult for me, Percy. I didn't appreciate it."

"You did this out of revenge?"

"It's like a debate. You know, point and counterpoint. They made their point. I just made mine with a little more force, Percy."

"My name is Percival."

He ignored the outburst, picked up the revolver and moseyed around the desk. "You know, doc, I don't know what you're all worked up about." He scratched his temple with the gun's barrel. "I mean, that paper's been pretty hard on your school from time to time, too." He stopped at the Book.

"That's no excuse…" Percival broke off as the cowboy opened the case and ran his fingers across the leather. The Uzi's shaking stopped. It pointed steadily at Jim Bob. "Don't touch that!"

"Why not? It's mine, ain't it?"

"It's not yours. You stole it. It belongs in a Church. Now get your hands off or I'll…"

"You'll what, doc? Shoot me? I don't think God would like you stooping to outright murder, do you?"

"What's one more sin at this point?" he whispered. He extended his arms, leveling the machinegun at the cowboy's head.

"You know, doc, I had hoped we could be friends. But I really don't like it when someone walks into my office and threatens me. Now you put that little gun down, and we can just pretend like this little thing never happened." Jim Bob cocked the hammer back. The click sounded loud in the still office. "Or I can plug your head with a couple of bullets, and burn your body somewhere out in the country." He reached into his front pocket, pulled out a lighter and started toying with the wheel. He glanced down at the Book. "It occurs to me old paper might make some really fine kindling."

"No!" Percival yelled. His finger spasmed on the trigger.

The rattling Uzi bucked in his hands. Jim Bob jerked under the deadly hail and collapsed. His body slammed into the case, shattering glass and flipping the Book into the air. It landed on his chest and fell open. Pages turned with a soft whisper. Dark writing flashed by, offering glimpses of what appeared to be hieroglyphics, Sanskrit and other characters he couldn't identify before it halted at a blank sheet. Red lines danced across the paper, darkening as soon as they appeared. The page flipped, and the drawing continued.

Percival dropped the gun. He sank to his knees and crawled forward until he crouched, trembling, over the Book. A comic book unfolded before his eyes. Every frame featured Jim Bob, showing his dark dealings and rise to power. *But the Quill is still in its holder. Where is the ink coming from?* The professor looked around the tome and gasped. Four crimson trickles flowed across the corners from Jim Bob's wounds. The stream thinned and stopped.

When he looked back, the drawing had ceased.

Two panels sat on the page. The top showed Percival pulling a scrap free of the Book. He glanced down and saw a small paper triangle peeking from the back pages. His hands shook as he hesitantly reached down and drew it out. It bore two words scrawled in shadowy ink: "Your own..."

"Dear Lord, was this Your will?" Percival murmured. His knees gave way and he fell, butt smacking the floor. "But why? Please help me understand." Eyes closed, Percival's head sank to his chest. He sat motionless for several minutes until a new thought arose: *The Book.*

Opening his eyes, he leaned forward and gazed at the bottom picture. It showed him removing the Quill. *Is this to be my atonement?* He reached out and tore the laces free. His hand paused over the ebony feather. *Your will must be done, Lord. No matter the cost.*

Percival snatched the Quill. Burning cold burrowed into his hand. He gasped as the spines grew and dug into his flesh. A page turned. The Quill jerked down to the paper and started writing in his own, neat hand. Blood trailed the nib. Once completed, each word writhed and darkened to a shadow that seemed to float above the white paper. Percival tried to pull free, but couldn't unclamp his hand or stop the movements of his arm. Already he felt drowsy and weak. He looked down at what had been written and groaned...

FIRST NIGHT IN JENNINGS GROVE

Vernon's grip tightened on the steering wheel. Vinyl creaked in protest. He tried to ignore the sound, with better success than his attempts to block out his wife's nagging, infant son's screaming and the CD of children's songs playing on the stereo for the tenth time. The sun hung just above the horizon, making him squint through the windshield to make anything out.

"Vern, slow down!" Cheryl yelled as he slalomed through yet another curve on Farm-to-Market Road 197.

He bit his tongue and just stopped himself from stomping on the brake pedal, although he did tap it hard enough that his wife's seatbelt locked as the station wagon lurched to a more moderate speed. Alexis laughed and clapped her hands. Raymond's screams continued unabated.

"Five minutes ago, you were telling me to go faster," he muttered.

"What was that?"

"Nothing." He sighed and ran a hand across his head. His fingers traveled halfway down the back of his skull before encountering a fringe of brown hair. "Can't you do anything about Ray?"

"He's hungry, and he wants out of his car seat. If you'll pull over, I can feed him..."

"No. We've been in this stupid car for seven hours already, and we've stopped a dozen times. We're nearly there; he can just wait."

An exasperated glottal hiss escaped from the back of Cheryl's throat, and she turned up the volume on the radio. "Down by the Station" was starting again. Vernon just knew little puffer bellies all in a row would haunt his every waking moment for the next week. The sacrifice was worth it, he guessed; Alexis had remained fairly quiet the whole trip, aside from complaining of hunger or a need to "go potty." Given the four-year-old's usual demeanor on road trips, that qualified as a minor miracle.

"Chug, chug, toot, toot, here we go!" his daughter belted, off-key as usual. Any other time, it would be cute. Now, it was just irritating. Vern turned the radio on. Static assaulted his ears, and he hit the scan button. Snippets of country music joined the attack.

"Daddy, I want kid songs!"

"Honey, I want to hear the radio for a while. You can listen to your kid songs later when you go to the store with Mommy."

"But I want it now!" She started to cry.

"Now, Vern, turn the CD back on. There's no need for this."

"Everybody, just shut up! I've had enough of your griping and your whining." *Man, what I wouldn't give right now to wake up in the morning and be single again.*

He punched the eject button on the stereo. He grabbed the offending disc and flung it to the back of the car like a Frisbee. Alexis' cry rose to a wail, which inspired her brother to even greater vocal feats. Vernon sniffed. Ray had dirtied his diaper. *Figures*, he thought. Cheryl folded her arms and glared at him through her oval-framed glasses. His right foot slowly pressed down, and the car picked up speed once more as he ground his teeth.

A metal building flashed by in a blur; he barely had time to register the words "Chicota Volunteer Fire Department." A sign pointing to County Road 36850 zipped past just as fast.

This time, he did slam on the brakes – which promptly locked up.

The station wagon, its rear loaded down with boxes, swerved and slid across the road. Trees spun past the windshield like an autumnal kaleidoscope. The Camry whipped around and skidded into a shallow ditch on the opposite side of the highway. It tilted slightly to the right before dropping back onto all four wheels amid a chorus of squeaks from the suspension. Inside, the car was deathly quiet. Then everyone started yelling at once.

Raymond, of course, resumed his screaming. He could barely hear Alexis saying, "That was *cool*, Daddy! I want to do it again!"

"Vernon Edward Hamilton, what on earth were you thinking?" Cheryl shouted. "You could have killed all of us!"

He slowly relaxed his death grip from the steering wheel, put the transmission into park and rubbed his eyes with trembling hands. He sat there, breathing in ragged gasps for several minutes. He turned to his daughter.

"Sweetie, please hush." Turning, he leveled a warning finger at his wife. "Nobody's dead. No one's even hurt. The car's running fine. Yeah, it was stupid, but until something actually happens, keep your comments to yourself."

He glanced at the dashboard clock. "Look, it's nearly six. These people will be getting out of church soon. Let's get home and try to calm down so we don't make a bad impression on our new neighbors."

He dropped the car into drive and eased back out on the asphalt. Black lines showed the path of his car's wild ride. Waiting at the intersection for a couple of battered pickups to go by, he offered a silent prayer of thanks that no one had been hurt. This move was hard enough on everyone as it was; he didn't need to add injuries to the stress.

Vernon had been quite happy in his previous job at a small plastics company on the Texas Gulf Coast. Everyone in the shop worked hard, often performing the duties of two or three people because the owner didn't want the expense of adding to his headcount. Vernon didn't mind. It made for long hours but decent pay and a fair measure of job security. Or so he thought until Herb Franklin announced he was bankrupt, the company was shutting its doors for good, and he planned to move to South America with his secretary and all the money he could squeeze out of his business — including, they found out later, the pension fund.

In the last six months, the Hamilton family had been forced to sell their home and move into a two-bedroom rat hole of an apartment while Vernon looked for another job and his wife bore their second child. With his experience, Houston should have been an easy place to land something. But, as Vernon gradually discovered, Franklin was not the most ethical of businessmen. Prospective employers took one look at his resume and moved on to the next candidate. The only consolation, small though it might be, was that his former coworkers were having similar difficulties.

As their money dwindled, they moved to a smaller rat hole and finally an efficiency that even rats turned their noses up at. Vernon started to wonder if their next home might be under an overpass when he got the call.

Ethan Roodschild, an old supervisor, had found work near the Oklahoma border at a place called Paris Industries. They made plastic swimming pools and fake Christmas trees. Ethan could use a good man on his crew.

"The pay's not as much as you're used to, but the cost of living is a lot lower up here," Ethan had said. "Are you interested?"

Vernon agreed to it on the spot. He'd start in three weeks, at the beginning of October. Cheryl wasn't thrilled, but she agreed they had to leave. It was only a matter of time before one of the gunshots they routinely heard at night put a bullet through their window. Ethan helped them find an old, two-bedroom farmhouse they could lease for only $300 a month. He even paid the deposit and first month's rent. Judging from the photos he sent, it wasn't much, but at least they had managed to take a step in the right direction.

Driving down this county road, Vernon listened to gravel crunching under his tires, smelled the dust his car kicked up and glanced sideways at his wife in the passenger seat. She chewed on a lock of her curly auburn hair, a sure sign of anxiety. The stress of the last half-year had taken its toll. A tall woman, she had always been thin and pale, but these days, Cheryl hovered on the verge of gaunt. Her usually penetrating stare had become a hollow-eyed gaze. She had her feet up on her seat, hugging her knees close to her chest as she hunched away from the screaming behind her.

I probably don't look any better, he thought. He had lost quite a bit of weight himself, but unlike his wife, his short, stocky frame had plenty to spare.

He reached over and patted her knee. "It'll be all right," he said softly. She shot a withering look at him. "Look, I'm sorry. I overreacted. You're right to be mad, and I'm a big, stupid jerk." Her face relaxed slightly, and she turned her frown back out the window. *How long has it been since I've seen her smile?*

They crested a hill and got their first look at their new home.

The community sat on the Red River, a collection of roughly a dozen homes and a small church tucked away on the northernmost point of Lamar County. The houses formed a large semicircle with Jennings Grove Primitive Baptist Church at its apex.

Vernon followed the looping road to the left, driving slowly as he looked for their house. Each residence had a large yard, at least an acre or more apiece. *Alexis'll love that,* he thought. A few sported tricycles, swing sets and other signs of children, but he couldn't see any people. *This place looks like a ghost town. He* shivered. He pushed a switch on his door handle, and the window hummed as it rolled down.

Only the church showed signs of life. Stained-glass windows glowed with various saints and biblical scenes as twilight approached. As he cocked his head out the window, Vernon made out muffled strains of "In the Sweet By and By." A sign out front proclaimed this week's message as "The Outer Darkness, Where there is Weeping and Gnashing of Teeth." *Well, now isn't that just cheerful?*

"There it is," Cheryl said, pointing past his ear. He nodded and pulled into a driveway just past the church.

Knuckling his back as he climbed out of the car, he looked at the white house and grunted. The porch had been rebuilt recently, and some of the windows replaced, but no amount of cosmetics could hide the fact that this was an old broad of a house.

"The pictures didn't do this place justice. I'll bet it's at least sixty years old. They should be paying us to live here."

His wife barked a laugh, pulled Raymond from his car seat and wrapped him in a yellow-and-blue-striped blanket.

"I've got to change Ray and feed him," she said, bouncing him on her shoulder. "Can you get Alexis and start unloading this stuff?"

"Sure." He opened his daughter's door and pushed the lever on her seatbelt. She squirmed in his grip. "Be still."

"I want Mommy," Alexis replied, arms folded and her bottom lip pooched out.

"Not right now. She's got to feed the baby."

"Aww, man." That was one of her new favorite phrases. "Can I go play on the swing?"

"What swing?"

"Over there, silly." She pointed behind the house, to the northwest corner of the property. Two ropes suspended a board from a branch of the biggest pecan tree he had ever seen. Even knowing it was there, he found the swing hard to pick out. The tree cast a nearly impenetrable shade in the dying daylight. *I bet that thing's great for sitting under in the summer.*

"Sure, sweetie. Just don't go anywhere else, and come up to the house if we call you, OK?"

"OK, daddy." She grabbed his leg in a bear hug before tearing across the yard to the tree and calling over her shoulder, "I love you."

"I love you, too."

When he got back to the house with an armload of books from the back of the car, Cheryl was sitting on the porch in a rocking chair, breastfeeding the baby.

"Cheryl, cover up or go inside. There's a church next door, for crying out loud."

"When someone complains, I'll cover up. There's no one around, Vern."

"Yeah, I noticed that. Kinda creepy, isn't it?"

"A little. Look, it's going to be dark soon. Could you hurry up and get that stuff out of the car?"

Shaking his head, Vernon walked up the porch. At least Cheryl had propped the door open and turned the lights on.

Floorboards creaked as he walked through the living room, only slightly muffled by a threadbare, green carpet. He could feel the hardened pad crumbling as he stepped. He wrinkled his nose at the dust and a musty odor that permeated the house, as if it had been shut up too long. Boxes and furniture covered most of the floor, often right in his path. He navigated the obstacle course and stepped through a curtained doorway on the far side of the room.

Pale yellow linoleum squeaked as he stepped into the kitchen. This room was slightly less cluttered, although several boxes marked "dishes" sat on the counter. He found a clear spot on the table and set his books down. He opened the refrigerator with some trepidation. The light came on and cold air drifted out, but as he suspected, it was empty. As he shut the fridge, its compressor kicked on, and the lights flickered.

What kind of wiring do they have in this place?

After the lights steadied, he noticed a cracked window between the fridge and stove that looked out onto another room. Puzzled, he walked in.

Someone had enclosed the back porch. Their washer and dryer sat in one corner, while their blue sleeper sofa and a desk bearing a TV and VCR occupied the far side. A door near the laundry area led into their only bathroom. A soft hiss and *fwoomp* made him jump. He turned to face a propane water heater in the near corner. Drawing a deep breath, he tried to steady himself. He blew sharply through his nose at the dull odor. It smelled like exhaust fumes he remembered from sitting on one of Houston's six-lane parking lots during rush hour.

He threaded his way through the two bedrooms that took up the rest of the house. Their beds had been set up and made, their dressers pushed against the wall, and boxes haphazardly perched on every flat surface available.

Ray slept in his mother's arms when Vernon walked back out on the porch.

"Don't spend any more time than you have to in the bathroom," he said. "The water heater's not venting right. I'll call the landlord tomorrow."

"Wonderful." She sighed, leaned back in her chair and closed her eyes.

He scratched his head. "Look, Cheryl, it was real nice of your brothers to load our stuff up and move it for us, but don't you think they could have been a little more careful about putting it up? And they ate everything we had in the fridge."

"You're right," she replied sharply. "It was nice of them. They didn't ask for any money, and if they want to take a little food, well, I think..."

What she thought remained a mystery as the bang of an opening door and a babble of voices cut her off. He glanced at his watch, which showed six.

"Church dismissed," he said. "You want to go meet the neighbors?"

"You go ahead, Vern. I'm tired, and I don't want to wake Ray up. I can meet them later."

"It's all right. I understand — neither one of us has gotten any sleep lately. I'll join you in a little bit." He walked down the gravel driveway and glanced over his shoulder. Cheryl had resumed rocking, and Alexis was still swinging, hair and red skirt flying as she moved through the air. He smiled.

The congregation hadn't wasted any time in dispersing. A few had already passed his house by the time he reached the road. He watched the people as they headed home. Senior citizens looked to account for most of the Jennings Grove's residents, with younger couples making up maybe a third. Regardless of age, everyone moved with the same brisk stride while eyeing the setting sun.

A man and woman in their mid-thirties strode by, the husband carrying a girl about Alexis' age. Vernon waved.

"Hey, how you doing? My name's Vern Hamilton. My wife and I just moved in." He turned and waved at the porch. "What's your daughter's name? We've got a little girl about her age." When he turned back, the couple had already moved on.

He waved at another pair walking with a sullen teenage boy in tow. The woman waved back, and her husband nodded in a friendly fashion, but neither halted or even slowed.

Four more people passed without even glancing his way. *That's it. I'm through being polite.* When a middle-aged man in a suit and fedora walked by his driveway, Vernon snagged his arm and spun him around.

"What is the meaning of this?" he demanded. "Release me at once. Can't you see how late it is?"

"Look, man, I'm sorry to be rude, but we just moved in and no one will so much as talk to me. I had heard this was a friendly little place, but so far, everyone's acting like we've got the plague or something."

"Ah, the new family — the Hamiltons, wasn't it?" His expression softened, and he smoothed his graying mustache with a thumb and forefinger. "My name is Travis Ware. I'm sort of the unofficial mayor around here. I'd be more than happy to speak with you in the morning, but I really must get inside. I suggest you do the same.

It's almost dark, you know." He put a special emphasis on the last. Vernon frowned, released Travis' arm and watched him disappear into the deepening murk.

The breeze grew as he walked back up the driveway. It sighed in his ears, almost seeming to form words. The hair on the back of his neck tried to stand. *Something's not right.*

"Alexis!" he bellowed. "Get in the house now!"

She didn't answer. He ran up the driveway and into the house. Cheryl sat on their bed, Raymond cradled in her arms. "Do you know where a flashlight is?" he asked.

"That big one of yours is on the kitchen counter. Why?"

"I gotta go get Alexis," he called as he made his way to the kitchen. "She wouldn't come when I called. I guess she's having too much fun on that swing."

What she called his big flashlight was nearly a hand-held spotlight. He pointed it upward and clicked it on. Even with the lights on in the house, the flashlight threatened to blind him. *Forgot I put new batteries in it before we moved.*

Rubbing his eyes, he stormed out of the house and over to the tree.

"Alexis Nichole, you get in that house right now or so help me..."

She wasn't there.

He slapped a hand down on the plank, stopping it in mid-swing. The wood still felt warm.

"Alexis?" he whispered.

Wind gusted. Branches creaked overhead with a sound like a menacing chuckle. He swished the light back and forth. The beam sliced through darkness, but seemed reluctant to illuminate anything. He should have been able to see the house clearly, but his light fell short, offering only the barest hint of bushes underneath bedroom windows that glowed in the twilight.

The breeze dwindled and died, trailing off with a faint sigh. "Bye-bye, Daddy."

Vernon broke into a run, swinging his flashlight in wild arcs that offered glimpses of his new yard. Dashing behind the house, he barely turned in time to avoid a barbed wire fence. His foot caught on concrete stairs, and he fell against a silver beast hunkering against the fence, light skittering off to one side and landed in the grass to shine on the steps. His body draped itself over cool metal, and his head smacked down with a hollow bong.

Turning over, he slid down the propane tank and sat on the ground, his head banging the side once more. He winced at the bolt of pain that stabbed through his temples. A sob ripped free of his chest as he groped for the flashlight. His fingers brushed plastic, pushing the light away. He froze. Something glowed softly just beyond the light splashed on the wall in front of him. It looked like a pair of legs incased in white hose.

"Alexis? Honey, you scared me." A faint titter of laughter floated on the night.

He grabbed the flashlight and turned it toward her. A flurry of movement resolved itself into a crepe myrtle, its pale branches dancing in the breeze.

"Alexis! You stop this right now!"

Laughter answered him once more.

He started to turn, then jumped to face the other way at a shuddering thump. He jogged around the corner as the sound turned into a steady hum emanating from a window in the back room. He relaxed. *Why is she running one of those air conditioners? It's not hot out here. Is she trying to waste electricity?*

Light dimmed, flickered and died. Vernon shook his head. *A blown fuse?* Well, she'll have to deal with it for now. He turned the light away from the window and started back to the front porch. Maybe Alexis went this way.

Cheryl screamed as Raymond started to wail. He froze, turning his head from porch to window and back. He ventured a half-step toward the front when his wife screamed again.

Cursing, he spun on one heel and ran back to the steps. The knob turned, but the door wouldn't move when he pushed. He threw his shoulder at it, stumbling into the house as the door opened with a sharp creak. He turned his flashlight toward the TV. In his panic, Vernon thought it looked as though the darkness resisted the beam before it grudgingly parted to show his wife crouched on the floor, her body curled around the still-screaming baby. Her shirt hung tattered on her back. She sat as he approached, turning to face the light. A long scratch ran down her cheek.

"I w-w-wanted t-to see if the air conditioner worked, but when I turned it on, the lights went out." Her voice rose to a shriek. "*Something* tried to grab Ray!" Her voice cracked. She began to sob hysterically and rock back and forth.

"Sweetie, settle down. You probably just jumped when the circuit breaker tripped. There's nothing in here to grab the baby. Look, I'll go find the breaker box, and we'll get these lights back on."

She sniffed and nodded. Vernon turned and played the light along the walls. He knew that box was around here somewhere. Had he seen it in the bathroom? He took perhaps a half-dozen steps before his wife started yelling again. He whirled and pointed his light back in the corner.

This time, there was no doubt about it. Shadows visibly retreated from the light, uncoiling tendrils of darkness that retreated beyond the edges of the beam, dragging yellow and blue cloth with them. He thought he heard a faint growl. His eyes bulged. *That was Ray's baby blanket! What is going on here?*

He strode back to his wife. "Are you all right?"

She nodded and clutched at his pants leg. "You can't leave us again. Promise you won't leave us!"

"I promise," he said.

He pulled her hand free and pushed her back into a corner. He placed the flashlight on the desk and wedged it in place with the television so that the light made a pool around them. He sat next to his wife and drew his knees to his chest. Got to stay in the light, he thought. As he squirmed into place, Cheryl's head snapped up and her eyes widened in panic.

"Where's Alexis? Where's my little girl?"

"I don't know," he replied grimly. "I couldn't find her. Unless you want to go out there and look" — she whipped her head side to side in denial — "we're just going to have to hope for the best and wait 'til morning. We won't do her any good if we let whatever's out there get us."

She huddled in closer and continued rocking the baby. Ray eventually quieted and drifted off to sleep. Vernon realized Cheryl had done the same as her trembling stilled and her breathing evened. He waited several moments, then pushed her upright. Crouching, he reached out along the wall and tried to stand. Something cold and implacable grabbed his wrist and jerked him off balance. Vernon pulled back, his mouth drawn in a grimace as the grip bit into his flesh. He heaved and fell over as his watchband broke, landing on top of Cheryl, who bolted upright and grabbed his shirt.

"What are you doing? You promised you wouldn't leave!"

"I was going to try to find Alexis..."

"She's fine. You said she'd be fine until we could find her in the morning. You can't leave us here alone!"

"All right, all right," Vernon said, making gentle shushing noises. Cheryl gradually calmed and slid back into a fitful sleep.

He wrapped his arms around what remained of his family. Trying to ignore the pain in his bleeding wrist, he glared at the darkness. *I never realized how bright Houston was.* Light was everywhere in the city. Even at midnight, streetlights glowed, cars drove by and a few neighbors remained awake. But out here, light only remained while you created it. Darkness reined supreme everywhere else. Why do people always want to leave the city and come out to the country?

Vernon began to see patterns as the darkness writhed around them. It flowed like a river of night that created alien alphabets and pictures in its whirls and eddies. He even saw faces in that blackness, but looked away hurriedly, afraid of seeing a small, familiar visage looking back at him. Occasionally, tendrils of shadow ventured toward them, only to whip back from the light.

Afterward, he could never pinpoint the moment he drifted off to sleep. One minute, he was listening to the slow, steady breathing of his wife and son while gazing at the midnight kaleidoscope around them, and the next, he was jerking his cheek off his wife's hair to look at the ring of light, certain it had grown smaller while they dozed. But everyone was still here. He leaned back and gazed at Cheryl. The light created a halo around her, outlining the edges of her body in a soft glow. His eyes followed the line from her head down her shoulder to her arm, which rested on one hip that led down her leg and to her foot...

Vernon's eyes widened. Her foot was gone, slipped into the shadows.

Slowly reaching across her, he grabbed Cheryl's knee and pulled. She stirred and murmured, but didn't awake. Sweat beaded on his forehead. Her foot wouldn't budge. With a grunt of effort, he pulled as hard as he could. He caught a glimpse of her ankle before her leg snapped straight and disappeared to the calf.

Eyes popping open, Cheryl screamed. She clutched Ray, muffling his own cries against her chest. Her leg sawed back and forth, dragging her a little further into the darkness with each pass. It twisted, and she flopped over onto her belly. She started sliding faster. She extended her arms, pushing the baby toward him. Arms wrapped around his torso, Vernon shook his head in mute denial.

"Take him! Take Raymond!" She jerked back until darkness hid everything below her armpits. "Don't let it get him! Take your son!"

His gaze flickered between his wife's anguished face and the squealing infant in her outstretched hands. He unclenched one fist gripping his shirt and hesitantly reached for Raymond. She slid back to her neck, and he jerked his hand back. She kept screaming for him to take his son. Raymond squalled. Vernon started to reach out again and froze as the night claimed its prize and wrenched her from sight. Her screams cut short.

Tears screaming down his cheeks, Vernon groped in his pool of light until a tiny hand grabbed his finger. He snatched his son against his chest and rocked until Ray's cries subsided.

"You got her!" he yelled. His voice cracked. "Isn't that enough? Leave us alone!"

The darkness, apparently unmoved, and still not sated, continued its black dance, circling his illuminating shelter like coyotes circling a campfire.

They came for him just after dawn, once the sun made it safe again.

Travis Ware and a group of men, all still dressed in their Sunday finest, poured in through the open back door. They stood in silence, staring at Vernon, who sat with the sleeping infant in one hand and the weakening flashlight clutched in the other.

"There, I told you at least one of them would make it," Travis said. "Congratulations, Mr. Hamilton. You survived your first night in Jennings Grove. Few who move here do."

One of the men — the one with the sullen teenager — stepped forward, hand extended. Vernon remained motionless until the man touched him. He swung the flashlight into his nose, which collapsed with a crunch, and lifted the light above his head once more. The man clutched his ruined nose with one hand and balled the other into a fist. Travis gripped his arm.

"Now, now, Marvin, that's no way to welcome a new neighbor. I believe a little understanding is in order. Remember the state we found you in after your first night?" Marvin nodded and stepped back. "Now, Mr. Hamilton, you can put that down. It's dawn. There's nothing to harm you any more."

Vernon slowly lowered the flashlight to the floor and stood, blinking, as he gazed at the men gathered around him.

"How? Why?" his voice trailed off, but Travis seemed to understand.

"Everyone asks that, but I doubt anyone really knows. Myself, I think this is just one of those places in the world where man hasn't tamed the darkness." He shrugged. "The night has always been a source of terror. The Bible speaks of 'outer darkness;' Shakespeare mentioned a 'wild night.' Here, we see the truth of it."

"But why do you stay?"

"Why? Because it's home." He seemed genuinely shocked. "Where else would we go?"

Vernon nodded. He looked down at the boy sleeping in his arms. Home. Having lost everything else, it might be nice to at least have that. "Will I..." He swallowed. "Will I ever see my wife and daughter again?"

"Probably, but it's best to ignore them.

"Look, Mr. Hamilton, you need to clean up and get some rest. I understand you work the night shift, and tonight will be your first on the job."

He ushered all the men out and turned to shut the door. "Mr. Hamilton, we will have an official celebration tomorrow at noon —

it's so seldom we get people who can live here — but I want to be the first to welcome you to Jennings Grove."

NOTHING TO BE AFRAID OF

Dark flooded the house. No TVs flickered. No computer screens glowed. No nightlights, no closet lights, no bathroom lights. Not anymore, Daddy said. Billy was a Big Boy now. There's nothing to be afraid of.

Quiet ruled the house. No crickets sang. No radios played. No ticks, no tocks, no gentle snoring. No one sleeping with him anymore, Mommy said. Billy was a Big Boy now. There's nothing to be afraid of.

But...

What was that tap-tapping on the closet door?

What smelled like that squirrel Buster had left on the porch?

What was that tug-tugging the blanket out of Billy's hands?

There's nothing to be afraid of. Daddy said so. Mommy said so. There's nothing to...

TRICKSTERS

Author's note: *The inspiration for this story is a real runestone to be found in eastern Oklahoma near Arkansas. There are many competing theories about the meaning of the runes to be found on the large stone slab – which stands 12 feet tall, 10 feet wide and 16 inches thick – but the one favored by locals is GLOMEDAL, "Glome's Valley." They say Norse explorers crossed the Atlantic, rounded Florida into the Gulf of Mexico, up the Mississippi River, the Arkansas River and finally the Poteau River around 750 A.D.*

Glome climbed out of the battered longboat and shifted the shield strapped to his back. Chainmail offered a muffled rattle under his coat. Behind him, the longship's hull scraped over rock as his men disembarked and lifted it free of the river to rest on the stony shore. Others gathered their gear and spread out along the shore. He removed his helmet, rested one hand on the sword hilt at his side and let the late afternoon sunlight wash over his face, savoring the forest scent around them. A light dusting of snow coated the short mountains around them and glowed in the shadows under the trees. Not as much as back home, but comfortably reassuring. *If this is the heart of winter here, these old bones will appreciate the coming spring and summer,* he thought. He turned at a sudden crash and the sound of splintering wood to see a pointed rock stabbed through the hull.

A black-haired bear of a man lumbered up beside him while glaring knives a youth who stared at the injured boat and rubbed his meager beard. "Medok lost his grip." Gruff Leif looked as close to sheepish as Glome had ever seen him. "We can repair the damage, but it will take time." He glanced upward. "At least there is plenty of lumber. I will see if the boy can fell a suitable tree without causing more trouble."

"Do not hurry, Leif. We have time." His friend nodded and turned. Glome caught his arm. "Be easy with your son. He is young and has much to learn."

A bent, white-haired man scuttled between them, bowing and smoothing his curled mustache and bushy beard. Leif snorted and stomped off, slipping an axe from his belt as he went.

"Gracious and wise as ever," Alrik said in a wheedling tone. Scars cut through his beard like a river through the desert, twisting his lips so he had to speak from the corner of his mouth. He swept a hand at the rolling mountains around them. "Did I not speak the truth? Is this not a pleasant place?"

"It is, old man."

"Then you will bring the rest of your clan?"

"Perhaps."

"But..."

"I said perhaps," he snapped. "There is much to see yet."

He set his helmet back on his head and waved the old man away and hid a smile in his iron gray beard. *They will come.* His mind's eye had already felled many of these majestic trees and hewn them into a great longhouse. *Our women and children will come. We will carve our new home out of this land, and I will rule a great clan.* He'd brought two dozen of his stoutest men for this journey. In all the years since his childhood that Glome had heard Alrik speak of this place, his father's friend warned constantly of the long and dangerous journey sailing around the coast of this new land and up mighty rivers. But the strange old man spoke so expansively of the beauty here that Glome felt he must ignore his father's warnings and see it for himself. *Too bad you died without making the trip yourself, Father. You should have listened. Alrik may be mad, as you believed, but he spoke the truth in this.*

He glanced up at a sharp *thwack*. Leif towered over Medok. He spoke low enough that no words could be made out, but his voice carried as a deep growl. Leif punctuated each comment with a blow to the top of his son's head with the axe handle. He raised his hand to strike again when Medok's throat exploded, spraying his father's face with blood.

A stone arrowhead protruded from the youth's neck as he collapsed into the river. Leif roared and leapt into the boat. Arrows zipped after him, thudding into the longship or splashing away in the water. Men shouted and fell, signaling that other arrows had found their targets.

Whirling, Glome yanked his shield around and crouched with it over his head. "Get down!" he shouted. "Take cover!" He slowly backed toward his ship and scanned the darkening forest, searching for the enemy.

Men grabbed their own round shields and hunkered around the boat. Leif ignored the order, standing tall near the mast with a drawn bow in his hands. He loosed arrows as quickly as he could notch them. Others glanced at him and scrambled for their own bows. A stream of arrows disappeared into the forest. A short, clipped cry was the only response for several moments. Then a rain of deadly hail fell upon them. Stone-tipped missiles slammed home. Glome's shield and ship protected him from the arrows, but did little to avert the spray of blood that fell in a grizzly rain from all sides. More bodies splashed into the water. Leif remained untouched through the onslaught. Arrows spent, he glared and shouted at the trees.

An unearthly whoop spiraled down to the river. Glome shivered as the sound traveled up his spine.

"Dökkálfar!" someone gasped.

"Silence!" Glome hissed. "There are no dark elves here, Yngvar. I have studied the maps. This corner of Midgard is far from Svartálfaheim."

"I care not," Leif growled. He held an axe in either hand. Blood ran down his cheeks. "Elf and man bleed alike. They both die." He jumped from the boat and stalked up the shore.

"No, you fool!" Glome lurched after Leif and grabbed his elbow. He brought the shield up just in time to deflect an axe blow, then used it to knock Leif to the ground. He knelt with one knee on his chest. "I'll let that slide, old friend, but do not test my patience again."

"He was my only son!" Leif tried to rise; Glome leaned on him harder.

"I know. I helped bury Runa after she gave birth, remember?" He shook his head. "If you wish to join Medok in Valhalla, I will not stop you. But if all you want is to throw your life away, I'll kill you myself. Would you rather meet your son in Odin's hall with your hands clean or washed in his killers' blood?"

His struggles slowed, then ceased. "Very well. I will wait until I can spit in these demons' eyes and rip their guts out." Glome helped him stand. "Do you have a plan for getting us face to face with them?"

"We stay near the boat until the sun is gone. The moon has been waning for several days; night should give us all the cover we need to make it to the forest." He nodded at a heavyset man lolling against the ship. "Jorund can track any creature that ever lived in all nine worlds. If they've gone, he will find them for us."

Leif grumbled and settled back, hacking chips out of the wooden hull. Every so often, one of his men would launch an arrow into the trees. No response came. *Have they gone already?* Glome frowned and counted his men. Little more than a dozen remained. *Surely they wouldn't have given up. They killed half my men, and we haven't even seen them yet.*

A twanging chorus echoed from somewhere inside the woods. Five bright points streaked overhead and struck the longboat fore, aft and sail. The smell of pitch and burning wood assaulted his nostrils. Fire raced along the ship, eating lumber and gobbling canvas. Glome jumped into the boat with a yell and started beating out flames. Leif, Yngvar and Jorund joined him. Another wave of fire arrows lanced toward them, spreading more flame faster than they could douse it. Two men fell into the snow and lay still as their clothes burned. Glome gave a disgusted growl and waved them out of the boat.

"Gather the dead and place them on board before she burns completely."

"Where are you going?" Jorund asked, his nasal voice giving him a goose-like honk.

"To find out why any of us are still alive."

Crossing half the distance to the treeline, Glome drew his sword and clashed it on his shield. The din shattered the quiet afternoon.

"We are here!" he roared. "We do not hide like children. Come out, cowards! Come out and fight if you dare!" Silence descended as the echoes died out. He laughed. "If you have no stomach for battle, what do you want with us?"

He stood for several long, quiet moments. Crackling flames offered the only sound. He ignored the smell of roasting meat. Finally, Glome spat on the ground and sheathed his sword.

A voice spoke then, creeping from the branches ahead and the rocks to his left and right. He understood none of the alien tongue, so full of deep, melodic resonances, but the taunting tone was unmistakable. Shaking his head, he spun on his heel and turned back to his men. He danced back just in time to avoid running over Alrik. *Where did he come from?* The old man had always been like that, disappearing and reappearing at odd moments. Only on board ship had he remained in one place for long, but even then he'd been hard to find if he wished to remain hidden.

"Perhaps I can help," he said, rubbing his scarred lips. He cocked his head. "He says you provide an easy target, strutting and roaring like an enraged bear. He wonders what trick you will perform next."

"And how is it you speak their tongue, old man?" Leif demanded. He struck Alrik on the back of his head.

Alrik shrugged, his typical response to any question that touched on his past. "I must have picked it up somewhere."

"We'll discuss this later," Glome interjected. "Who is this coward who hides behind the trees?"

Clearing his throat, Alrik called out in a deep tone so unlike his normal whine that Glome's eyes widened. Laughter tinged the response. "He gives his name as Coyote. He says you amuse him and wishes to know if he may grant you a gift."

"The only thing I want from him is his head, and I plan to take that for myself."

Alrik nodded and spoke briefly. No answer came. The men looked at each other and squinted at the trees as the sun started to slip below the horizon. Finally, a sound broke the silence, the soft crunch of light footsteps on snow. An animal emerged from the trees. The gray beast looked somewhere between fox and wolf. It sat on its haunches and grinned at them with its tongue hanging from its jaws.

"A dog? Do they think to mock us?" Leif notched an arrow and fired. It burst into flame and disappeared halfway to its target.

The coyote rose on its hind legs, growing as it stood. Its hair darkened and dwindled, the limbs lengthening and thickening. Its muzzle melted. Soon a dark-skinned, dark-haired man stood before them clad in tan shirt and breeches. *No.* Glome shook his head. *This creature may wear a man's skin, but he's no man.* Coyote wore a small smile. He waved them forward and uttered a few unintelligible words, then spread his arms and vanished in a puff of smoke that raced back to the forest.

"What did he say?" Alrik stood, staring thoughtfully at the space where Coyote had stood. Glome punched his shoulder. "What did he say?"

"Come and take it at the top of the mountain, if you dare."

"We dare," Leif said.

"Do we?" Yngvar asked. "You saw that thing. We have no magic on our side, no gods to fight with us. How do we stand against such power?"

Leif snarled and turned away, but many of the remaining men nodded.

"Most wise," Alrik said. "I've heard of this Coyote, I think. He is one of these people's gods, a tricky sort like mighty Loki. Much better to leave this place and find land somewhere else, or perhaps return home." He glanced at Leif. "I'm certain your son would understand. What use in fighting a hopeless battle? Certainly, no one will think you coward."

Glome's face darkened by the word. "No!" he barked. "I came here to find a new home for our clan. I will not flee with my tail between my legs. I will give them such a battle that the poets will sing of it for generations."

Alrik bowed. "As you wish."

Nodding, Glome turned to Jorund. "Lead the way." Alrik stepped aside as if to let the other men pass before him. Glome halted him with his shield. "You go in front with him, I'll not have you disappearing when we need you to speak for us." The old man bent his neck in acquiescence and fell in line. Glome marched beside him, scanning the trees as they stepped into twilight, following a narrow trail that snaked its way up the mountainside.

Evergreens dotted the incline, but most of the trees seemed to be oaks waiting for spring to clothe them. He caught sight of color on a few, bright green bunches of mistletoe clinging to naked branches. The sight of something so familiar cheered him immensely. *If Baldr's bane can thrive here, so might we.* He turned to point it out to the men behind him and caught sight of Alrik already staring at the white berries. A snarl had etched itself into his normally placid features, and he trembled with what Glome could only call revulsion. Spittle frothed his beard as he clawed the scars on his face.

"Get moving." Leif shoved Alrik from behind, throwing his gaze back at the ground. He scrambled forward and fell into pace behind Jorund, who bent double in his climb up the slope.

Glome turned back toward the mountaintop. A flicker of motion caught his attention. His eyes narrowed. A dozen throats whooped, and the trees disgorged a host of enemies.

He fought back-to-back with Leif. His friend grunted and swung his axes in a rapid, nonstop rhythm. Every blow ended with a wet, meaty *thunk.* Glome found himself facing a tall, dark-skinned foe with bright feathers that fluttered in his black hair as he thrust a spear. Glome caught the lance on his shield and turned it aside. His sword swept up, slicing through the haft and then the attacker's throat. The man fell, gurgling and spraying blood. Glome grunted in satisfaction, grinning through the wet spray.

Pain exploded along his left ribcage, and the mail rattled under a heavy blow. He turned to see another dark-haired adversary wielding a wicked stone axe and a surprised expression.

"Weren't counting on that one, were you?" He rammed the rim of his shield into the man's face. Bone crunched under the blow, and he spat teeth into the snow. Glome lopped off the axe hand with a slash that buried his blade in his opponent's thigh. The man fell screaming with hands wrapped around his leg in a futile effort to stem the crimson tide spurting into the snow.

Breathing heavily and wincing at the pain in his side, he turned in a circle with the sword held before him. The battle had ended. Their number had been reduced to ten, but better than twice that many of the enemy lay dead. Leif limped to his side.

"They bleed a great deal. I wonder if any of them was the one who killed Medok?" He had lost his right ear; blood flowed down his cheek and stained his coat.

"There is no way to tell, old friend."

Leif nodded. He ripped a bandage from his shirt and wound it round his head. "Then we'll just have to kill more until we are certain." He sat with his back to a tree, lifted a flat stone from the ground and pulled a metal rod from his pack. He grabbed another rock and started pecking runes into the stone.

The tapping followed Glome as he walked among his men. All had sustained some sort of injury, and a couple looked barely able to stand. He doubted they would last until morning. Jorund he found laying face down with one hand wrapped around one man's throat and the other thrusting a dagger through another's jaw.

Noise nearby drew his attention. Glome turned downslope and found Yngvar gasping his last. A broken spear protruded from a ragged wound in his belly. Four lay dead around him. Glome knelt beside the wounded man and patted his shoulder. Yngvar's mouth worked, and Glome leaned in. "Dökkálfar," he whispered.

"So it would seem." Glome clasped his hand. "You fought well. I will see you again in Odin's hall, my friend." Yngvar smiled and fell still. *We may all see Valhalla before this night is done.*

He followed Leif's hammering back up the mountainside. He leaned against the tree and looked over his friend's shoulder at his handiwork. Leif had pecked his son's name into the rock.

"This stone is hard," he said. "It will hold the names of our fallen until Ragnarök."

"Add Jorund and Yngvar to your list."

A mocking voice floated down at them. Looking up, he saw someone had started a fire at the top. Leif growled and stood. "Where is Alrik?"

"Here," the old man called from further down the slope. He walked swiftly toward them, as if he moved along a flat meadow instead of climbing a rocky mountainside. Glome frowned. "The one called Coyote asked how long you planned to rest."

"I care nothing for that fool's words." Leif grabbed his shirt and slammed him into a tree. He drew an axe and held it a fingerbreadth from Alrik's wide eyes. "Where were you, old man?"

"I got out of your way. These old hands lack the strength of such a mighty warrior..." The axe chopped away a branch beside his left ear. A dangerous glint entered Alrik's eyes. "You would do well to watch yourself."

"I think I would do better to watch you. Old hands or not, your place is here with us. A battle is no time to decide to take a stroll. Next time, I'll make sure you never walk again."

"Leif, put the axe away." He glared at Glome, and Alrik smiled. "You're right; he should remain with us." Alrik's grin withered. "But this is not the time to be fighting amongst ourselves. We have another enemy up there."

He pointed up the mountain and paused. A stream of warriors headed toward them. They ran silently, hefting spears and drawing bows as they came. "They're coming again!" he shouted. "Take cover!" Men ducked behind rocks and trees. Alrik sidled away, but Glome grabbed his arm. "You stay with me." His eyes narrowed, but he followed Glome behind a boulder.

Arrows and spears skipped off the rock and thudded into trees. He glanced around the stone and saw a man try to peer past a tree, only to take an arrow in the eye. A spear skewered another hiding behind a slender pine when the shaft went through the trunk. "Hold your ground! Let them come to us!" He looked again; the missiles had stopped and the enemy was nearly upon them.

"I thought you did not hide like little children." Coyote's voice boomed down the mountain. Glome found his words oddly accented, but perfectly understandable. "Where are the mighty warriors now? My head is still attached, and yet I have taken your friends, your kin...your sons."

Alrik popped up and cupped his hands around his mouth. "Yes," he cried shrilly. "These are the devils who slew Medok. What happened to your vengeance?"

Roaring, Leif left the cover of an oak and charged. He crashed into the enemy with both axes swinging. Many fell before the horde swallowed him and silenced his battle cries.

Glome grabbed Alrik's sleeve and jerked him into the boulder. His head smacked against the rock, which cracked. Blood spilled from a small gash above his eye. Alrik shoved Glome to the ground. "Your father knew his place better than you, boy. No man lays a hand on me. You would do well to remember that." He gazed at the bonfire flickering above them. "Time to meet this Coyote for myself."

The old man straightened and walked up the mountain. The earth trembled with each step. The advancing warriors looked at his face and quailed. Those who did not run fell to the ground, convulsing and bleeding from ears and nose.

Grasping the rock, Glome climbed to his feet and gave chase, motioning for his men to stay put. Men groaned and gurgled on the ground and the very air smelled of death, but no one barred his path. He had nearly crested the top when thunder shook the very mountain, knocking Glome to his knees. He slid several feet back down the slope. Boulders rolled away to his left and right and crashed into trees, crushing living and dead alike, but he heard nothing aside from a loud ringing.

Glome crawled back upward. Sound returned as the ringing faded, leaving behind pain in his temples. He caught voices raised in argument, regained his feet and crept stealthily forward.

"...cannot allow this to continue." It took him a moment to recognize Alrik's voice, which had dropped all trace of subservience. Glome slipped around a rock and saw him circling Coyote, who matched him step for step and glare for glare. "The *jötnar wait in Utgard for me to lead them across the Bifröst bridge* and storm the gates of Valhalla."

"I know all of this, and I look forward to it as much as you," Coyote replied.

"Then return to me. We cannot cast down Asgard until I recover all the shards of myself that scattered across Midgard when I struggled free of my chains."

Coyote shook his head. "I am not ready. I find that I enjoy this new land and these people's stories that give me shape." He waved a hand. "I am not the only piece you seek. There are others in the world – Eshu, Kokopelli, Bamapana, Seth. There is still a piece of us chained to those rocks under the serpent. You must find them, as well."

"I don't know where they are. All I have are names. I found you first. And you are one of the greatest. My power will grow greatly when we join together, make it easier to find and recapture the others."

Coyote tapped a finger on his lips. "Then join with me."

"What?"

"You join with me. I cannot be our only aspect to be found in this land. Make Coyote stronger, and we will find all those who are here."

"I will not! I am Loki, not Coyote." He raised both fists. Lightning spiraled around his hands. "You will come with me." Coyote backed away, eyes narrowed and arms crossed before his chest.

Glome yelled and leapt from his hiding place. His sword whipped around, halting a hair from Alrik's throat. *No, not Alrik. Loki.* The Sly-God looked at the steel and paled. *Could he truly be so weak as to be scared of a mortal blade?* "You led us here to die for some foolish quest? Why not come yourself and leave us in peace?"

"Because I couldn't," he snapped. "I have no life, no existence outside my people. You think I would have wasted two generations with your family if I could have come on my own?"

"Then you have no life." He shifted the sword until the point rested in the hollow of Loki's throat. "This ends here."

"I agree," Coyote said from behind them.

Glome turned to see what mischief the other god might be up to. He felt an iron grip seize his arm and throw him against the edge of a huge, flat rock. His sword clattered away. Glome tumbled to the ground with his face pressed against the stone. The mountain trembled with Loki's approaching footsteps, but Glome couldn't move or feel much of anything beyond a mass of pain in his back. A hand lifted him in the air. His head lolled on his neck until Loki's familiar face came into view. Behind him, Coyote slipped forward, carrying a large tree branch.

"I told you before, no man touches me." He raised his other hand, which held Glome's sword. He thrust the blade deep into Glome's gut. He gasped at the sudden discovery he could feel more than his back. Agony tore through his abdomen. Loki dropped him to the floor, which twisted the blade further. He moaned. "Now to deal with the other..."

Coyote threw the branch spear-like at Loki's back. The wood shivered as it flew, shedding bark in favor of scales and a triangular, hissing head. The serpent coiled itself around his arms and waist and lowered open jaws over his head, dripping venom across his face. Loki screamed and thrashed. Coyote planted a foot on his chest, grabbed the snake's head with one hand and reached the other toward Loki's mouth. His arm wavered and turned hazy.

The smoke cloud drifted into the Sly-God's nostrils and parted his lips. Coyote's eyes widened. He threw his head back with a grimace, slowly dissolved and vanished. The serpent vanished. Loki coughed, rolled over and pushed himself up on his hands and knees. He saw Glome struggling to breathe and smiled. He stood and coughed into his fist.

"I would wager you thought he had me, didn't you?" Loki wiped blood from his fist onto his breeches. He coughed again and spat on the ground. Red splattered across the rock. He knelt beside Glome and lifted his head by the hair. "Before you die, I want you to know I'm going to find the last of your men and kill them. Then I will find every last member of your clan and torture them all to death. It's a pity your own wife is dead, but I believe you have children and grandchildren, do you not?"

Glome snarled and tried to move. Loki laughed. His mirth drowned in a coughing fit that bent him double, then drove him to his knees. Wide-eyed, he hacked up blood and tried to catch his breath. His face turned red, then darkened to a more natural tan. His beard fell out, and the hair on his head turned black.

"No," he whispered, staring at his darkening hands. He collapsed, coughing and shaking, and rolled away.

Glome stared at the trembling form and slid toward darkness. The god's trembling increased, and his coughs took on a higher note. It took him a moment to realize it had changed to laughter.

Coyote rolled over and lay on his side, head propped on his hand.

"Thank you for distracting him. Or should I say me?" He laughed again. "Now I can remain here for a time, until I grow bored with this new land and move on." Coyote sat up and frowned. "Loki was right about one thing, however. Your men must die. No tale of this must ever reach Asgard, not until I am strong enough to tear out Odin's other eye and wear it on a golden chain around my neck." He paused. "Still, you fought well. It is a pity no song will ever be made of it. I suppose you deserve some recognition for that."

Turning to the stone slab, the trickster jabbed his finger into the stone over and over like a mad woodpecker. Finally, he stepped back and nodded to himself. He lifted Glome gently and turned him to face the rock. There, in the runes of his people, he could read "GLOMEDAL."

"This will be Glome's Valley for all time. A weak memorial, but better than none." Coyote laid him back on the ground. "Ragnarök will come soon, I think. You've shown me what mighty warriors live here. More from your lands will come to this side of Midgard. With a little prodding, I can use these natives to create – how did the poets put it? – 'an axe age, a sword age, shields are cleft asunder, a storm age, a wolf age, before the world plunges headlong.' Yes, it will come. Yggdrasil itself will burn, and you've shown me the way."

Glome found his voice. "...will kill you..."

Coyote laughed. "I think not, old friend. You will head for Odin's hall soon."

"No...at Ragnarök...swear it by Odin's good eye..."

"I have no doubt you will try." He frowned. "And I do not like such threats. You spoil my mood, warrior. Remember this as you enter the gates of Valhalla," he said, voice bubbling as his form melted and ran, "none of your family will join you there." The voice took on a wheedling note, and Alrik stood over him once more.

"Before Coyote walks this wide land freely, Loki's last promise will be kept. Your family will die, but I will make sure every last one meets a painful end far from battle. Think on that while you feast at Odin's side."

Snarling, Glome slipped away to the sound of laughter.

AFTER, LIFE

Death. Darkness. Ralph's entire world revolved around those two things. It had always been so, and he saw no reason to believe it would ever be otherwise. And yet, he expected more. He needed more. There had to be something beyond the corpse stench, the eternal night filling everything. Hadn't there been more, once... before?

Before what? He shook his head. If this had always been, how could there be a before? Ralph hammered a fist in frustration. A muffled thud answered. *Shouldn't that hurt?* But what did it mean to hurt? Memory stirred, rose and sank beneath dark waves, offering only a bright glimpse of a brown-haired woman weeping at his side. He clutched his chest and nodded. That flare of remembered agony. That was pain.

Who was the woman?

He growled and tried to lash out. Questions provided their own pain. They droned and needled incessantly, but nothing he did could drive them away.

Something kept him from venting his anger. Every blow landed on a soft, yielding surface that boxed him in on every side. His hard-soled shoes drummed top and bottom. His fists beat a steady tattoo to either side. Even his head knocked on something when he tried to sit up. No matter how hard he struck, it failed to yield more than a soft thud. He tried to weep, but no tears came.

Vanessa cried enough for us both.

He twitched at the thought. Vanessa... was that the woman? It felt right. Another memory surfaced. The woman — Vanessa — sobbing and begging: "Don't leave me, Ralph. Never leave me."

He could hear his own voice, frail and barely audible: "I won't."

That vow burned through him. It spoke of a world beyond the darkness. It promised him more. If only he could reach her.

Roaring, Ralph rammed both feet against the top of his prison. It refused to budge. He struck it again. Again. Again. The wall creaked. He rained blow after blow until wood splintered and shattered. Flesh tore under the onslaught, but he didn't care. He felt no pain. Indeed, he felt little beyond a growing need to be out in whatever world existed beyond this box. And underneath the panic, hunger.

He found dirt. It poured inside. He clawed his way through thick, gooey earth, frantic to climb free. Hunger and alarm grew with every stroke. Vanessa's tear-streaked face filled his vision. She begged him over and over again not to leave her. She needed him. He'd promised. So he dug.

His right hand broke through first, followed by his left. He emerged and looked around. He had never dreamed of such space. A bright circle overhead spread silver light over an otherwise darkened world. Stone crucifixes and other markers surrounded him. Ralph climbed unsteadily to his feet. Now freed, hunger gnawed at him, driving him forward. His steps hurried. He stumbled over tree roots and headstones, but he had to keep moving.

Vanessa needed him. And he needed her.

PART II

We Went Mad Together

LIKE FATHER, LIKE DAUGHTER

Author's Note: *This story was part of the shared world anthology* Courting Morpheus, *where a town full of horror writers all stopped being able to sleep as their creations came to life.*

Fog crept through the farmer's market as a canary yellow LUV rolled down Main Street. A few tendrils tested the twilight air, but most of the mist seemed content to lurk among the empty benches and stalls. Squealing brakes brought the truck to a halt at the Anders Avenue traffic light. Silence descended once more, broken only by the pickup's clattering, choppy engine.

"Green would be nice," TJ McCollough muttered at the red light glowing above her. The temptation to run the stoplight was strong – she couldn't see anyone around – but Mom had always warned her about the sneaky cops of the New Bedlam Police Department. The last thing she needed right now was a traffic ticket she couldn't afford.

Looking around, TJ frowned. New Bedlam was hardly party central, but even a small town that rolled its streets up at dusk should be jumping at least a little. If not for the lights from the inn and businesses along Main, she might have thought the town deserted. She saw more people in the University of Houston library on a Friday night. Motion to the right caught her attention. She squinted, trying to make sense of the shadows frolicking in the patchy fog. *Probably high school kids out for spring break.* She rolled down the window and leaned out, squinting at the mist.

Despite its ghost-town appearance, the city was alive with an odd assortment of stealthy sounds. Whispers, snatches of conversation, footsteps and an occasional moan drifted on the breeze with the gathering mist. TJ shivered despite the warm spring air. Some of those noises sounded somehow *wrong. Get hold of yourself, girl,* she thought with a mental shake. *This has always been a creepy little town. Don't let your imagination run away with you.*

TJ had planned to stay at school over spring break and catch up on a couple of major projects. At least, that's what she told her parents. She did have a lot of homework piling up, but truth was, she didn't want to come. Dad had insisted on moving to this backwater just before her senior year of high school. He had found some wonderful haven for professional writers, a nice, out-of-the-way town where he could write in peace and network with fellow scribes. Mom had loved the idea of moving back north. Raised in Nebraska, she found the Galveston climate oppressive. Even her twin brother Horatio seemed pumped. But TJ refused to leave. She had friends in Texas she could stay with and a scholarship lined up for college. Besides, the town was just too creepy. She found herself a little overwhelmed by the star power gathered here, but the city itself was too Lovecraftian, full of old buildings, shadows and fog. And she barely recognized her family when she visited. Horatio had fallen with some Goths. Mom seemed happier than she had been in years, but her smile had an odd brittleness about it. Dad had retreated almost entirely into his work. They used to stay up late into the night discussing the horror genre and writing in general, but she could barely pry him out of his study to say hello and goodbye.

Plans of staying in Houston evaporated with her mother's call the other day. She could still hear the barely controlled panic in Mom's voice. *"It's the writer's block,"* she said. *"You've got to come, TJ. I've got to get out of here before he drives me crazy. He won't sleep. He barely eats. All he does is walk around the house yammering about darkness and making sure all the lights are on. I swear, I think if I flipped a switch off, he'd kill me. Please, TJ. Talk to him, you know, writer to writer. You've got to do something."*

The traffic light finally changed. Pushing in the clutch, TJ wrestled the transmission into first gear amid a grinding, metallic chorus. The Chevy lurched forward, threatened to die and lurched again. Cursing, she stomped down on the clutch, gunned the gas and popped her left foot free. Rear tires spun a moment before catching asphalt.

Writer to writer, she thought with a smirk. *Now that she wants something, suddenly I'm a writer.* Dad had encouraged her literary ambitions, but the best Mom managed was to tolerate them. When a major horror magazine bought her story "A Doll's Eyes" earlier in the semester, she had called them, eager to share the news. Dad wouldn't come out of his study. Horatio was at the local coffee shop. All Mom would say was, "Don't get your hopes too high, dear." That off-handed condensation kept TJ at a slow boil for weeks. When her mother called, she had nearly refused. But she had to. Her father needed her.

A wall of brownish-gray fur flashed past her headlights, jerking her back to the present. TJ slammed on the brakes, but whatever it was had already disappeared into the mist beyond. *A dog. It was just a dog,* she told herself. *But what kind of dog is that big? Why couldn't I see it any better?* Glancing upward, she saw a darkened streetlight. She turned. It looked as if maybe one of every three lights was lit. As she watched, another flickered and died.

Shuddering, TJ turned left on King Avenue, past the book and antique shops and into residential neighborhoods. Lights burned in nearly every house she passed. One particularly bright oasis glowed a little down the street on the left. She tried to count the houses. *Surely not...* Protestations died as she pulled into the driveway at 1418 King, parking where her mother's Camry normally sat. The sprawling McCollough residence had lots of windows, and every single one shone brilliantly. Rows of lights lit up the yard. *What on Earth is going on here?*

She grabbed her backpack, slid out of the truck and trotted up a gravel walkway to the front door. There she saw not every light was on; the ornate glasswork set in the door was dark. She tried the knob and found it unlocked, just as Mom had promised. TJ walked in. Light blazed everywhere except the stairway in front of her.

A glassy-eyed, gaunt figure shambled out of the shadows, pale hands outstretched. Stained, wrinkled clothing hung loosely on its frame. It moaned as it approached. TJ screamed and backed away, fumbling with her keychain, trying to find the pepper spray she kept there. It was only after she hit the wall that she realized the groans were actually words.

"Lights out. Too dark. Got to get the light back on."

"*Daddy?*"

He ignored her. Reaching overhead, he grabbed the bare bulb and quickly unscrewed it, tossed it at her and inserted a replacement. TJ hissed in pain and dropped the hot light bulb. *How long had that thing been burned out? A couple of seconds?* Light restored, her father blinked and peered at her.

"Hi, TJ. It's good to see you." He gave her an awkward hug. "I don't know where your mother's gotten to, but I could use some help checking the other lights. Do you mind?"

"Sure."

TJ followed in a daze. Every Frederick McCollough fan knew him as a tall, fat man who smiled a lot. The same picture appeared on the back of every book cover, from his early *Outer Darkness* to his latest, *The Living Night*. The last time she had seen him, he still resembled that photo, even if he didn't smile as much. *Now he looks like something out of "Dawn of the Dead."*

"Daddy, are you OK?" He didn't answer, or even pause in his constant muttering of "lights" and "dark" and something about the "end word." She opened her mouth to repeat herself when he replied.

"I'm fine, sweetie. Just... tired." He never stopped his slow, shuffling gait. "It's a lot of lights to keep up with, you know?"

Chewing on her lip, she lapsed into silence once more. He threaded a random path through the house, but he seemed determined to check every last bulb. As they wound their way from room to room, she noticed that every lampshade and light fixture had been removed. *Easier access to the bulbs*, she thought. This house — an antiquated, sprawling domicile that must have been home to generations of farmers before New Bedlam swallowed it — had been one of the few bright spots of her visits. TJ had found herself unable to contain a sense of childlike wonder at the way rooms seemed to magically appear when you were convinced you had reached the outer wall. Now, she just found it exhausting.

After they completed their circuit of the first floor and headed upstairs, TJ decided to call it a night. "I'm going to bed now. I'll see you in the morning." She grabbed his arm and pulled him into a tight hug. After a moment's hesitation, he returned the embrace. "It's good to see you, Daddy." He smiled faintly, restless eyes scanning the walls. Something about his behavior seemed oddly familiar, but she couldn't put her finger on it.

"Good night. Don't turn any lights off, OK?" He turned and resumed his inspection, calling over his shoulder: "Sleep while you can."

Frowning at the floor, she turned down a side hall and went to her room. *What's that supposed to mean?* She shut the door and slipped her boots off. *I'll ask him about it in the morning.* Backpack hit the floor with a soft thump. TJ yawned and turned toward her bed.

A hundred glinting eyes stared back at her.

She yelped and took a half-step backward. The china dolls, apparently unmoved, continued their silent gaze from atop her bed. Hand pressed to her chest, TJ gave a shaky laugh and took a deep breath.

"What are you guys doing here?" The last she had seen of them, her collection had been safely stowed in glass cabinets in the room across the hall. They were too fragile to leave out in the open like this. She grabbed a couple and carried them back to their room.

It was full of light bulbs.

Small cardboard boxes filled the room from floor to ceiling, leaving only enough space to open the door and a small path to the window.

She backed out slowly, finally understanding the depth of her mother's panic. Weight loss, muttering, checking lights over and over again — all that was worrying enough, but someone obsessed enough to buy what looked like every bulb in New Bedlam clearly wasn't going to just snap out of it.

Back in her bedroom, TJ swung the door closed, set the pair of dolls on her dresser and carefully transferred their bedmates over to join them. When that filled up, she put them on a pair of chairs. The last few went in the closet, except for Percy.

An antique German doll, Percy was a blond schoolboy given to her by her grandmother shortly before she died. He marked the beginning of her collection, which now numbered more than a hundred. Only a couple others were actual antiques, and none as old as Percy, but even the newest were worth several hundred. And they all freaked her out.

It was mostly the eyes, she thought, the way they always seemed to be staring at her. Oh, sure, they had other creepy features – their rosy cheeks and exquisite detail coupled with the ceramic sheen gave them the appearance of very small, healthy, laminated immortals. But the eyes were the worst. *Once you start collecting something, people won't ever stop giving them to you*, she thought as she placed the German doll on the nightstand. *Of course, if they hadn't, I would never have published that story.* "A Doll's Eyes" featured a teenage girl terrorized by her dolls. The idea came from a recurring nightmare she had had since childhood. She shuddered and turned Percy so he faced the wall.

Snapping the overhead light off, she climbed into bed without bothering to change her clothes and turned off the bedside lamp. Darkness didn't descend so much as hover in the corners. Light streaming in through the windows and under the door held most of the night at bay. *With all that, he'll never notice one dark room.* A yawn forced her jaws wide. TJ rolled onto her side, snuggled into her pillow and drew the covers up to her chin.

She closed her eyes.

And waited.

And tossed.

And turned.

And waited some more.

She opened her eyes.

Red numbers on the bedside clock showed the hour had reached nearly midnight. *I've been lying here three hours?* She sat up and stretched with a yawn. *It must be worry about Dad. The way he's acting would make anyone have trouble sleeping.* Her head whipped around at a soft *snick*.

The closet door swung open slowly. Shadows oozed out. The light dimmed. TJ drew the blanket to her chin with trembling hands, eyes bulging as darkness rolled across the floor. It drifted around her room like the ground fog outside, skirting the brighter patches of light. Soon it surrounded her bed and blocked the floor from sight. Then it started to rise.

It was like watching the tide come in at night, wave after wave slapping against the bed, each slightly higher than the last. *What happens when it gets to the top?* she thought, unable to tear her eyes away. *This can't be real. It's like a scene from one of Dad's books.* Hardly a comforting thought, given what usually happened to people in horror novels. The wave crested at the foot of her bed, and the dark tide started to move in. She could *feel* it moving, like a heaving quilt dragging across her blanket. *What do I do? How do you fight the dark?* She looked around, struggling to make sense of shapes in the blackness. Her gaze traced the contours on her night stand. *Of course.*

With a quick snap of her arm, she reached out and turned the lamp on.

Light spread across her room, but slowly, as if the darkness fought being pushed back. She thought she heard a faint, angry hiss. TJ bounded out of bed and rushed to the wall, flipping the switch back on. The light grew stronger. Shadows banished, she sighed with relief and went back to bed. She sat on the edge, face in her hands.

"I'm cracking up," she muttered. "I've been here a few hours, and I'm already going nuts. Insanity loves company." She giggled and clapped a hand over her mouth. Looking up, TJ found herself staring dozens of dolls in the eye. She stood once more and shut the closet door. "No way. I'm not looking at those things tonight."

She stood in the middle of the room, pondering whether or not she should turn off the light. It might make getting to sleep easier, but only if she could shake whatever delusion she had caught from her father. *Are you sure it's a delusion?* a voice whispered in the back of her mind. She wanted to tell it to shut up, but she couldn't shake the memory of the weight of those shadows sliding across her bed. *That's it; the lights stay on, even if I am going crazy.* Besides, it wasn't like it would make going to sleep that much more difficult. Her roommate kept odd hours and often stayed up well into the night studying and doing homework. TJ was used to sleeping with lights on.

Bedsprings creaked as she slid in between the sheets and rolled onto her side. A few more squeaks sounded as she struggled to find a comfortable position. She closed her eyes. It took everything she had to keep her back to the closet door. Skin crawled between her shoulders as if someone stared at her, and her ears strained to catch any sound of it opening. *Stop it! It was just the house settling. Dad always said these old pier-and-beam foundations walk around.* That little voice piped up again, reminding her that Dad had spent a great deal of money getting the foundation shored up so it wouldn't move any more. *Besides*, it whispered, *the door didn't just swing open. You heard the latch.* TJ chuckled at that. *Sure, the dark came to life and opened my closet, just like in* The Living Night. *Dad would love that one...* Her eyes snapped open.

"It can't be."

But she knew that story all too well. When the producers had started seriously talking about a movie based on her father's book, she had scrutinized it from cover to cover, trying to picture how each scene would look. The one where the shadows took the little girl had stood out more than any other. Of course, the protagonist's slow slide into madness and obsession with keeping lights on had been powerful as well. TJ's eyes widened. *No wonder Dad's weirdness seemed so familiar.*

A soft sliding sound and brief *clink* interrupted her thoughts. She bolted upright and turned toward the closet. The door remained closed. *Girl, you have got to calm down. Keep this up, and you'll be a nervous wreck by dawn.* She lay back down and rubbed her forehead. *How far off is dawn, anyway?* She looked at the clock. Percy stared back at her.

"Impossible," she whispered. A small whimper escaped her throat. One hand crept out from under the blanket and paused about halfway to the doll. *Nope. No way I'm touching that thing.* She chewed on her bottom lip. *But I don't want him staring at me all night.* She tucked the hand under her head as she pondered. It slipped inside her pillowcase. *That might work.*

She grabbed her pillow and the pillowcase with her other hand. Pulling it over her head, she started to jerk them apart, pausing every few tugs to make sure Percy hadn't moved. Once they came free, she tossed the pillow on her bed and slipped the bag over her china doll. The cloth ballooned then slowly settled over the still schoolboy. It made Percy look like some odd, floral ghost, but it was better than having him stare at her. *Unless it makes him mad.* She shook her head angrily. *Shut up, already! It's just a doll, for crying out loud.*

"Yeah, but dolls don't turn themselves around, either." She jumped at the sound of her voice. *I have got to stop talking to myself.* She lay back down and forced her eyes to close and her breathing to even. She couldn't do much about her racing heart, however. After several minutes, she allowed one eye to open. The shrouded doll hadn't moved. She opened the other eye and stared for a long time. Percy didn't move. Finally, her pulse slowed to a more normal rhythm, and her eyes drooped closed of their own accord.

She dozed fitfully, her sleep filled with vague dreams of soft whispers, bumps and clinks. At least, she hoped they were dreams. At the first of the noises, she pulled the blanket over her head clutched it hard to keep the covers from slipping off. *Got to stay under the covers*, she thought wildly. *Nothing can get you under the covers.* Her grip tightened at each sound. Tension ate at her even while she slept. Finally, as the first glimmers of dawn filtered into the room, she threw the covers back and sat up.

"Shut up!" she screamed. "Just leave me alone."

The dresser was empty. TJ glanced to her left. Percy had gone, as well. The pillowcase sat on the nightstand like a discarded grocery bag. She slipped out of bed and tiptoed over to the closet. Taking deep breath, she grabbed the knob, turned it slowly and paused. She exhaled and threw the door open in a rush, jumping back with a small scream. Empty.

"Gone." She giggled and closed the door. She turned to open the bedroom door. "They're all gone! They're all..."

A porcelain clown sat on the threshold. Bells in its hat jangled merrily.

Fists pressed to her mouth, TJ backed away. *No, no, no, no, no. It's not fair. They were all gone.* She bumped against the window. Birdsong filtered through the glass. *Outside. That's it. Outside is safe. I've got to get out!*

She lowered her fists and took a hesitant step forward. The clown didn't move. It remained still even when she rushed forward and stopped just short of the door. Keeping her eyes fixed on the doll, TJ took a large, exaggerated step over. It didn't budge. She dashed down the hall, laughing. *Free! I'm free...* Laughter dried up as she turned to look back. The clown, still in the doorway of her bedroom, had turned to face her. She fled.

Halls and doors passed in a blur as she ran, turning at random whenever dolls barred her path. Her flight eventually brought her round to the main landing. A miniature bride blocked her way, a small bouquet clutched before her and train spilling down the stairs. She could hear Dad shuffling around downstairs and the occasional squeak of a light bulb being screwed into place. TJ fell back against a door. *They're everywhere. Why on earth would people give me so many of these things? Did they want me to get caught?* Groping behind her, she found the knob and turned it. The door opened, spilling her into her father's study.

She ran around the room, looking franticly in every nook and cranny. No dolls. She relaxed and slumped into his comfortable leather office chair. TJ had not spent much time in here; Daddy always had to have one place in his house that was off limits, somewhere he could be undisturbed. It was a fairly large room, but the large desk in front of her and books filling the walls from floor to ceiling elsewhere made it feel cozy.

Turning slowly in the chair, TJ hung her head over the back and let her heavy eyelids fall halfway shut, watching blurry shapes spin by. A glowing oblong hunk of silver caught her attention. She stopped, sat up and rubbed her eyes. It was an aluminum baseball bat resting on a couple of hooks screwed into a wall plaque. Standing on her toes, she reached up and grabbed the bat. TJ ran her hands over the rubber grip, recalling her father's beaming smile as Horatio hit the winning home run in that Little League championship game. It was about the last time she could recall seeing the two together. The bat had spent years collecting dust in their garage in Galveston. Daddy must have mounted it in here when they moved.

She sat back down, propping the bat up between her crossed legs. She watched the light play over its gleaming surface while she spun around. The rest of the room faded into a blur of color. A new color suddenly joined the background as she completed another circuit. TJ stomped down, halting the chair in mid-twirl. There, on the floor, near the door, stood a pale Queen Elizabeth, a gift from Aunt Susan in England. They stared at each other for long moments. Eyes narrowing, TJ tapped her foot and sent the chair into a slow spin, stopping after one turn.

The queen stood a couple of feet closer.

Without thinking, she swung the bat. Elizabeth exploded in a cloud of ceramic dust. Her royal gown fluttered to the floor.

TJ spun around once more. The small pile of clothes remained where they had landed.

She leapt to her feet, wobbled slightly, and ran to the door. She wrenched it open and stalked toward the waiting bride. The groom had joined her. TJ grimaced and swung at the tuxedoed gentleman golf-style. Porcelain fragments rained down the stairs. She clubbed the bride directly on the head, sending up a small puff of white dust. With a primeval scream of triumph, she dashed down the stairs two at a time.

I can get out! There's nothing they can do to stop me! They're just clay.

A blond-headed schoolboy stood in front of the door.

"Out of my way, Percy." He didn't move. "I'm not kidding. I want out of this stupid house and this stupid town. I'm not going to let some little German kid stop me."

She raised the bat.

She lowered it.

He was grandma's, the only thing she ever had from her parents. She told me to take care of him. TJ lowered her head and wept. The bat clattered to the floor. She buried her hands in her face and sobbed.

Something nudged her shoe.

TJ blinked back her tears and wiped her eyes with the heels of her hands. Percy stood practically on top of her foot. With a cry of revulsion, she lashed out. The kick caught the doll in the chest and hurled it into the door. He crashed to the floor, ceramic features cracking. TJ groped around on the floor until she found the bat. She swung it high overhead and brought it crashing down onto the doll's head. She kept bashing until even the clothing lay in tatters. She jerked the front door open and stepped out on the porch. Stretching, she smiled at the sun. "Good-bye, New Bedlam. I am out of here."

She made it down two steps before another thought stopped her. *What about Daddy? He's so concerned about the lights, he'll never even notice the dolls.*

I can't leave him. Hefting the bat, she stalked back into the house and kicked the door shut. *I've got to find them all. Got to smash them. Then I can leave.*

TJ froze at the sound of the locks snapping back. After two days of this, she had learned just how sneaky the little devils could be. The first few were easy enough; they showed up whenever she turned a corner. But they soon learned to fear the bat and resorted to other tactics, moving to places she had already checked, appearing underfoot just as she turned a corner. She rubbed her sore neck. That tumble down the stairs had been rough. Still, she figured at least a third of her dolls were gone. She would get the rest of them. She had to.

The door swung open. TJ ducked into a corner and raised her bat. What was it this time?

Marguerite McCollough walked in the house, smiling and humming to herself. She held a bundle wrapped in brown paper under one arm. Mom's smile faded a bit when she saw light streaming from every socket available. When her footsteps crunched, she looked at the floor, frowning at the ceramic shards scattered everywhere. She bent down and picked up one piece bearing a bright blue eye and the end of one blond curl.

TJ turned and resumed her hunt while Dad nearly bowled Mom over as he lurched into the living room to get to a darkened lamp in the corner. "Burnt out," he muttered. "Got to get the light back on."

Frederick looked worse than ever. His skin hung off his bones, and he looked ready to fall over at the slightest touch. Only his eyes held any life, a feverish animation that darted to every corner of the room in search of any offending darkness. She glanced at the fragment in her hand.

"Frederick, what is the meaning of this?" Mom followed him out of the room, shaking the porcelain shard at his retreating back. "This was your daughter's prize position. It was her last gift from my mother. How could you smash it, and all these others?"

He turned briefly. "Wasn't me. Got to go. Talk about it later. Got to check the lights upstairs."

Ceramic pieces ground underfoot as he climbed the steps. Mom stood in the entryway in a sort of daze. She stood in TJ's path. *No time to be polite*, she thought and rushed past, knocking Mom to the floor. Her purse and brown bundle spilled on the linoleum.

"Now see here, young lady! This is my house, not a barn. I will not be treated like this."

"Can't talk now, Mom. I got to find them. I know they're hiding here somewhere." She glanced at her mother and started to step past the staircase toward the dining room, but halted suddenly and pivoted on one heel. That package she was carrying. Something about its shape disturbed her. She leveled the bat and spoke in a low, harsh voice. "What is that?"

Turning, Marguerite looked to see. A smile blossomed on her face. "It's for you, honey. I know you didn't want to come up here, and I'm sure it wasn't easy spending all this time with your father, so I thought I'd pick up something for you." She picked up the gift and started unwrapping it. "I couldn't believe it when I spotted this in an antique shop window. Your father won't be happy when he finds out how much it cost, but I just had to get it for you." Brown paper littered the floor; in her hand stood a perfect replica of Percy.

TJ's arms went limp. The bat thumped to the floor, only the small end still grasped in a weak grip. The other hand crept to her mouth. "I killed you," she whispered. Her fist tightened, and she hefted the bat. "Go away! Why won't you go away?"

Doll and hand shattered in a mist of porcelain, blood and bone. Mom screamed. She turned pleading eyes to her, mouth working soundlessly. TJ stared down impassively at her glassy eyes, those pale, delicate features. Those *porcelain* features. Her white-knuckled grip on the bat tightened even further.

"You're with *them*, aren't you? Why else would you bring one of them here?" TJ's voice took on an edge. She lifted the bat in both hands high over her head. "Got to find them all. Got to smash them."

The bat fell.

STONE HEART, VINYL FLOORS

Author's note: *This story was originally published in* Harvest Hill, *a town that exists in one of the world's thin places. Every Halloween, that barrier fades completely and horrors come to life.*

Dappled sunlight played over the gray stone house. An idling engine and birdsong were the only sounds audible in the October morning until the front door crashed open and Byron somersaulted across the concrete porch, through the arched entryway and landed on the cobblestone sidewalk. Groaning, he sat up and scooted to a nearby pillar. A metal brace on his left leg scraped against the stone. Byron dragged himself upright and turned to the still-open door.

"I need to go. Can I have it now?" No answer. He sighed. "Please?"

There was a sound like a snapping flag, and a metal crutch flew out to land on the immaculate lawn. The door slammed shut. Grimacing, Byron staggered across the sidewalk and bent down to pick it up. He slipped his left arm into the cuff and closed his fist around the rubber grip. Steady at last, he brushed off his slacks and jacket and straightened his tie as he turned to face the house.

Byron never understood why people so often called her "ugly" and "depressing," as if she were nothing more than a monochrome pile of rock. They refused to see the lovely varied shades of gray in her tile roof and the stone fitting together like a jigsaw puzzle to form the walls, chimney and wide curving windows. There was color here as well. Junipers obscured the foundation and English ivy climbed the walls. And for some reason, almost no one noticed the crown jewel — a stained-glass circle just above the porch in scarlet, cobalt, emerald and yellow. The butterfly in the window usually seemed about to take off at any moment. This morning its wings had folded and were barely visible; she was angry he planned to work late.

A car horn blared behind him. Byron ignored it. The bushes on the eastern side had gotten a bit unruly. The carpool could wait long enough for a little trimming. He started up the driveway toward a stone carriage house set at the back of the property. He favored his left leg as he walked; the fall had aggravated his knee. *That'll all be a thing of the past soon.*

The horn sounded again, several long, harsh blasts that made him stumble. He turned halfway, but kept his gaze locked on the garage. He chewed his lip. The engine revved behind him. Byron sighed and limped to the sedan. He climbed in the back seat next to Bridget, who tried to conceal a smile behind her hand.

"Old lady throw you out again?" Frank asked as he put the car in reverse to back down the long drive. Charles laughed from the passenger seat.

Byron ignored them. He didn't know why they thought he had a wife, and he didn't care. There could be no one else in his life. There was only his Butterfly.

As usual he rode in silence while the others talked around him. He watched the neighborhood's garish Halloween decorations while they chatted about ballgames and dates of the weekend just past. Finally the car reached the accounting firm of Superville & Bobbitt, located on the top floor of a historic building downtown. The four climbed out and went inside.

"See you this afternoon," Frank called from the elevator.

Byron shook his head. "I've got to work late. I'll take a cab home." Frank waved and let the door slide shut. Byron headed for the stairs. *Got to keep exercising, no matter how much it hurts.* His knee felt like a ball of fire by the time he reached the fourth floor. Gritting his teeth, he staggered to his office, ready to collapse in a chair – which he found already occupied.

A young woman wearing a black pantsuit sat at his desk peering at his laptop. She was pretty, with long curly black hair and a light tan. She might come to his chin if she stood. He noticed the digital picture frame on his desk had gone dark. The memory card poked from a reader next to the computer, and images of his house flickered across the screen. As she watched, a wild, overgrown lot became a lawn and a decaying stone house emerged from the receding greenery. Indignation drove all thoughts of pain away. Byron closed the distance to his desk in two limping strides and slapped the laptop shut.

"Can I help you?" he snapped.

She looked up, a puzzled expression on her face. "My uncle said he told you I was going to be here today."

He frowned in return. "Uncle?"

"Melvin Superville."

"He said I was supposed to train a new hire this week. You?"

"Me." Her nose and the corners of her eyes crinkled as she smiled, exposing even, white teeth. She extended a hand. "Melanie Superville."

"Byron Wise," he said, shaking her hand. "Pleased to meet you."

"Likewise." Melanie tapped the laptop with one green-painted fingernail. "Did you really do all that work yourself?"

"Most of it." He cocked an eyebrow. This was a new tact. Most simply asked why he was so obsessed.

"It's beautiful. No wonder you want to spend all your time there."

"Thank you." He eased himself down onto the desk, rubbed the tender knee and grimaced at its misshapen feel. After ten 10 years, he usually didn't notice, but he felt a mounting sense of impatience with his surgery so close. "I take it you've been talking with the rest of the staff."

She stood up and rolled the chair toward him. Byron sank into it with an appreciative grunt. "When Uncle Melvin told me I was getting a mentor, I decided to see what I could find out about who he was saddling me with." She leaned against the desk. "I've got to say, you're not what I expected."

"Meaning?"

"You're not boring." Melanie laughed. "Most accountants your age I've ever met are about as stiff and boring as a two-by-four."

"I'm not that old." He scrubbed a hand through his short gray hair, a gift from his mother's side of the family. "I'm only 46."

"Well, you've still got 20 years on me." She winked, flipped the laptop open and pointed at the screen. "But you've actually got a life."

"Boring her with your house instead of working, Wise?"

Byron jumped at the stern voice and swiveled in the chair to see a fat balding man scowling from the doorway. "No, sir, Mr. Superville. Just making a little small talk, getting to know each other." He fumbled for his crutch. "Sorry. Took the stairs this morning, and my knee's acting up."

Melvin Superville motioned him back down. "Sit, sit. Good heavens, man, we have an elevator for a reason. I can't imagine your doctor told you to kill yourself."

"Really, I'm fine, sir."

"Ever the trooper, eh, Wise? Good. Hate to think we were considering a slacker for management."

Byron's mouth worked without a sound. Melvin laughed and clapped him on the shoulder. "We'll talk about it on the first. I assume you're taking tomorrow off, as always." He waddled off.

Byron sat still. *Me? A manager?* He'd never considered the possibility. Once he had blown all his money on Butterfly, it had been something of a minor miracle to find a decent accounting firm in a town the size of Harvest Hill. In such a small town, he figured the local boys would be the ones to get promoted. Not that he'd complain; the money that came with a promotion would come in handy. Butterfly always needed attention, and he wouldn't have much free income for a while after the knee replacement.

Melanie poked him on the shoulder. "Congratulations."

"Thanks."

He spent the morning showing her the office layout and procedures and introducing her to the staff. Noon rolled around by the time they'd finished, and Melanie went out to lunch while Byron ate at his desk. He'd nearly finished his sandwich when an e-mail came through. His pulse quickened when he saw the IP address. *What does Butterfly want? Has she forgiven me?*

Two webcam photos popped up on his screen. The first showed the kitchen. Unidentifiable chunks floated in pinkish-gray water in the sink. In the other picture, paint peeled in long strips from the walls and ceiling of the living room. *She's still not happy, but at least I know how to make it up to her.* He had been getting tired of the white walls anyway. He glanced at the photograph. *I guess we both were.*

Melanie returned soon, and he spent the rest of the afternoon watching the clock and his new protégé prepare taxes for a local upholstery shop. He offered a few comments, but not many. She proved a fast learner and even offered a couple of suggestions of her own. As she poured over paperwork, he looked at his watch again. It was half-past 6. He looked up to find Melanie grinning at him.

"Got a hot date?"

He shook his head. "Just need to go to the hardware store to get a couple of things on the way home. I need to call a cab to make it before they close."

"Oh, don't do that. I've got a pickup; let me take you."

"I don't want to be a bother."

"Please. I just moved here. All I've got to look forward to is unpacking boxes and warming something in the microwave." She pointed to the digital frame with its rotating pictures. "Besides, I'd really love to see that house."

He hesitated. He wasn't sure how Butterfly would react to unannounced company. But Melanie seemed so sincere; he couldn't remember the last time someone had shown that much interest. "I suppose it wouldn't hurt."

"Yay." She bounced on her toes, clapping softly. Byron grinned, grabbed his crutch and motioned for her to lead the way.

They rode the elevator down and strode through the lobby into the parking lot, where Byron waited beside a battered white Nissan pickup while Melanie dug keys from her tan leather purse. He offered directions, but otherwise rode in silence. He tapped an irregular beat on the leg brace and watched the town slide by. *What color would she like for the living room?* He thought a light blue might be nice, but Butterfly often had her own ideas.

Squeaking brakes derailed his train of thought as they came to a stop outside the store. Byron climbed out and walked inside, Melanie in tow. A bell dinged overhead and the rubber tip of his crutch squeaked on worn linoleum as they entered. He smiled at the smell of old paint and sawdust. One of those jewels only found in small towns like Harvest Hill, Dixon's Hardware & Lumber had been good to Butterfly over the years. A short gray-headed man emerged from behind a counter and approached with a warm smile.

"Hey, Mr. Wise!" he said. "Who's your friend?"

"Tom Dixon, meet Melanie Superville. She's a new employee at the office."

"And a real looker, too." Tom shook her hand and offered a wolf whistle. Melanie blushed. "I was starting to get a little worried about you, Mr. Wise. Haven't seen you in a couple of weeks, thought you might have finally decided that house of yours was finished."

"There's always something to do with Butterfly, Mr. Dixon. I've just been kind of busy lately."

"I know how it is." He nodded. "What can I do for you today?"

"I need to buy a few paint samples and the biggest garbage disposal you've got."

"You already tore up that one-horsepower job you bought last year?"

"Apparently so."

Tom scratched his head, brow furrowed in thought. Then the lines eased and his face brightened. "I got just the thing." He scurried off into the store's dim recesses.

Melanie turned to Byron. "I've been meaning to ask — 'Butterfly'?"

"I named her for the stained glass window above the porch." He ducked his head and scuffed the floor with the tip of one loafer. "When I found her, she was falling apart — you saw the photos — but she's overcome all that to become something beautiful, like a butterfly emerging from its cocoon."

Face flushing, Byron turned to the colored cards showing what sorts of paint Tom had available. Melanie joined him without a word. She scanned the rack and now and then handed him a card. Byron had a half dozen in his hand by the time Tom returned with a cart carrying a large box. He wheeled it next to the counter and wiped his brow.

"Anything tears this baby up, and I'll eat it," he said.

"What is that?" Melanie asked.

"It's a commercial disposal. Guy from a new restaurant ordered it last month and went out of business before he could pick it up." He thumped the box. "This thing's got a 10-horsepower induction motor. Get a big enough drain, and you could probably run a horse through it, bones and all." He pointed to an illustration on one corner of the box. "Got to warn you, though — it's got its own water flow system. You're going to have to install some new pipes and wire up the controls."

"That's fine. I've done that kind of work before," Byron said and held up the cards, fanning out shades of blue, green, rose, white, orange and yellow. "I'd like small cans of these, please." Tom took the cards and led Byron to a paint mixer in the back.

Melanie leaned in and spoke in a conspiratorial whisper. "You know, you could just take those cards home. They're free."

"You never know how it'll look on the wall by those things." Byron shook his head. "I want to make sure it's perfect before I paint an entire room."

They caught up with Tom at the mixer. He pulled each finished can off the machine, tapped it shut with a mallet and handed it over.

"Thanks," Byron said as he paid for the items. "I'll stop by in a couple of days to let you know which one I'm going to need." Tom nodded and waved.

Melanie hauled the cart to her pickup and manhandled the box into the bed. Byron sat in the cab and placed the bag of paint cans on the floor. Melanie slid into the driver's seat.

"Tell you what, neither one of us has much planned tonight, it seems. Why don't you let me take you out to dinner?"

"I can't. I need to get to work on this stuff."

"Tonight? You don't waste any time, do you?"

"There's always so much to do for Butterfly, I hate to let things slip."

"Alright, but I'm not taking 'no' for an answer. This is just a rain check."

He laughed. "You got it."

They talked as Melanie drove through town. His end of the conversation died as they approached Church Street and turned onto his driveway.

Melanie grinned at him. "What, no decorations?"

"They're ugly. Besides, I don't encourage company this time of year." He shrugged and fell silent.

She looked at him with a cocked eyebrow and stopped next to the house, dark except for a light burning in the entryway. Staring, Melanie killed the engine. She leaned on the steering wheel and let out a low whistle. "The pictures didn't do it justice. You've done some great work here."

"Thanks." Byron smiled. She grinned back and opened her door. He grabbed the bag and climbed out.

By the time he got around the pickup, Melanie had lifted the garbage disposal and headed for the door. She moved quickly despite her burden and soon disappeared beneath the arch. He caught up with her in the entryway. Melanie set the box down and leaned against the door. The light flickered overhead.

Byron shook his head. He should have known better. "I'll take it from here."

"You sure? I was kind of hoping to see the inside."

"I'd really like that." The light flickered again, buzzing like an agitated bee. He put a hand behind her back and nudged her back the driveway. "But not tonight. I've got a lot of cleaning to do. I want your first sight of Butterfly to be perfect."

"Okay, Byron, but remember: You promised." She leaned over and kissed his cheek. The light overhead flared and died with a loud *pop.* "You really need to look at that."

Byron watched her walk away, one hand on his cheek. He stood there even after the Nissan disappeared down the street. The doorbell sounded behind him. He jumped, shook his head and turned to the door. It opened, but he hesitated on the threshold, left hand twisting the grip on his crutch while the other bounced the keys. Cold air flowed from the darkened interior.

"I decided to come home early." The sound fell flat. "I've got some paint samples and a new disposal." A light came on somewhere toward the back of the house. "She's just a girl from work. The boss asked me to help train her this week." Another light flipped on at the top of the stairs in front of him. "Look, I'm sorry. I should have talked to you first. It won't happen again. I promise. Can I come in?"

Lights sprang to life all over the house, reflecting in polished oak floors. A long runner slid down the wooden steps to the front door and rose to face level. He flinched. She'd used that same rug to throw him out this morning. It snapped, popping his face with the tassels, then folded over to caress his cheek. Byron tilted his head into its weave. She always did grow more frisky around Halloween.

"It's good to be home." A length of the rug wrapped itself around the box and dragged it into the house as Byron stepped inside. The door closed behind him. Having deposited the box in the kitchen, the rug snaked back up the stairs. He tossed his jacket on the nearest step. "What do you say we get to work?"

The room shuddered. Flakes of paint fell from the walls and ceiling like so much dandruff. He pulled a vacuum from a closet under the backside of the stairway and set about cleaning paint from the floor and furniture. Chairs and tables tilted themselves out of the way, sometimes barking a shin or thudding into his hip. Byron smiled and shook his head. If Butterfly wanted to let him know he hadn't quite worked his way back into her good graces, that was fine. He always got there again. Once he finished, the furniture walked to the center of the room. The leather couch bumped into his back, sending Byron into the wall.

He stood there for a few minutes and waited for his knee to stop throbbing. When he could move again, he hobbled to the closet and opened a second, smaller door in the back. He used his crutch to hook a large bundle of paint-splattered plastic. Working awkwardly, he draped the sheet over the furniture and floor.

Byron pried the lid off the first small can, exposing lime green. He slung paint across the nearest wall. The color ran and disappeared as it absorbed into the plaster. He repeated the process five more times, ending with a pearlescent rose.

"I'll leave you to think about that while I get started in the kitchen. Could you cut the water off for me?" The doorbell rang in response. "Thanks."

He went into the kitchen, shoes squeaking on yellow vinyl. A putrid smell slapped him in the face, making him gag. One hand over his mouth, Byron pulled a strainer from an overhead cabinet and fished the solid chunks out of the sink. It appeared to be meat and small white pieces he couldn't identify, along with an occasional patch of gray hair. Byron dumped the mess in the trashcan in the utility room. He found his toolbox, set it inside a bucket and dragged it back to the kitchen.

Byron opened the box, pulled out sections of pipe and laid them on the floor. Electrical components went on the counter. He wrestled the garbage disposal near the sink. Then he lowered himself to the floor and opened the cabinet doors. He set his toolbox on the floor and shoved the bucket under the piping.

A few quick turns with his pipe wrench loosened the J-trap. Foul water rushed down the pipes and into the bucket. He turned the trap over and tapped it on the side of the pail. What fell out looked like hair and ground meat, with more white chunks mixed in. *Is that bone?* He lifted a shaking hand to the disposal and worked the pipes loose, followed by the ring that held it to the sink.

His trembling increased as he worked. By the time he got the disposal free, he just could hold it still. He had lowered it about halfway when it slipped from his hands and crashed to the floor. A gray oblong shape fell free, squelching as it bounced and landed on his pants. Byron yelled and jerked his leg, trying to get it free.

It was a rat's head, eyes bulging and its teeth bared in an agonized snarl. Its neck ended in a ragged, bloody stump.

The head fell from his lap as he leaned over and vomited into the bucket. His abdomen heaved until it ached, and then he fell back against the cabinets. He reached up and felt in the sink for the strainer. He scooped up the grizzly ball and dropped it, strainer and all, into the bucket. Byron grabbed the countertop and leveraged himself back to his feet. *I'll be glad when I can just stand up again.* Panting, he slid his arm into the crutch and grabbed the bucket. He hauled it out to the back yard and dumped the contents near a tree. He set the bucket on the patio on his way back inside.

Shuddering, Byron shoved the old disposal away with his crutch, lowered himself to the floor and grabbed his tools. Butterfly still needed the new one.

He worked through the night, installing pipes and electronics. It wasn't until the sun's first rays touched the Formica countertop that he had everything done. Byron looked over the new assortment of gadgets and pipes leading to what looked like a small barrel mounted underneath the sink. The instructions said the control system made sure the disposal had enough water at all times.

Byron looked around the kitchen. *I really need to get this mess cleaned up.* He yawned and leaned back against a cabinet. *I'll do it in a minute.*

He awoke to someone prodding his shoulder.

"Wow. You're a mess. Why didn't you just call a plumber?"

"I don't like anyone touching her," Byron mumbled and groaned at the pain in his neck. "What?" He blinked and tried to focus on the shadow above him. "What time is it?"

"Nearly 4:30." It was a woman's voice filled with amusement. "You sure know how to party, don't you?" The face came into focus.

"Melanie?" She wore jeans and a T-shirt. As he struggled to rise, she put her hands under his arms and pulled. He leaned back against the counter and grabbed his crutch. "What are you doing here?"

"You didn't show up for work today. I got worried. No one else seemed too concerned, but I wanted to check on you."

"I always take off on Halloween. It's a good day to spend with Butterfly." He trailed off. "Did you say 4:30?" *I've lost the entire day!*

"I did." She smiled again. "Don't think you're going to get out of taking me to dinner just because you slept through your day off. So go get cleaned up. And while you're at it, you can tell me why there's a smiley face and a bunch of frowny faces on the wall in there." She jerked a thumb over her shoulder.

He shambled to the living room. A large rose-colored circle had appeared on the left-hand wall, beaming at him with white eyes and a smiling mouth. On the right, a series of frowning circles showed Butterfly's displeasure with his other color choices. "It's just a way to let me know which one works best."

"Pink? I think the blue would look better. But, hey, it's your house." She shrugged and nudged his shoulder. "What about that dinner?"

"Yeah, sure thing. Just let me take a shower."

Byron picked up his jacket on his way up the stairs. He stopped when the master bedroom wouldn't open. He hit the door with his shoulder and earned himself a bruise, but it refused to budge.

"Come on, Butterfly," he whispered. "I'm just going to go out, grab a bite to eat and get the paint so I can finish the living room tonight. I won't be gone more than a couple of hours." He pushed. The door opened a crack before slamming shut. "Don't be like this. Please? Look, she's the boss's niece. If I don't go, it could create problems at work. I can't take care of you without a job. That's all I want. I love you." Hinges creaked as the door opened.

In the bedroom, he stripped off his soiled clothes and tossed them on the floor. He brushed his teeth and shaved in cold water. Nothing came out of the hot tap. *Should have known she'd find some way to let me know she's not happy.* He limped to the shower and sat in the chair he had installed there. Bracing himself, he shut the door and turned on the water. A frigid blast hit him in the face. Byron let out a small yelp and washed with haste. He dried and dressed even faster, still shivering as he limped down the stairs. He stopped at the bottom and tucked his green shirt into his jeans.

Melanie stood in the living room, arranging a paint roller, brushes and tray on the floor. She straightened at the sound of his crutch hitting the plastic sheet. "I was putting your tools up and spotted the paint stuff in the utility room. I kind of figured this was what you'd be doing next."

"I appreciate that."

"I also checked out your new garbage disposal."

"You what?" He hurried across the plastic-covered floor, slipping and staggering his way to the kitchen. "I haven't had a chance to double-check the fittings yet."

"Man, you need to chill before you blow a gasket. I just dropped a couple of potatoes in there. Worked like a champ." Melanie giggled. "That thing chewed them up without even slowing down. I think the guy at the hardware store was right."

"Glad to hear it." He peered under the sink. No signs of water leaking. In fact the kitchen looked spotless. "Did you mop in here?"

"No. I just ran a rag over the counters. Why?"

"Oh, nothing." He smiled. Even with her little tantrums, Butterfly liked to look her best for company. "Nice work," he whispered to the ceiling. The light fixture blinked. He walked back into the living room. "Shall we go?"

She drove them back to Dixon's, where he purchased five cans of the pink paint. Then he directed her to a small Mexican restaurant just off downtown.

Melanie let him order for both of them. She talked about college and her dreams of establishing her own CPA firm one day. Byron told her how he'd bought Butterfly off the delinquent tax rolls and lived in a tent on the lot for two years before the house was habitable.

"That was about the time I got hurt," he said, touching the leg brace. "Today's the anniversary, in fact."

"What happened?"

"I hired a contractor to install the tile roof. Once they were gone, I climbed up on the roof to check it out for myself because..." He trailed off, embarrassed. He'd never discussed this with anyone.

"Because you don't like anyone else touching her." She gripped his hand. "I get it. There's a reason they call it a labor of love."

"Thanks," he mumbled, staring at their hands. His cheeks burned. *She understands! How many people just call me crazy?* "Anyway, it had just rained, and the roof was slick. I slid off and hit the driveway. Destroyed the knee. Doctor said I needed a complete replacement."

"Wouldn't the insurance cover it? I thought the company had decent coverage."

"We do, but I'd opted out at the time. I hardly ever got sick, and Butterfly took every spare cent I had." His lips twisted in a crooked smile. "I signed up after that, but by then it was a pre-existing condition."

"So you just have to live with it?"

"Not anymore," he said. Leaning forward, he continued in a whisper: "I've saved up the money. I go in for surgery next week."

"You saved enough money for a knee replacement? What is that? Ten grand?"

"Twenty-five, actually — had to set aside some for physical therapy, too." He frowned. "I hated doing it. There's so many things I need to do for her."

"Yes, but think of how much more you can get done if you're healthy." She lifted his chin until their eyes locked. She gave him an intimate smile. "Besides, not everything has to revolve around that house. I know it's important to you, but you're important, too."

A clearing throat interrupted them. Byron looked up at the waiter holding out their check, cheeks heating. Melanie kept her gaze on him, and that made him flush even harder. He stammered a thank you and handed the waiter a credit card.

"Look, I really need to get home. I've got work to do, and it's probably going to take all night."

"I know."

He started. "You do?"

She laughed. "Why else would you buy all that paint? I already told Uncle Melvin that you would probably be out tomorrow. He didn't seem surprised." She grabbed her purse. "I'm going to help."

"Are you sure?" Byron felt torn. Melanie seemed so enthusiastic, totally unlike anyone he'd met. But this was Butterfly. This time of year was their special time. "I mean, it's late, and painting's hardly the most enjoyable thing in the world."

"Oh, I don't know. I find anything can be fun with the right company." She slid out of the booth and stepped around the waiter returning his card. "Coming?"

"You're not going to let this go, are you?"

"Nope."

"Then I guess I don't really have any choice."

"Great!" She extended a hand and helped him to his feet. He held it until they reached her truck.

Byron leaned back in the seat and closed his eyes. He grinned in the dark cab. He never thought he'd meet someone like Melanie. *Take it easy. You just met. It might not work out.* Perhaps, but if one person could come to love Butterfly, then another could. She would come around. She loved him; she would want him to be happy. Surely she hadn't saved his life just to hold him all to herself.

His knee ached at that memory. He had no idea how long he had lain in the driveway, unable to move or even think beyond the blinding pain. No one knew where he was. Sometime in the middle of the day, Byron figured the end had come. He closed his eyes and whispered his affection for Butterfly and an apology for failing to finish their work. He woke up in the hospital. All they could tell him was 911 had received a call about noon. No one had said anything on his end, but the open line allowed them to get a fix on his address. "You got some friendly ghosts living there, pal," one of the officers had told him.

"Wake up. We're here!"

He sat up. "I wasn't asleep. Just reminiscing."

"Care to share?"

"Some other time, perhaps." He opened the door and leveraged himself out of the pickup. "Let's paint."

They walked up the cobblestone path to the front door. He inserted the key in the lock, but it didn't want to turn. "Don't do this to me."

He thumped his head against the door and tried again. He strained until the tumblers snapped into place. Even then, the heavy door fought his entrance. Melanie put her shoulder to the wood and helped shove. It opened grudgingly, and they fell inside. Byron sprawled on the stairs while Melanie caught herself on the doorframe. She flipped the lights on and stood there, panting. "You might want to look at that door."

Squeaking hinges offered the briefest of warnings. Byron lunged for Melanie's hand and jerked her to the stairs just as the door slammed shut. She looked at him with wide eyes. "That was creepy."

He forced a weak laugh. "Welcome to the joys of an old house."

She stood and offered him a hand as he struggled to regain his feet. Byron waved her away. Using the crutch and banister, he pulled himself upright, overbalanced and bumped his head into the door facing.

"That hurt just to watch," Melanie said. "No wonder you've been squirreling away money for that operation."

Byron put a finger to his lips and tried to shush her. As she finished talking, every light in the room flared and winked out. Water started running in the kitchen, followed by a series of pops.

"What on Earth?" Head cocked, Melanie picked her way across the living room.

Byron followed, whispering over and over, "Don't, Butterfly, please."

The vinyl had pulled free of the floor, curling at the edges with bubbles rising and falling across the room like a pot set to boil. Melanie turned to him with wide eyes. "What's going on here?"

"She's upset."

"She who?"

"Butterfly."

Something slammed into them from behind. Melanie staggered forward. Byron fell. He rolled over and tried to stand, but the couch had pinned his crutch to the wall. The metal shaft bent at a sharp angle. He wrenched his arm free, grabbed the wall and climbed to his feet. Walking proved impossible. Every time he moved his foot, the roiling floor threw him back against the wall.

Melanie staggered across the kitchen, arms wheeling as she struggled to stay upright. She stumbled past the refrigerator. The door flew open and hit her in the back, and that sent her headlong into the sink. She placed one hand on the edge and one in the basin to push herself upright.

"What do you want?" she screamed at the ceiling.

Byron heard a sudden whirr, a click and water rushing underneath. The sprayer whipped out and wrapped itself around Melanie's arm in the sink. The hose tightened and drew her hand toward the hole where the garbage disposal waited.

"NO!" She tried to pull away. "I'll leave. I'll go right now and never come back. I promise. Please! Please! Pl—"

Her words cut off to a shriek as her hand dropped into the drain. Blood splattered her face, the counter and surrounding cabinets. Melanie shrieked and thrashed as more of her arm disappeared. Then she fell quiet. The floor stilled. Soon the only sounds were the grinding disposal and Byron's whimpers.

Color drained from Melanie's face and she slumped forward. The sink distended to catch her, the drain widening to incredible proportions. *You can run anything through it with a wide enough drain,* Tom said. The disposal ran like a champ until her foot disappeared.

"Butterfly, how could you? She cared about me. About us..."

He frowned. What had she said at the end? *I'll go right now and never come back.* He shook his head. If she had *really* loved them, nothing could have made her leave. Just like Butterfly. He patted the wall and looked around the room. The surgery could wait. All he really needed was a new crutch. Butterfly needed a lot more. Tonight he'd get the bleach and clean this mess. Tomorrow he would go and order some new granite countertops and tile flooring. He'd do the work himself. He couldn't trust anyone else to do it right.

Byron nodded. There could be no one else.

There was only his Butterfly.

PERFECT CLASS

Author's Note: *"Perfect Class" was to appear in* Dead Bells, *an anthology where Earth's few survivors wake up one morning to find that everyone else has been mummified overnight. The anthology hit a few snags and got canceled, but I was too proud of the results to let them fade entirely.*

Squinting in the candlelight, Aaron Parker wiped the fog of his breath off the mirror and scraped the few last white streaks of shaving cream off his upper lip. He plucked a rag from the bucket beside his sink and wiped his face clean. He yelped as the frigid washcloth hit his raw skin, driving away the last vestiges of sleep that had fuzzed his brain since he awoke half an hour earlier. He stared at his reflection. He'd never had much spare flesh to speak of, but if he lost too much more, he would be down to bare bone. His bald head gleamed softly as it rose above a fringe of hair that was more salt than pepper these days.

"I need to fatten you up, son," he muttered and tossed the rag back in the bucket. It slapped the water, and ice rattled against the plastic sides. "Guess we need to find a warmer place to hang out for the winter, too." *Dee's not going to like that. She always hated moving.* He buttoned up his shirt. His cold fingers fumbled with the top button. He growled at it until it slipped through the hole. *Oh, well. That's life. We have to just deal with it as it comes.*

Aaron walked out the bathroom and down a short hall into the small apartment's only bedroom. He opened the closet, revealing rows of pressed, white shirts lined up on wire hangers. Black suits hung along the other side like giant bats roosting alongside a rack of bowties. He fingered the ties a moment before drawing out a clip-on with a grimace. He hated those things; it felt like cheating. *Why'd the electricity have to go out? I could tie a proper bowtie if my fingers hadn't gone numb.* Still, it was a small price to pay for what had become a nearly perfect world. He glanced at his wrist. "Holy cow, I'm going to be late!"

Hooking the clasp around his throat, Aaron straightened the bowtie and quickly flipped his collar down, smoothing it as he scurried out the door, through the living room and into the kitchen. A thin woman dressed in a faded, threadbare yellow bathrobe sat motionless at the table. She kept her back to him, her gaze fixed on the rising sun outside the window. Aaron smoothed his wife's dull, brittle hair and planted a kiss on her dry, leathery cheek.

"Good morning, honey." His breath fogged the air around her ear. No response. But then, there hadn't been since the first of the year. *At least she's not nagging me anymore.* Aaron chuckled. *Dee'll come around. She can't give me the cold shoulder forever.* "Don't worry about breakfast. I'm running late for work. I've got to go." She offered no sign of movement as he straightened as he walked to the front door. He picked a coat up off the couch, bent down to retrieve a satchel beside the door and walked out. Her eyes remained fixed on the horizon even when the door slammed behind her husband.

Cold air slapped him in the face in the apartment building's stairwell. It swirled around his head and slipped down the collar of his coat. Aaron shivered and hurried down the stairs, dodging an oak tree branch poking through the window on the second-floor landing. Paris got cold in the winter, but this one had been particularly harsh. The small northeast Texas town had already braved one ice storm between Christmas and New Year when a second hit within the last week — just in time for the power to fail. *So much has changed since the year rolled over. We lost all our electricity. Dee's stopped nagging me.* He shook his head, uncertain whether to be relieved or worried about his wife's silence. *Surely everything's fine. She's tired the cold shoulder before.* A voice yammered for attention in the back of his head, trying to tell him that everything was *not* fine, no one sat at the table without talking for a week. Aaron ignored the voice and forced it down. It went easily enough; he'd had a lot of practice in the last few days.

Once outside, Aaron dug in his pockets for a set of unfamiliar keys. His gloved hands slipped on the ring, but managed to snag the key fob and drew it out. He paused, listening to the silence. No people yelling. No stereos blaring. No cars zooming down the street. Nothing but wind and the occasional rattle as an animal found something interesting in a garbage can. *Perfect,* he thought and gazed out at the parking lot. *It was a Suburban. Red, wasn't it?* Not that that did much good. At least six sat out there. He sniffed and winced as cold bit into his nose. Pointing the black plastic rectangle out at the packed parking lot and pushed a large, red exclamation point. Lights flashed on a large SUV three rows in, and the horn started blaring. He shuffled off the sidewalk, punching the button again as he headed toward the vehicle. He breathed a thankful sigh as the noise cut off. It took much longer for the calm feeling to return.

Climbing inside the roomy cab did little to lift Aaron's mood. The engine roared to life on the first try, and the heater warmed up after only a few minutes — both drastic improvements over his old car. But he couldn't help a wistful glance out at the vintage Super Beetle encased in ice near the edge of the parking lot. He had bought the car new when he first started teaching high school English, back when he had still thought it possible to have a perfect class free of all the heathens and hooligans he'd been forced to put up with since. *Why is it so hard to find students who will sit still, be quite and actually listen? More than thirty years doing this, and I doubt I've found a classroom full all told. Just a bunch of big, loud idiots.* Aaron thumped the steering wheel in frustration. *Just like this thing.*

He tried to drive his Bug for a day or two, but the clogged streets allowed only limited progress. It was as if the people who had double and triple parked their cars the night before had never come down to move them. Route after route proved impassible. So Aaron parked the Volkswagen and wandered around the cars outside. Most were locked. He had nearly given up when he found this Suburban, which had belonged to the apartment manager, not only open but with the keys still in the ignition. With the SUV, Aaron could shove smaller cars aside and tow larger ones out of the way. He could also watch the gas needle creep a little further toward empty with every trip. It currently stood at about an eighth of a tank. *I'm going to have siphon some gas out of the other cars again.* He shuddered and spat on the floor. He could still smell the fumes, taste the cold liquid hitting his mouth and face. He had thought he would never get the stink out off his skin despite several icy baths.

Turning left on Southeast 10th Street, Aaron pulled up next to an old, red house and put the transmission in park. He checked a list of handwritten addresses on the seat beside him. All but this one had checkmarks beside them. *Five oh one. That's it. My last stop.* He'd been putting this one off, but he couldn't anymore. All his other students were accounted for. He glanced at his watch. School would start in half an hour. *Time to get to it.* Aaron slid out of the driver's seat, gasping in shock as the cold air slapped him in the face. *You would think I'd be used to it by now.* He walked to the back of the vehicle, opened the liftgate and shuffled up the sidewalk. Ice made the wooden steps treacherous, but he managed to climb them with one hand on the nearest post. Once he was sure of his footing on the porch, he checked the doorknob. Unlocked. *One less thing to worry about, anyway.* He took a deep breath, turned the knob and opened the door. The house gasped a puff of stale air. The smell was just like all the other houses he had visited: cold and stale with a hint of something that reminded him of parchment or old paper. Aaron left the door open; he'd be headed back out in a few minutes.

A man and woman sat on the couch, dried husks huddled under a blanket with their faces toward the TV. Aaron ignored them. He wasn't interested in Cynthia's parents. He made a quick circuit of the downstairs, darting through the frigid den, dining room and kitchen before taking a quick, reluctant peek into the bathroom. All empty. He glanced up the stairs and sighed. *Figures she'd be up there. How on earth did she manage?* The stairway didn't look wide enough to accommodate her bulk. *Maybe she went up sideways or something.* Another sigh, and he trudged up the stairs. He glanced in a couple of empty rooms and hurried on. A look at his watch showed he only had twenty minutes to get to school. The third door showed him what he was looking for.

Cynthia sat on her bed, dressed as if for a party. Lipstick and eyeliner stood out on her leathery features like clown makeup. Aaron shook his head sadly. She'd probably been up here watching the ball drop on New Year's Eve and drifted off while waiting for the phone beside her pink-ruffled bed to ring. Easily twice as large as any of her classmates, she'd never been one of the popular students even though she was one of the sweetest girls he'd ever met. She did tend to keep to herself most of the time. *Not that that made her any smaller.* Aaron mentally berated himself for the unkind thought, but the facts wouldn't change. He had put this one off because he wasn't sure how he was going to get her into the Suburban and to school. He walked to the bed and looked down. *Can't put it off any longer.* He squatted, put one arm under her knees and the other around most of her waist. Muttering under his breath, Aaron braced his legs and closed his eyes in anticipation of the effort to come. A deep breath, and he heaved. And nearly fell over.

It was like hefting a large rock only to find it made of Styrofoam. He staggered under the lack of weight, trying to regain his balance and maintain his grip. Aaron backed against a wall and stood there while his equilibrium recovered. He looked at the still figure in his arms and smiled. "Finally lost some weight? Good for you!" He patted her waist awkwardly with a sound like someone smacking a sack full of leaves. Cynthia made no response. He shrugged and manhandled her out of the room.

The stairs proved the trickiest part. Cynthia was a great deal lighter than she had been, but still heavier than any of the others. They had been proved no more difficult than shifting foam mannequins. He figured this girl weighed about the same as the desks in his classroom — not really heavy compared with most furniture, but awkward and hard to move around. He stepped out on the porch, tread softly down the stairs, then slipped and slid his way down the sidewalk to the SUV. His breath came in harsh, painful gasps of icy air by the time he made it to the curb. After supporting him through so much, Aaron's footing finally betrayed him as he stepped down onto the street. He stumbled and managed to half-lurch, half-fall onto the Suburban. Cynthia tumbled into the vehicle, jarring to a halt against the back seat.

Panting, Aaron scrambled inside and checked to make sure she hadn't been injured. He breathed a sigh of relief when her arms and legs bent normally and nothing seemed out of place. She stayed quiet. *Probably just in shock. She'll recover.* He crawled back out, shut the gate and walked around to climb into the front seat. He was still breathing heavily when he started the vehicle and pulled out onto the street. He glanced at his watch. Ten minutes. He punched the gas.

The world smeared white as the rear tires slipped on the treacherous pavement. Aaron turned the steering wheel, trying to regain control while he stomped on the brakes. *Stupid!* he thought as a slight bump told him the wheels had stopped spinning even if the SUV hadn't. He whipped his hands off the wheel, holding them up as if someone had pulled a gun. A grunt ripped free as the heavy Suburban slammed into a parked pickup and snapped him against the seatbelt. Metal squealed on metal, then the vehicle bounced off like a ponderous Ping-Pong ball. It pirouetted and fetched up against the curb. Aaron grabbed the wheel again, whimpering as the Suburban rocked to the left and settled back on its springs. It slipped backward on the pavement, finally coming to a halt with a bone-jarring thud against a downed tree. Shaking, he ran a hand across his body to make sure there wasn't anything more wrong with him than a headache, then turned around.

"You OK back there?" he said, his voice quavering. No response from Cythia, who had bounced to the other side of the cab and now lay on her side. "Well, you're not screaming, so you must be alright," he muttered.

Once his nerves had steadied, Aaron pulled out onto the street and crept forward. There was no way he could make it in the four minutes his watch said he had left, but he doubted the principal would care much. *I haven't even seen Mr. Hathcock in weeks. I wonder what he's up to these days.* He shrugged and returned his attention to the street. His foot depressed slightly, allowing the speedometer to climb to twenty-five miles per hour. He squinted at the white roadways while his white-knuckled hands maneuvered through Paris. Finally, half an hour later, he pulled into the parking lot and killed the engine. He unclenched his fingers from around the wheel and massaged his aching head. Then he sat back with a sigh and muttered, "Let's get to class."

Cynthia still lay on her side in the back, but she seemed fine aside from her odd silence. *Now that I think of it, they've all been really quiet lately. I wonder if they're sick.* That small voice tried to pipe up again in the back of his head, asking if they were even breathing. Aaron tried to ignore it. He chewed his lip as he carried the large girl into the school. He shuffled across the courtyard and in through the back door. His shoes squeaked on linoleum as he stepped inside. His breath fogged the air before them. Without lights, the hallways remained dark, but he had grown quite familiar with the layout over the course of the last several years. "What period are you in again?" he asked Cynthia. Still no answer, but he didn't really need one. "Second, wasn't it?" He walked down his hallway and took her to the second classroom.

A motley collection of leather-faced teenagers filled all but three of the thirty desks. They wore an odd assortment of clothing, from pajamas and night gowns to formal eveningwear. Not a single one moved. After depositing her at a table near the teacher's desk, he nodded in approval and walked out, down the hall into the first room. *Nice of the other teachers to let me use their classrooms. I couldn't have gotten all of them in my room.* He chuckled. *Moving them around certainly wouldn't be any fun, either.*

A similar, mismatched crowd sat in the classroom, with only two fewer than his second period. He surveyed the group, then walked to a cabinet. Unlocking the door, he pulled out an armful of textbooks and started placing them on desks. He carried five at a time, opening them to *Macbeth* as he walked around. He felt winded by the time he grabbed the last bunch and carried them to the opposite side of the room. Three remained in his grip when he tripped over an errant desk leg. He threw his hands out to keep from falling. The books went flying. Two landed on the floor like dead birds killed in flight. The third smacked against Nicolas Lane's head, snapping it back to rest against his spine.

Eyes wide, Aaron rushed over. "Are you OK?" He grabbed a handful of brittle hair and hauled the head up. It flopped forward, turning slightly. "What have I done? What am I going to do?" He ran a hand across his pate and muttered: "I'm in trouble?"

For what? the voice in his head snapped, finally capturing his attention. *Look at them! They haven't moved in a week. They haven't eaten anything. They're dead already.* Eyes wide, he went to his desk and sat, resting his chin on his hands while he gazed out at the dried-out shells of his former students. Nick's wrinkled face looked back at him, shriveled lips pulled back in a macabre grin as if he got the joke even if his teacher didn't. Aaron stared for awhile, fingers drumming on his desk as his eyes wandered from one desiccated student to the next. Even if they were dead, did it really matter? They were quiet. They were still. They were attentive. Aaron nodded and stood.

Finally, a perfect class.

"Shall we begin?" When no one objected, he turned to the board and began writing.

LITTLE MONSTERS

Author's Note: *"Little Monsters" was published in the online* The New Bedlam Project *zine. The name should sound familiar by now; it's based on the Courting Morpheus anthology.*

Rubbing her eyes, Patricia stifled a yawn and tried to focus on the pastel smear thrust in her face. The colors swam and blurred, but she couldn't force them to sharpen. How long since she had been home, much less slept? Days, surely. Perhaps even weeks. "Very nice, Timmy." She could have left it at that and let him go back to his seat, but prudence wouldn't quite let her. *I've got to know what it is. Can't afford not to.* The first time she'd tried that had nearly cost her her life. *Not that I haven't lost enough already.* A twinge of pain shot from the hand under her left armpit. Tilting the hat back on her head, Patricia jammed the thumb and forefinger of her free hand into her eyes. The pain was sharp and intense and, once the spots cleared from her vision, brought the world into sharp focus.

Blues and greens featured prominently in the creature scribbled onto the construction paper the red-haired boy held up for her perusal. It looked like some weird lizard-mammal hybrid, with what appeared to be fur and a ridge marching along its back. Triangular teeth munched on black lines that had small lightning bolts shooting up around them. Circles around its feet held bite marks, as did something behind it that looked like a TV. "What is it?"

"It's a greflin," Timmy said, tucking the paper under his arm. "My daddy told me about them. He said they eat 'puters."

Patricia nodded as he walked back to his seat. He stopped to grab more paper and crayons on the way. Somewhere behind her desk, she could already hear something chomping on the computer lines. She seemed to recall that Timmy's father wrote technological horrors. *So much for surfing the Internet or trying to write. She sighed. At least it only eats electronics. Not like that werewolf Bobby drew that day.* A shudder ripped through her body. She avoided looking at the bloody smears across three empty desks that had once held the classroom bullies. A smaller splash marred the cage that had once held Gerald, the class' pet mouse. It had made the mistake of biting Bobby when he squeezed it too hard. She glanced over in the corner where he sat, his blond hair bouncing as he scribbled furiously at a piece of paper. He'd been working on it silently for days now. Patricia wondered what would happen when he finished. She stood up.

"Going somewhere, Miss Henderson?"

She cringed at the cute, little girl voice. From the sound, it belonged in a Shirley Temple movie. But the mind behind it was pure New Bedlam. Patricia turned to the left to look at the six-year-old girl drawing on the chalkboard. "No, Rose. I just had to get out of that seat for a few minutes. My rear's starting to hurt."

Rose giggled. "That's OK, Miss Henderson." She turned back to the board.

Chewing on her bottom lip, Patricia forced herself to move closer. Her throat constricted at every step; for a second, she thought she might vomit in revulsion. She closed her eyes and swallowed. Once the nausea passed, she opened her eyes. "What are you working on, Rose? Can I see it?" She hated the meek tone, but survival demanded it.

"Not yet," she said. "It's not ready."

"Not even a peek? Please?" Leaning in, Patricia could make out an oblong shape, pointed at one end, and something oval in front of it. She wasn't entirely sure she *wanted* to know, but not knowing wasn't an option these days. "Just a little one?"

Black curls bobbed as Rose looked up, a scowl twisting her pretty features. "I said no!" She covered the drawing with one arm. With the other hand, she picked up an eraser and cleared a space to her left, obliterating one of dozens of large and small pictures showing a stick figure in various poses. They all looked like the symbol on a women's restroom door, straight lines with a circle for a head and a triangle for a dress. Some had her carrying trays of food, or reading a book or sitting still on a chair. One had a hand caught in long hair flowing off the top of her head. The largest drawing was much more detailed, showing a hand and fingers on a rectangle with a curve coming down at the side. Patricia bit her lip, shoved her hand further under her armpit and looked back at Rose's latest handiwork. This time, the stick figure's face was visible. It wore a frown with a large X over the mouth. "I think you need a time out, Miss Henderson." She tapped on the picture twice.

Patricia's feet swung her around and marched her to the desk, where she sat and stared at the class. She tried to open her mouth, but her jaws refused to cooperate. Not that she expected anything different by this point. She laid her head on the desk and listened to the chomping sounds coming from the computer. *Why couldn't this have happened during the summer?*

When the sleepless nights started, Patricia thought she might go crazy for a while. It had been more than a decade since the all-nighters in college, and her body had gotten used to a full night's sleep. Still, she dragged herself to New Bedlam Elementary School every morning and tried to keep up with her first graders. A bone-crushing weariness set in, but she found it easier to cope as the nights crawled by. Caught up in her own misery, Patricia never noticed the dark circles and dragging steps of the town's other residents until she overheard the children talking about how their mommies and daddies stayed up all night. Shortly after that, nightmares started walking the streets, and they realized the whole town had gone crazy.

Writing may have made the whole thing bearable — it had always provided an outlet in the past — but she couldn't seem to jot down so much as a journal entry these days. No one could. The only consolation was that if all these spooky writers in town couldn't put two words together, at least they weren't creating any new monsters. *Too bad we never thought about the monsters we'd already created,* she thought, cutting her eyes at Rose. *Especially the little ones. Writer's block! That's a laugh.* It certainly wasn't much of a problem when the most creative minds in town couldn't even write. Whatever ailment plagued the rest of New Bedlam, it didn't seem to hamper the children's drawing skills. And with all the raw talent sloshing around this town, it was only natural a fair amount of it would get into the gene pool. It had been a source of pride in state testing, especially in reading and comprehension. These days, however, it trapped Patricia in her own private hell. She couldn't quite pinpoint when their drawings held more life than colored wax. Careful questioning hadn't revealed anything, either. Their young minds had simply found a new creative outlet and took advantage of it. She glanced at Rose again. *They call me "Miss Henderson," but she's the one in charge. Has been for some time.*

Patricia struggled to speak, to force her jaws apart. All her efforts gained was a general tremor that shook her head side to side. The hat fell off. She caught sight of her reflection in a small mirror on the desk and whimpered. A few individual strands of black hair were all that remained of what had once been a combing nightmare. One of Rose's more effective punishments. A few children pointed and laughed. Blushing, she leaned over and tried to pick up the hat. It required her to reach across her body with the free hand, which fell short. *Can't stand up.* Rose's drawing showed her seated, and she wouldn't get up any time soon. Grimacing, she pulled the other hand out and reached down to snag the brim with two fingers. A red-stained bandage wrapped around her palm, nearly obscuring the fact she didn't have a thumb. She fought down another urge to puke. She settled the hat on her head and the hand back under her arm. Patricia kept her eyes focused on the desk. If she looked at the paper cutter right now, she *would* throw up. *I can't take this anymore.*

Swallowing, she raised her hand. Rose ignored it. She waived it back and forth and dredged up a coughing noise from the back of her throat. Finally, the girl turned toward her, hiding her drawing behind her back. "Do you need something, Miss Henderson?" Patricia wanted to slap that smug little face. Instead, she nodded. "Well? What is it?" The teacher tried to speak, but still couldn't part her jaws. "Oh, sorry. I forgot about that." A quick swipe with the eraser banished the controlling mage. "Is that better?"

"Yes, Rose. Thank you very much." She worked her jaw from side to side. "I was just wondering: Do you think now would be a good time for nap time?" *If they can take a nap today. Sometimes they can, sometimes they can't.*

The little girl tapped her lips with a piece of chalk for a moment before shaking her head. "Not right now." She turned back to the board.

"Rose, please," Patricia gasped. "They're obviously tired—"

"I said no, Miss Henderson."

"It doesn't have to be long, Rose, just a little one." She stood up. "Surely you need a rest after all the pretty drawing you've done."

Rose sighed. "You just have to push it, don't you, Miss Henderson?" A mischievous smile broke across her lips. "I was afraid this might happen. You know what this means, don't you?"

Patricia sobbed and dropped to her knees. "No, Rose, please. Don't. Just forget I said anything. I won't mention it again—" She stretched her arms out, not bothering to hide the maimed hand as she pleaded with the little girl. "I promise."

"I wish I could believe you. I really do. But I just don't see how I can." Rose stepped to one side, revealing the drawing she had been working on so hard. Patricia's eyes widened as she took in the image. Her scream caught in her throat, emerging as a panicked croak. Her head whipped side to side. Rose laughed and nodded. "I'm afraid so, Miss Henderson." She lifted the chalk to tap on the picture.

The teacher lunged forward, hands outstretched. A distant voice clamored in her head that she was only making things worse, that the punishment would be *really* bad this time. She ignored it. *If I can stop it this time, that's all I need.* She almost made it, but fell short as the chalk made its second hit against the board, leaving a white trail across the drawing of a finger and pencil sharpener. *Should have realized she'd be getting better,* Patricia thought as her body straightened of its own accord and her feet started toward the corner of the room. *After all, she's had lots of practice, and her mother's an award-winning artist.* A shrill sound reached her ears. It took her a moment to realize she was giggling. The laughs became yelps as her dragging steps approached the corner.

Why did I have to buy that thing? It had seemed such a cute, whimsical thing at the time. How often did you see a pencil sharpener that would actually fit those huge pencils kids always seemed to write with? Now, it was just a hand-operated meat grinder. Muscles in her arm knotted as Patricia tried to halt her hand's progression. But inch by inch, it crept forward. The hand folded itself into a fist with the index finger pointed out, like a teacher scolding a wayward student. With a final lunge, her finger jammed into the pencil sharpener. Her maimed hand rested on the crank. *Maybe it won't work. Can't sharpen a pencil without a thumb.* She giggled again. But hope shattered as she discovered that the position might be awkward, but it would work quite well.

Even as her hand began to turn and she felt the nail inside start to crack and break, Rose spoke up behind her: "When you're done there, Miss Henderson, would you read us a story?"

FINAL EDITION

Author's Note: *"Final Edition" was my first shared world story and remains one of my personal favorites. It appeared in* Grants Pass, *an anthology built around a story where a girl named Kayley blogs about what she'd do after the apocalypse. "When the end of the world comes, meet me in Grants Pass, Oregon."*

Dusk settled on Paris, Texas. The sun, hidden all day behind dark clouds, took advantage of its last few moments to create a nearly perfect Texas sunset, painting the cloudbank in glowing blues, reds, oranges and yellows.

It was, as Matt Godwin's father liked to say, enough to knock your eyeballs out. It was also a wasted effort, as Matt's own eyeballs remained firmly fixed on the ground spinning slowly beneath him. The sun slipped below the horizon, stealing its momentary beauty along the way. Sullen, leaden clouds hastened night's approach.

Matt stopped turning the merry-go-round. He lay there a moment. His chin hanging over the edge as his hand traced random glyphs in the pine bark mulch some city official or other thought would make the playground safer for children. Scooting back, he rolled over and rested his head on the metal surface. His five-foot-six frame barely dangled off the other end. His girth just fit between hoops meant to hold children despite his weight loss in the last few months.

He lifted his left hand and turned his wrist this way and that in an effort to determine the time. The hour and minute hands showed 4:27, and the minute hand hung motionless. Matt cursed the watch for a few moments, but stopped with a wry chuckle. What was the point? Time meant little anymore. It was morning, noon, dusk or night; what else did you need to know these days? He unfastened the band and slipped the watch off his wrist. He hefted it for a moment, and then tossed the offending timepiece into the night.

"Hey, squirrels! Do you know what time it is?" he called, laughing once more.

As usual, no one answered except a passing breeze laden with the scent of more rain. The wind ruffled his close-cropped black hair as it played across seesaws stuck somewhere between teeter and totter and pushed swings that might never again hear kids demanding to go higher, Daddy, higher.

A soft crunching noise cut his laughter short. He raised his head, casting about for the source. Surely Bill wouldn't have followed him here...

The noise came again. Head swivelling like a radar array, Matt's attention centred on a corner of the fence surrounding the playground. He sighed with relief, and his entire body sagged with departing tension as a bois d'arc dropped a third green, wrinkly apple on the ground.

Thunder boomed across the yard, warning anyone outside to get indoors.

Matt stood, wincing as tight muscles protested a new position. Had he been on that merry-go-round all day? His stomach rumbled, a small echo of the thunder overhead. He supposed he had been. Matt stumbled around the carousel, disoriented after hours of slow turning.

"Where did I leave my backpack?" he muttered.

His feet found it first, stumbling over the black fabric. Hoisting the bag onto one shoulder, Matt headed out the gate. He needed to catch a City Council meeting.

Mayor Gary Hamilton pounded his gavel on the table.

"That is enough out of you, councilman! I will not tolerate such rudeness at my meetings! Do you understand me?" He glared at an alderman, who sat stiffly in his seat, hands poised a few inches off the tabletop.

The mayor swept his glower around the horseshoe, pointing at each seated figure with the gavel. Flickering light from several oil lamps gave him the look of a stern mediaeval judge. Satisfied an outburst was not forthcoming, he turned to the audience.

"I'm sorry you had to witness that, ladies and gentlemen. Sometimes the democratic process gets a little heated." Gary ventured a small laugh. "I hope this won't make top of the fold in tomorrow's edition, Mr. Godwin."

Matt smiled, shook his head and kept writing in his reporter's notebook. The last edition of *The Paris News* lay weeks in the past. But so long as anything happened here, it was his duty to record it. He was the city reporter, after all. Of all the changes seen here since the Crash — as people around here called it — three months ago, Gary offered one of the strangest.

Voters elected this slender, balding black man to represent one of the city's two minority districts last May. Timid and soft-spoken, he always made Matt think of a mouse. That changed once the councilman realised he was the only surviving member of Paris city government. As Gary saw it, that made him mayor — and that put him in charge. Power transformed this small, mousy man into a thunderous orator who held the reins of power tight. That the reins controlled nothing meant little to Gary. He just forged ahead, calling nightly City Council sessions to deal with what he saw as pressing problems.

"Now on to our last order of business," he said, reading from an agenda he painstakingly copied by hand each morning for the council and the dozens who attended the sessions. "Ducks in Lake Crook were staring at me again yesterday. This sort of impertinence simply cannot be allowed. I propose we form a subcommittee to enter into discussions with them. Perhaps we can find a mutually agreeable solution. If not, I'm afraid the police will simply have to arrest all of them."

The mayor adjourned the meeting with a quick rap of his gavel. He stood and walked over to the council member who had so recently been the target of his wrath.

"No hard feelings, I hope, Frank. You raise some good points; I just wish you would learn to curb your enthusiasm a little. It's unbecoming in a man of your position." He leaned over to shake Frank's hand, which came off in his grip.

"Well now, that's embarrassing," Gary said with a chuckle as he pushed the mannequin's hand back into place.

Matt stood and walked out of the council chambers, leaving the only empty seat in the house. He still couldn't believe Gary found enough mannequins in Paris to fill six City Council seats and dozens of chairs in the audience. He must have raided every department store in the city. That would also explain why they all wore different clothes every time he came here.

He turned back for a moment. Gary wondered among the rows of chairs, grinning and patting shoulders as he schmoozed with his 'constituents'. Matt shuddered and walked down the stairs and out into the night, eager to be gone despite the rain. The sight of all those dummies no longer disturbed him as much as it once had, but it still creeped him out. And he could only take so much of an unhinged, small-town politician. At least Gary's obsession gave him the illusion of productivity, even if it did centre on ducks and dress-store dummies.

Bill was a different matter altogether.

Matt supposed he should have seen it coming. "Big Bill" Vance of Clarksville was the most persistent letter writer *The Paris News* had seen in years. Even with the newspaper's policy that nobody had a letter printed more than once a month, Bill's name showed up more than any other on the opinion page. The policy didn't stop him from sending his missives every week, either. The subject changed from rant to rant, but each contained the same two themes: The government did it, and the media couldn't be trusted. Had the various local, state and federal agencies paid Matt all the money Bill claimed, he could have retired two years ago before he even reached thirty.

It probably shouldn't have come as any surprise that Bill would focus all that mistrust on Matt. After all, he was likely the last member of the media left in Northeast Texas. But who would have thought he would turn violent?

Looking back now, Matt could see the first warning signs. He could even pinpoint the time — 5:30 p.m. on June 24 — since he set the meeting. That was the benefit of hindsight. At the time, everyone worried too much about survival to think of anything else.

Sure Big Bill had been edgy, but so was everyone gathered there. And why wouldn't they be?

Even now, three months later, Matt saw the small crowd with crystal clarity. It was a pitiful group of shell-shocked survivors from three counties. These three dozen or so men, women and children were all who responded to Matt's message in the last edition of the paper. It was a single sheet, front and back, detailing what he knew about the happenings of the last few weeks. He closed with a request: Everyone still up and about should meet at newspaper office on Loop 286 to discuss what they should do.

The meeting started with a rehash of what people knew, which wasn't much.

America was more or less gone, both in government and people. The dreaded Big One had finally hit California, followed by smaller ones that shook the entire West Coast. Hundreds of millions were dead or dying of some particularly nasty germs.

Elsewhere, the world fared much the same. No matter where you looked, everything trembled on the point of unravelling. The same diseases had run rampant in every nation, decimating populations before medics had time to blink.

That led to personal stories. Everyone knew several people — mostly loved ones — who were dead. Matt listened with as much patience as he could muster, but it was hard. They weren't here to tell war stories. But he knew if he interrupted too soon, they would turn on him. As if he hadn't suffered! A souped-up version of the Black Death that appeared to have originated in Austin took his fiancée. Matt had held her hand as she wheezed and rattled her last few breaths. His sister had died of the Super Flu, for crying out loud! A cousin succumbed to some bizarre strain of Ebola or something like it. And what about his parents? Dead in one of a pair of twisters that hit Paris in the last month — the first the town had seen in two decades. Did Matt whine about it? Of course not; he went to work so this bunch of babies would know what was going on.

Eventually, his patience came to an end.

"All right, people. That's enough," Matt said, standing on a desk. His voice rose over the inevitable protest. "Enough! We can talk about this later, but right now, we've got more important stuff to think about, like what do we do now? Where do we go?"

The small crowd erupted. Where could they go? Why would they go anywhere? The cities were desolate wastelands, home to only the rotting dead. At least they knew the land here. So what if a couple of tornadoes had taken out a few buildings? Most of them still stood; even if the Love Civic Centre and Paris' landmark Eiffel Tower had been obliterated, at least its giant red cowboy hat had survived to adorn a Cadillac in the parking lot. Others pointed out that this town was just as empty as any of the bigger metro areas. Were forty people going to keep a town alive that once had about twenty-six thousand? Besides, most of those here lived outside Paris. Did they plan to leave their homes and move here?

Where — that was the question everyone shouted eventually. Matt wanted that question; he needed it to make this meeting work. He had an answer. He raised his hands and yelled, "Hey!" until the clamour quieted.

"Actually, I have a suggestion," he said. "I agree we can't stay here. There just aren't enough of us. I also understand your reluctance to leave this area. I share it. This has been my family's home for generations. But if we are to survive, we're going to have to find other people. I think I know where some are headed."

"And how would you know that?" Heads turned to identify the speaker. Matt could have told them who it was. He heard that voice at least once a week over the phone. Bill stood near the back, leaning against a door with arms folded across his barrel chest. He was an imposing figure, a foot taller than Matt and big enough to fill the doorway. Gray hair and beard did nothing to soften his look. "Big Bill" was tough, and he knew it.

"It's my job to know," Matt shot back. He instantly regretted the quip. This had to be handled delicately, but the man grated on him. He forced himself to soften his tone. "Look, I shouldn't have said it like that, but you know it's true. I was researching an article about how people felt about the end of the world — it seemed to be coming up on us real quick — after I saw a preacher on TV talking about a blog post from a girl named Kayley. He spent a lot of time talking about it; it even made some of the national news casts."

"What'd they say?" a woman asked from the back.

Matt paused. He hadn't counted on questions. He was surprised they didn't know already, even if most of them had been too wrapped up in their own affairs to pay much attention to the world outside Lamar County. He figured they'd have heard the televangelist, at any rate. But if they didn't know, he wasn't about to tell them that he'd seen the preacher holding up a crumpled sheet of paper and quivering with such righteous indignation that even his immaculately styled grey hair trembled in rage while he denounced those "attempting to flee God's righteous judgement" . *What was that passage he quoted? "Then they will say to the mountains, 'Cover us!' and to the hills, 'Fall on us!'"* Matt had laughed and started searching immediately for the posting. He printed out his own copy to reference, which proved fortuitous. Traffic to the blog grew so heavy in the following days he'd found it nearly impossible to access it.

His mind racing, Matt shook his head. "That's not important right now. What is important is that she was planning for this. She knew the importance of gathering people together in one place. She wanted them to join her so that maybe something could survive."

Not that he planned to tell them what the preacher had thought of her plans.

"You knew this and didn't tell anyone? Why didn't you put it in that rag of yours instead of calling us all here?" Bill demanded. "I knew we couldn't trust you reporters. You're in cahoots with those government people, the ones who started these super germs in the first place. I bet you're still hiding stuff from us!"

Matt indeed hid more information than he offered. The region's Congressman had confessed a great deal over the phone shortly before his death. Terrorists had finally mounted a major offensive, but not with airplanes or nuclear bombs, as everyone had feared. They'd managed to get their hands on some of those "super germs" from the well-guarded stores of several world powers. The old politician had been delirious with fever, but Matt thought he had told the truth. His raving quietened toward the end of the interview, winding down until he gasped, "You're not recording this, are you?" Then he hung up. Matt had been trying to confirm some of the details for a major story when everything fell apart. Not that he planned to tell these yokels that. It'd only play into Bill's hands at this point. And he certainly wouldn't tell them Kayley said her online note was as much a mental exercise as a practical solution.

Instead, he said: "I didn't put it in the *News* because people don't need to go off willy nilly. We need to band together. Do you want old Mr. Ferguson there trying to make the trip by himself? Or what about Sally here, with her three kids? People out there are scared, and fear turns men into animals. I've seen it time and time again."

"Well, you just got an answer for everything don't you? So where is this magical place?"

"You're not going to like this part," Matt warned. "It's a town called Grants Pass in Oregon." The protest rose once more, louder than before. Leave Paris to become a Yankee? It took several minutes to die down enough for him to continue. "Look, people. I told you that you wouldn't like it. But just hear me out. It's a nice place, and not all that different from Paris."

He told them what little he found out before the Web imploded. Grants Pass nestled in the mountains of southern Oregon about an hour north of the California border at the intersection of I-5 and U.S. Highway 199. The town sat on the Rogue River; Paris lay between the Sulphur and Red rivers. They both had about the same population. He told them about the giant redwoods and the so-called House of Mystery at The Oregon Vortex, where people supposedly changed height.

"No one said we had to stay there. It might not be more than a staging area. But we can't stay here, and we can't roam aimlessly around the United States just hoping to come across some other people," Matt said.

"We need a target, and this is as good as any. Better, really. Before it went down, people were searching the Internet for anything they could find about the end of the world or the apocalypse. This page was near the top of every search.

"'*When the end of the world comes, meet me in Grants Pass, Oregon,*' Kayley wrote. If this isn't the end of world end, what is?"

Bill walked out first, glaring murder at Matt as he shoved his way past the reporter. Seven or eight more looked at each other, shrugged and filed out at erratic intervals. The rest exchanged glances, but remained and planned. They would leave in a month.

Matt laughed. A *month!* Another month proved pestilence still walked the land. By the end of July, he was sure everyone else was dead until he wandered downtown and saw flickering lamplight — electricity had died weeks before — in a second-floor window of City Hall and witnessed his first meeting of the new City Council.

A week after that, he wished everyone else had died after Bill tried to blow his head off with a shotgun. Matt lost count of the number of close calls in the last two months as Bill tried to shoot him and run him over. The last incident, about two weeks ago, was certainly more memorable. Bill decided to take a more biblical approach and stone him to death. Fortunately, few rocks hit their target. Even in this new world where Matt could say with some confidence he was the best journalist alive, no one would pick Bill to pitch for the Texas Rangers. Since then, Matt hadn't seen hide nor hair of his would-be assassin. He hoped Bill had given up and gone back to Clarksville for good. If not, maybe he should head to Oregon by himself.

The rain slackened as Matt walked up the street to the newspaper offices, before dying altogether as he turned the key in its lock. The long walk from City Hall to the paper gave him much needed exercise, plus the building offered plenty of room and hiding places should Bill ever try to force his way in. More importantly, the lights still worked.

It had taken him several days to find the generator. He knew the paper had one to keep computers running in case of an outage, but he never thought to ask where. Once located, a length of hose, gas can and wagon pilfered from the local Wal-Mart let him keep the generator running with fuel siphoned from cars in town. Matt figured there was probably a way to get it out of the ground storage tanks at nearby gas stations, but he could not puzzle out how.

The generator couldn't power the building's air conditioning system but proved sufficient to run a few lights and his Macintosh.

Exhaustion threatened to pull him under, but Matt had a job to do. He needed to get the day's story filed before he went to sleep. He did not want to get stuck in a backlog where he had to spend all day writing just to catch up.

An hour and a half later by the clock on the wall, Matt saved his story with the hundred or so others he had accumulated in the last three months. He turned out the light and made his way to a pallet on the floor of the editor's office. Sleep claimed its due, pulling him under almost before his head hit the pillow. The night passed peacefully.

The morning brought a gun to his face.

Matt blinked once and scrambled back, hitting his head on the editor's desk. The shotgun barrel followed, tracking every movement of his head in perfect synchronisation.

"Time to wake up, news boy," Bill said.

Matt looked about wildly. The side doors locked automatically and he chained the double doors in front every morning.

"How?" he said.

"You shouldn't put chains on the outside if you really want to keep somebody out," Bill said with a chuckle. "A hacksaw doesn't make much noise, you know."

He straddled Matt and dropped the rifle slightly as he leaned over. "This is all your fault. If it weren't for you and the government, my Betty would still be alive. Our kids would still be alive. Do you have any idea what it's like to bury your wife and children in the back yard, news boy?"

Matt didn't bother trying to answer. His foot shot upward, straight into Bill's crotch.

Big Bill fell hard with a strangled croak. The shotgun clattered to the floor as he clutched himself. Matt scrambled to his feet, grabbed the gun and smashed the butt into Bill's head, who fell limp as a boned fish.

Matt dashed out the front door. One foot kicked the cut chain and sent it slithering into the grass. The city's new fire truck sat in the parking lot, a red behemoth blocking his path. Matt barely paused as he skidded into a turn and ran around. Panic held him in its grip and refused to let go. He barrelled down Lamar Avenue and headed west.

His flight carried him nearly to downtown before his body decided to call a halt. Matt sank to his hands and knees, gulping air in great gasps. His heart galloped in his chest, and black spots danced in and out of his vision. Matt thought he might either have a heart attack or vomit. After a few moments, he decided on the latter. He remained staring at the remains of last night's dinner until loud growls and wild howls reached his ears.

Turning, Matt saw the fire truck racing up the street, careening off parked cars and utility poles. Its engine growled in protest at the pace Bill forced it to while its sirens howled with murderous intent. To bad he didn't have a camera; this would make a spectacular photograph.

"What is your deal, dude?" Matt yelled.

He climbed to his feet and started an unsteady trot west. Maybe he could lose Bill among the buildings that remained downtown – if he could reach downtown. He crossed the road and dashed through yards and onto a side street. Lamar Avenue was a major thoroughfare, but many of the residential lanes were much smaller. Given Bill's difficulty just keeping the fire truck on the road, these smaller streets with cars lining the curbs might well prove impassable.

Following a path of turns, dead ends and backtracks, Matt soon lost sight of his pursuer. Bill never fell out of earshot, however. The engine and sirens rose and fell. Metal screeched in protest a few blocks over, followed shortly by a loud boom as he ran into something he could not simply push out of the way. Once or twice, Matt even caught a whiff of the fire truck's diesel engine.

His shambling flight eventually brought him to First Street. Turning north, he started toward City Hall, taking advantage of buildings, piles of rubble, trees and any other hiding place he could find. He stopped in a doorway across the street. The storms had carved erratic paths through downtown, flattening some buildings while leaving structures like Culbertson Fountain on the Plaza and the Peristyle in Bywaters Park intact. City Hall stood alone, exposed.

Matt paused, uncertain, until Bill made his mind up for him.

The fire truck raced past in a red blur. Matt jumped, and ran from his hiding place. Tires screeched behind him as he wrenched open a door and ran up the stairs.

Matt crouched, half-crawling his way to a corner office. Reaching the window, he pulled himself up to peer over the ledge. He saw no sign of Bill or his fire truck, but he could hear the siren warbling somewhere behind City Hall.

The noise grew louder. Matt stood and leaned out the window, straining for some sight of his attacker. The fire truck barrelled through an intersection and leapt up the square, smashing into the marble fountain. Matt stared for several minutes at the mangled rescue vehicle. Surely no one could have survived the impact.

The driver's door opened, indicating Bill indeed lived, if not in perfect health. He limped across the street with blood streaming down his face. He paused at the corner, looking around. Matt pulled back. The motion caught Bill's attention. He grinned and pointed up at the reporter before resuming his limping march. The swish of the front doors announced his entrance into City Hall.

Matt's head swung side to side. What was he going to do? He could hear Bill's stuttering gait coming up the stairs. He took off his shoes and ran silently across the hall into the City Council chambers.

As expected, he found the council in session. Apparently not everyone agreed with the mayor's approach to the duck problem. Matt ran to the horseshoe-shaped bench and crouched behind it. Gary squawked in surprise.

"Mr. Godwin, what do you think you are doing? You know better than to just barge in here!" Matt tried to shush the mayor, to no effect. "Get out of there! If you don't get up right now, I'll..."

Bill kicked open the doors. "You in here, news boy?" he shouted. "I hear clucking, so this must be where all the chickens are!"

Gary stood as he turned from Matt to the new intruder. His eyes bulged and a vein started throbbing in his forehead at sight of the shotgun cradled in Bill's arm.

"Firearms are *not* allowed in here! Signs are clearly posted at the entrance!"

"Shut up," Bill replied.

He swung the shotgun around and pulled the trigger. A mannequin's head disintegrated. The second blast caught Gary in the gut, knocking him back against the wall and out of sight.

Matt took advantage of the commotion to scramble from behind the table and rush along a wall toward the door. The shotgun roared to life and punched a hole through a dummy's chest. The next shot blew the arm off another, which caught between Matt's legs. As he struggled for balance, Bill caught up and swung the shotgun in a wide arc. The impact buckled Matt's knee and dropped him to the floor. He managed to push himself onto his elbows before Bill planted a boot on his groin. The big man slowly rocked forward, grinding all his weight down on the ball of his foot. Pain exploded through his abdomen.

When Matt could focus on anything again, he found himself staring down the barrel of a gun for the second time that day. Bill's finger tightened on the trigger. Damp warmth spread across Matt's jeans.

Click!

"Aww, crap!" Bill yelled. "You reporters are just like cockroaches, aren't you? You just won't die!" He grinned savagely. "Well, my mamma always said the best way to kill a roach is to crush it."

Bill turned the shotgun in his hands and held it like a club over his head.

"It's all your fault," he whispered.

Matt closed his eyes.

"OUT OF ORDER!"

The voice sounded familiar, but surely Bill's massive chest never issued such a high-pitched sound. Matt's eyes popped open.

The mayor stood behind Bill, one arm clutched around his stomach. The other rose over his head, gavel clutched in his fist. The hammer fell with a muffled crack. Bill's eyes rolled back in his head and he fell to one side, knocking over several chairs. Gary went down with him, still swinging. He kept hammering, grunting with every wet *smack*, until the head snapped off the gavel. Gary pitched forward over Bill's motionless body. He lay there, breathing shallowly.

"Firearms not allowed," he muttered. "Killed Frank... ruined my gavel... not on the agenda..." He trailed off into incoherence.

Matt sat still, staring at the pair until the mayor stopped breathing. As the sunlight started to wane, he finally grabbed a chair and pulled himself upright, standing still for several moments before limping out.

A double murder at City Hall, and he witnessed the whole thing! This was going to make a great story. He just needed to get one of the paper's digital cameras and come back. Maybe if he shut off everything else, the generator could power the press. He'd get another if necessary. Matt paused. Newspaper policy forbade photos of dead bodies on the front page. He turned back, surveyed the scene once more and nodded to himself. Screw the policy.

"I'm editor now," he said, rubbing his hands together. He planned to make the final edition of *The Paris News* the best this town had ever seen!

After that, who knew? Maybe Grants Pass needed an editor.

PART III

Worlds Other Than These

WHERE THE SUN DON'T SHINE

Resting on a slender twig, the mosquito barely had time to register a small pop before a tiny harpoon skewered it through both eyes.

"Gotcha!" Boddyjon yelled with a cackle.

A sudden swat sent his conical hat flying. He turned, frown withering under the captain's scowling visage.

"Stop playin' with the bugs and get back there!" Dimknock growled. He pointed to the rear of the ship. The rest of the crew wrestled with a propeller several times their size that had embedded itself in the wood when they landed.

"Aye, Gob." He snatched up his red hat and scurried aft.

I ought to leave that one out for the sun. He'd be more useful as a pebble. At least then we could get some work out of him as an anchor, the captain thought while cutting the line loose. Dimknock smoothed his bristling beard. A glance east showed they were nearly out of time. "The sun! Put your backs to it, lads!"

Several terrified squeaks sounded, and their efforts intensified. Dimknock limped to the railing, his enamel peg leg thumping on the deck. He kept an eye on the approaching sun and another on the back of the ship. He chewed on his white beard.

A rounded sliver of orange appeared on the eastern horizon. The propeller shivered, turned and halted, making the boat shudder. The sun's first rays touched the world. With a lurch, *Windbreaker* broke free.

Purple smoke belched from a large stack amidships as it rose into the air. It nudged the dead moth, sending the corpse falling to the earth below.

"Which way, Gob?" Nacklebell asked as he dashed to the bridge.

"West, you great pile of flyspeck! West!"

Blades whining, the propeller pushed the ship through the air as it rushed toward the departing night. Dimknock stamped toward the rest of his crew, who leaned against the stern.

"Minniwocket! Zookto! Get yer lazy bones over here!" A pair of slumped figures with oversized feet shambled forward, both twisting their hats in large hands. "You two will feel the lash once we make port. Ten apiece!"

Minniwocket's mouth worked as he fingered a patch over his left eye. Several scars crisscrossed his face and hands. Zookto, who stood a head shorter, kept his eyes fixed on the deck.

The captain halted any protest with the lift of a bushy eyebrow. "Care to make it twenty apiece?"

"No, Gob," they muttered in sullen unison.

"It be your fault we're in this mess, boys. Didn't I tell you not to be greedy? There was plenty to plunder for everyone, but you had to get into her heart. She died too soon, and now we be runnin' for our lives. By rights, I ought to leave you out for the sun. So be glad all you'll be gettin' is a few kisses from Duvakor's whip." He nodded at the bosun, a huge, slow brute whose cone-shaped hat seemed ridiculously small on his large head. Duvakor chuckled, a sound like the earth moving. "All right, lads. Get on yer feet and get starboard. You know what we be lookin' for. Find it or else you're all stone!"

They scampered to the rail, eyeing sheer cliffs of wood, stone and glass as they whizzed by. Dimknock cursed the summer heat that had these humans buttoning up their houses. With enough time, they could find a way into any dwelling, but they needed a quick entrance. *Be this the day we return to the earth?* It wasn't a cheerful thought, but one every pirate faced.

"Turn back! Turn back!"

The captain started at the squeaky voice. He glanced up at the lookout barrel atop the mast. Ranzle was bouncing and pointing off the stern. "What's got you all excited, boy?"

"Open window, Gob!"

"Thank Mother Earth!" He raised his voice. "Nacklebell! Hard about! The lookout spotted an open window." The captain fell to the deck as the ship lurched to port, one hand gripping the rail. She slowly righted herself and buzzed to the window. Dimknock offered a salute to the diminutive lad, still young enough that his beard barely reached his chest.

The room they flew into was blessedly dark, the heavy drapes barely parted to allow passing breezes through. The crew converged at the bow, looking around. Boddyjon spotted their target first. "Sleeper, ho!" he called, pointing off the port bow. A giant snored in the distance, wrapped in a sheet.

Nacklebell nodded and turned the wheel. The propeller's whine dropped as they slowed for a cautious approach. Dimknock pulled a telescope from a case on his belt and put it to his eye. Running his glass across the slumbering figure, he searched for a way in. *Patience*, he reminded himself. *They always open up eventually.* He swept it back and forth, pausing when a bare foot presented itself. "There's your path, mate," he said. The ship surged forward, purple smoke all but invisible in the dim cavern.

They ran through a gap in the sheet beside the foot, following the contours of one hairy leg. Two huge mountains of flesh appeared ahead of them. The pilot aimed straight for the cleft between them.

"Get to work, lads!" Dimknock called. "You know what to do – load the harpoon. Ready the ropes." *A shame we can't stay for long,* he thought as warm dampness enveloped them, cutting off all light. *But he won't live long. They never do. Until then...* "We're home, mates."

Brian rubbed his jaw and shifted uncomfortably in the waiting room. It felt like he was getting hemorrhoids or something. He awoke with an itching sensation a few days ago that had only gotten worse. Then his teeth started hurting. On top of that, his boss was hammering him to finish a major presentation a month early. He had worked late every night for two weeks and it looked like he would have to work all weekend. *That's probably what did this to me,* he thought. *Didn't I read somewhere that sitting too much could give you 'roids?* The stress had made him irregular, and he was having trouble sleeping. What else could go wrong?

"Dr. Smith will see you now, Mr. Peterson," the receptionist said with a bright smile. "Third door on the left." In the distance, a drill started up with a high-pitched whine and someone yelled.

Wonderful.

Standing, Brian tossed the magazine back on the table and took a deep breath. He was starting to wish he had gone with sedation dentistry despite the added expense. *I hate the dentist. If my teeth didn't hurt so much, I'd turn around and walk out of here.* His jaw clenched at the thought of that hook scraping around in his mouth. He winced and walked into the exam room. Dr. Randal Smith stood next to a tray, arranging his tools.

"Brian, good to see you again," he said. His mouth twisted in disapproval. "It's been too long since your last appointment, you know."

"I know. Too much going on at work, barely time to sleep. You know how it is."

"If you made the time, perhaps you wouldn't have to visit on these emergencies." Dr. Smith motioned him into the chair. "What do you say we get a look at those sore teeth?"

As Brian sat, the dentist clipped a paper napkin around his neck and grabbed his pick and dental mirror.

"So what exactly seems to be the problem?"

"I don't know. It just started the other day. One minute I'm eating lunch, the next it feels like someone's digging at my teeth."

"Is it a constant pain?"

"It always hurts, but every now and then, it gets worse for no apparent reason." He winced and clutched his jaw.

"Like now?" Dr. Smith asked. Brian nodded. "Open wide."

Jaws spread, he nervously eyed the tools going in his mouth. He could feel the round edge of the mirror make its way around the gumline. Dr. Smith frowned over his examination with an occasional *hmm* or *ahh*.

"I see a great deal of tartar buildup. You haven't been flossing, have you?" Brian made an incoherent hoot. "I thought not." The mirror moved to the backside of his teeth. "Hmm. You have some very strange scoring back here. I know I've seen it before, but where?"

He pushed back on his stool and sat with one fist on his hip and the other on his chin. Brian worked his jaw side to side and started to ask a question when a bolt of pain shot through his head. He could *hear* something scraping along one of his molars; the sound seemed to ride along the inside of his skull to his ears. He yelled and clamped both hands to his face. Tears trickled down his face.

In a flash, Dr. Smith had rolled his stool back to the examining chair. He whipped a pair of odd-looking glasses with loupes on the lenses from a pocket and settled them on his nose. Gently prying Brian's mouth open, he jabbed the mirror inside.

"Where?"

Brian pointed to the back side of his left cheek, squinting in agony. The mirror pushed his tongue aside and slowly moved along the row of teeth. It stopped somewhere near the back molar. Dr. Smith leaned forward, peering through his lenses. He remained still for several moments before reaching in with his hooked pick and taking a vicious swipe that scraped his tooth and took a chunk out of his gums. He yelped.

"Sorry about that."

The dentist turned and walked to a stereo microscope in one corner. Brian sat up and watched him wipe both sides of the pick on a glass slide, place a cover slip on top and slap it under the microscope. He studied whatever was under the lens for some time, then turned and walked out of the exam room. *Where is he going?* Scowling, he lay back on the chair and closed his eyes as the pain began to fade. *I wonder what's got him all excited.* A yawn escaped. He extended his arms above his head, then paused mid-stretch. *What if it's cancer?* The thought seemed ridiculous, but it wouldn't go away. What else could make him jump like that?

He sat up.

The microscope still held the slide.

He looked around. The doorway remained empty.

Brian stood and walked to the corner, looking over his shoulder every few steps. Once he reached the table, he peered into the dual eyepieces.

All he could see was a red and green blob.

Cursing, he bent over to look for the focusing knobs. He found them and returned his eyes to the microscope. The image slowly focused as he turned the knobs, resolving itself into something vaguely star-shaped.

"Tell me, Brian, have you had trouble going to the bathroom lately?"

He jerked upright. Dr. Smith had come back in the room. He was reading a large tome. *Some sort of medical textbook?* Brian thought. *Must be an old one.* Its leather cover was brittle and cracked, its pages yellowed. "Uh, yeah, actually, I have. What does that have to do with my teeth?"

He ignored the question. "I've called an associate, a gastroenterologist. You're scheduled for a colonoscopy on Monday."

"Wait, wait, wait. I came in here to have you look at my teeth, and you're sending me to have someone shove a camera up my butt? What have you been smoking? I can't take off Monday. I've got work to do. I barely got time off to come here."

"Brian, I suspect you have a very serious condition. You need to have it checked out. I think your employer will understand." He handed over a business card and a brochure. "This is Dr. Frederick Wesson's address. Your appointment is written on the back.

"The brochure will tell you how to prepare for the procedure. You're going to need to follow a liquid diet over the weekend. Only clear liquids, mind — nothing with any coloring in it. You can take water, plain coffee or tea, gelatin or broth. Sunday night, be sure to take a laxative so you're colon's completely empty."

"Uh, yeah, OK."

"Be sure to see Nancy on your way out to schedule another appointment two weeks from today."

"Sure thing." He walked out in a daze, barely remembering to stop at the receptionist's desk.

"Elnock's gone, Gob." Vand slumped at attention, downcast eyes fixed on the deck. Even the pickax on his shoulder appeared to droop. "We was up yonder mining teeth when the mouth opened all sudden like and this giant steel monster swooped in and snatched him. I waited and called, but he never came back." He snatched his red hat, blew his bulbous nose with a great honk and slapped it back on his head. "Poor ol' Elnock."

"You done well, lad. At least you brought the enamel back with you." Dimknock clapped him on the arm and turned away with the end of his long, white beard clamped between his teeth. He paced the deck, lost in thought until he bumped into something. Looking up, he saw he had run into his first mate.

"You look worried, sir," Nacklebell said, falling in step with the captain. "What's on your mind?"

"I'm wonderin' how long it'll be before we have to head out. Vand's tale tells me someone knows we be here."

"Aye, Gob, they may. But you know these humans. It'll be some time before they do anything about it. We've got hundreds of heartbeats before we have to leave."

"Aye." Dimknock laughed. "You've got the truth of it, mate." Raising his voice, he turned to the rest of the crew. "Minniwocket, Zookto, Boddyjon, you three stay with the ship. The rest of us will take the pram to check the net to make sure it's still holding, then we'll head to the heart. I be feeling a mite peckish."

The three to remain behind grumbled and stamped off to various points of the ship. The others grinned and cheered; a few smacked their lips. They gathered on the starboard side below a wide, flat-bottomed boat dangling from a hoist near the stern. Duvakor hit the pulley brake, and the pram dropped to hover level with the deck. After they boarded, Raulnab shouldered his squat frame to the rear and grabbed a tall, shimmering teardrop of blue metal at the back and spun it with one hand. It fanned out in a spiral with a sharp snap. Another push, and it started spinning.

Nacklebell guided the boat up and around their ship, anchored to a fold on the intestinal wall. Dimknock eyed it with a measure of pride. So long as they took care of her, *Windbreaker* served them well, no matter the host. Minniwocket and Zookto scrubbed the deck, shifting uncomfortably every now and then as their shirts rubbed against their still-fresh welts. Boddyjon polished the harpoon gun in the prow.

Their first stop was at the great net, a tight web of spider-silk ropes fastened to harpoons driven into the wall. Each projectile was charged with a simple spell that allowed the puncture to close around it. *At least they used the right ones this time*, Dimknock thought. Three or four hosts back, an overeager Boddyjon had fired the wrong harpoons for the net. Their host had died before they could settle in. He eyed each knot and connection with care. If it failed, they'd be forced out before they were ready. It happened to every crew, but seldom more than once. Most careless enough to build more than one slipshod net found themselves left in the sun. He spotted a couple of minor gaps, simple repairs from a length of rope stowed in the pram. Satisfied all was in order, Dimknock gave the order to sail for the chest.

He felt his mouth water as the steady beat grew stronger. They lived with that tempting throb constantly, but only ventured inside to harvest the delicacy.

"Thar she is, lads," he said, admiring the pulsing muscle around them. Their beards swayed back and forth, the only sign of the red current flowing past them.

Nacklebell tied the boat off on a small spike driven carefully in the ventricle's side wall. He took a pair of sacks from underneath his bench and handed one to the captain. "A good bit of news, Gob. I spotted fat deposits on the outside. She'll be tender for sure."

"Aye, mate, and this is a young fella from the looks of it. He should feed us well." The captain turned to the others. "Nacklebell an' I will work here." A curt gesture cut off their grumbling. "We're the most experienced. I aim to have a feast tonight, not flee because one of you gets too greedy like those last two bumbling idiots. You lads make the rounds and come back here in about ten thousand beats."

"Aye, Gob," they murmured in unison before untying the boat and glumly sailing away.

Dimknock drew his sword and grinned at his first mate, who did the same. They clanged blades and set to. He soon lost himself in the work, picking a likely spot, then shaving the wall and putting the meat in his sack before starting all over again. The trick was knowing when to stop and move on to another location, something Minniwocket and Zookto had never learned. He glanced at Nacklebell, eyes widening when he saw a half-full bag strapped to his side. *Mother Earth, he's working fast! And here I've only got...* He nearly fell from his perch in shock when he looked down. His own bag held even more. *Work you enjoy always goes faster.* Chuckling, he turned back to the wall of muscle and started slicing.

By the time the crew returned, the pair sat on full bags, laughing and swapping tales. Dimknock nodded with approval at their own collection, jars of bile and bags of bone, marrow and tissue. Vand sat atop an irregular, canvas-covered mound, beaming proudly. The captain looked at him, eyebrows raised, but the miner waved it away.

"Later."

He frowned, then shrugged and hoisted his sack onto the pram. Nacklebell followed. As soon as they had seated themselves, Raulnab spun the propeller with a flick of his wrist and set the boat moving. Everyone remained quiet on the trip back to the ship, wilted and tired but smiling. *The lads have done well. They deserve a celebration.*

Peg leg pinging on the deck, Dimknock was first back on board *Windbreaker* when they docked. Once everyone had disembarked from the pram and Duvakor hoisted it on board, the captain called the crew around him.

"Lads, you've done me proud. You've earned a bit of merriment. What do you say we get to it?" The men cheered and started passing the jars and bags around.

Their high spirits faltered and devolved into confusion as Vand strode in the midst of the crowd with a piercing whistle. He leaned on his pick and waited, smiling, until every eye focused on him. He remained silent for a few moments longer, then straightened and spread his arms.

"Mates, I won't take long, but I guts a bit o' news for ya." He waved at the covered mound in the pram. Duvakor reached in with one huge paw and whipped the canvass off. Underneath lay a pile of irregular stones ranging from dark green to a refractive white. The crew released a collective hiss.

"Gallstones *and* kidney stones?" Dimknock said in a low voice. He limped to the pram and fingered the pile with an impressed whistle. "Master Vand, you get the first pick of the heart and bile." He turned with a huge smile spreading across his face. "What are ya waitin' for, lads? Dig in!"

Cheeks burning with embarrassment, Brian lay on his left side on an examining table. He had been given some drugs when he came in, but they either hadn't kicked in yet or they weren't going to help as much as he had hoped. *Maybe I should have gone for general anesthesia after all.* He'd never liked the idea of being put under, but it sounded like a good idea right about now. A pretty nurse checking his vital signs smiled at him. He groaned. *Please, just kill me now.*

"Mr. Peterson, you really need to relax," the doctor said behind him. "This won't take long, only an hour or so. Just take a few deep breaths and try to calm down."

"Easy for you to say," he muttered. But he did as he was told. Surprisingly, it worked. A little.

"That's better."

He heard the doctor adjusting the controls on the colonoscope. When Dr. Wesson had first showed it to him, Brian thought he was going to pass out. The thing looked like some sort of evil, black plumber's snake. He felt himself tensing up at the memory and tried to think of something else. *My heartburn and lower back pain are gone,* he thought. *Whatever else might be wrong with me, that's good.* He let his eyes slide shut.

A sudden pain ripped through his gut, followed by another. He could feel the scope moving around inside. He grabbed the side of the table and struggled to remain still.

"What's going on?" he asked through clenched teeth.

"Not now, Mr. Peterson," the doctor snapped. Another jerk of the scope and the doctor muttered, "You little butt pirate."

"Excuse me?" Brian yelled. He struggled to rise, but the sedatives made moving difficult. The nurse held him down.

"What? Oh. I wasn't talking to you. Now, please be still, Mr. Peterson. I will be with you in a moment."

He withdrew the scope and set it aside. Brian heard him walk off, followed by running water and some splashing. By the time he returned, the nurse had rolled Brian to his right side, facing the now-blank monitor. The doctor sat in a chair and peered at Brian for some time before speaking.

"Are you OK?"

"I'm fine." He grimaced. "Just a little shook up. It felt like someone was riding a roller coaster in there."

"I understand," Dr. Wesson said. His voice took on an urgent note. "Mr. Peterson, you have a very serious condition. You need treatment immediately."

"What is it? It's cancer, isn't it?"

"No. In some ways, that might be easier to treat. What you have is a particularly nasty infestation."

"Infestation?"

The doctor nodded. He reached into the pocket of his lab coat and pulled out a CD case. Turning, he opened a door on the cabinet beside him to reveal a computer. He placed the disc inside. The computer whirred and beeped for a moment before the monitor sprang to life.

Unable to help himself, Brian laughed. The image was of a short man with a red, conical hat and green coat and pants. A white beard hung to his waist. He lay spread-eagle and looked flattened, as if stepped on by an elephant. A pick lay just beyond one out-flung hand.

"Thanks, doc. I needed a laugh. Now, what's this about an infestation?"

"This is it," he said gravely.

"Oh, come on. Enough with the jokes already."

"I'm not joking, Mr. Peterson." He pointed at the screen. "That is a picture of what Dr. Smith found inside your mouth."

"He found a garden gnome digging at my teeth. Right." He struggled to a sitting position. "Look, Dr. Wesson, if you're going to keep pulling my leg like this, I'm leaving. I don't have time for this..."

"You're not going anywhere until the medication wears off, Mr. Peterson, so you might as well sit still and listen." He took a deep breath and punched a few keys on a tray underneath the desk. Brian found himself looking at an odd sort of tunnel, sort of like an earthworm turned inside out. "This is the recording of your colonoscopy." He hit a few more keys. The image jerked and steadied, revealing what looked like a giant cobweb. "This is what's blocking your colon."

The camera zoomed in until the web became a fine network of knotted ropes. The image slammed to the right, then backed up. The image jerked side to side and steadied as a pearlescent mass filled the screen. As the camera backed up further, the shape resolved itself into an odd ship with a large smokestack belching purple fumes and an ugly-looking harpoon gun up front. It reminded him of the pictures of old whalers he had seen at the museum. Shapes milled about the deck, gesturing at the scope. Then something flashed and the screen went black.

"That's where they shot the camera," he said. He tapped a few keys. The recording rewound and paused. If he squinted, Brian could just make out gnomes of various shapes and sizes, their faces twisted in rage.

"So you're telling me I've got an infestation of gnomes in a ship sailing around my colon," Brian said, his voice flat.

The gastroenterologist nodded. "*Pirata annulus*," he said. "More commonly known as butt pirates. It's a breed of micro-gnome." He stood and walked to a bookshelf on the far wall. "All gnomes have to avoid sunlight. It turns them into stone. Most live in the earth, but a few have adapted to live in other environments. *Pirata annulus* is one of the nastier ones. They sail in through the rectum at night, travel up the colon until they find a place to dock and set up a web to block the colon so they don't get pushed out." He returned carrying a large, ancient book.

"Dr. Smith had a book like that. I thought it was from medical school or something."

"Or something," Dr. Wesson said with a smile. "It's a grimoire. There's always few medical professionals who get a little bit of extra training in these matters; not many are interested in the arcane branches of medicine. We use this to identify the more... unusual conditions."

"What do they want?" Brian asked, curious despite himself. *It can't be that serious if he's keeping the joke up like this.*

"The same thing most living things want: Shelter." He paused. "Food." Brian gulped. "Indeed. They also mine the teeth and will take any gallstones and kidney stones they find. They seem to have a special fondness for cardiac muscle. The most common cause of death from this particular condition is a heart wall so weakened that it blows out. Any chest pains, Mr. Peterson?"

"A little," he whispered, trembling.

"Well, you're young, and they can't have been in there long. I'm sure you'll be just fine so long as we get them out of there soon."

"How?"

"With these." He reached into another pocket and removed a vial that rattled as it shifted and handed it out.

Taking the glass tube, Brian squinted inside. "Looks like rocks," he said, giving it back.

"In a manner of speaking. They're nanotrolls, the gnomes' natural enemy. We administer them via suppository and wait while they fight it out."

"You're going to start a war down there?"

"It's the only way to be sure we get them all. I could probably destroy the net and flush the ship out, but what if the gnomes are elsewhere? They'd die eventually, but not without taking you with them." He paused. "Mr. Peterson — Brian — I won't lie to you. This is a risky procedure. Trolls and gnomes are nasty fighters. You'll likely suffer some serious internal injuries. But we can probably repair those. We can't bring you back from the dead."

Brian shook his head. *What's going on here? Why am I listening to this quack? Gnomes? Trolls? Get real!* "That's enough." He slid off the table and stood on wobbly legs. "I don't know why I'm even listening to this. I've got to get home and find a real doctor." He scooped up his clothes and made his way out of the exam room, clutching the wall for support. "Then I'm going to call a lawyer. You'll be lucky to keep your license after this."

He staggered through the waiting room, still clothed in the hospital gown.

Dimknock watched the giant serpent retreat. His beard bristled with anger as he turned to Boddyjon and clapped the gunner on the back. "Nice work, mate." Boddyjon nodded and reloaded the harpoon gun. Letting rage fuel his voice to a roar, the captain addressed the rest of the crew: "They know we're here, lads. They've already tried to destroy the net. It'll be the trolls next, mark my word!"

"What'll we do, Gob?" Ranzle squeaked from the lookout.

"We grab everything we can and set sail before they get here." He jabbed his fingers at the crewmen. "Boddyjon, man the gun in case they send anything else after us. Ranzle, you let him know if anything's coming. Vand, get as much enamel as you can. Minniwocket, Zookto, Raulnab, you boys make the rounds and set to carving. Nacklebell and Duvakor will take you around in the *Windbreaker* and come back to pick you up and load the booty."

"Where are you going, Gob?" Nacklebell asked.

"I be headin' to the heart." He drew his sword and limped to the pram. "Move, lads. I'll meet you back here when I'm done."

He pushed off, barely acknowledging their salutes as he sped away. He seethed at the thought of having to depart another host prematurely. *We may be leaving, but we be leaving rich.* A savage grin spread across his face, and he urged the pram to greater speed. He crossed paths with *Windbreaker* several times; each pass showed a growing pile of booty and food on the deck.

Once he reached the heart, Dimknock beached the hull against the muscle and set to slashing with his sword, taking care even in his haste not to cut too deep in any one spot.

The measured beats continued steady for some time with a ponderous *lub-dub, lub-dub.* As he continued, the great muscle sped up, gradually at first, then with greater urgency until the beats ran together — *lub-dub, lub-dublub-dublubdublubdub.*

"You know I'm here, don't you? Scared? Good." He stabbed and fell over when his blade pierced all the way through. "Well, now. You've been a fine host, mate, but I see it be time to go." He made a mock bow, sheathed his sword and jumped in the boat, dragging a sack of flesh behind him.

The beating faltered and resumed with an odd, swishing note. Dimknock raced through the host, looking for his ship. He saw signs of his crew's activity — a cored bone here, a slashed organ there — but no sign of the men themselves. *Maybe they're waiting for me near the net.* He increased the pram's speed until it shuddered. *Got to get out before he dies.* Finally, the net came into view. He slowed as he approached the meeting place.

No one was there.

His head swiveled, searching for any glimpse of *Windbreaker*. *Did the dogs leave without me? No. They wouldn't dare.*

The heartbeat stuttered, picked up again and died. Dimknock felt the flesh around him shudder and sag. *Not much time left. Where are they?*

A sudden popping sound jerked his attention upward. More staccato bursts followed. A piece of webbing drifted down and landed in his lap.

The net was failing.

The wall in front of him creaked and bulged slightly. Growling under his breath, he reached back with one hand and started the propeller spinning. He crouched low in the boat as it lifted and started down the long tunnel. *Tonight, I find another host. Give me a few beats, and I'll find another ship — one not crewed by a bunch of panicked fleas that hop away at the first sign of trouble. I'll...*

Something rocketed past him, upsetting the boat and nearly knocking him out. *Did the net fail already?* He looked up, straight into Duvakor's broad, blank features. The bosun grabbed the pram and hauled it on board with a mighty heave. The boat crashed into the deck, spilling Dimknock to dash against the mast. Raulnab helped him up with a gap-toothed grin.

"Didja think we'd left ya, Gob?"

"Aye. But yer here now; I take back most of the nasty things I thought about you." He slapped him on the back and stamped over to Nacklebell at the helm. "Cuttin' things a tad close, don't you think, mate?"

Eyes fixed on the path ahead, the first mate didn't answer beyond jerking his head at something behind Dimknock. He turned and saw Vand wearing a sickly grin and wringing his hat.

"That'd be my fault, Gob. I found another cache of stones in the other kidney. I couldn't just leave 'em behind."

The captain scowled. Vand sweated. Face twitching, Dimknock let his expression dissolve into a smile. "So long as you had a good reason, mate."

A great ripping noise behind them brought every head to attention. They knew what that sound meant. "Net's gone, Nacklebell. Get us out of here!"

147

He nodded. "Hang on."

Windbreaker leapt forward. Purple smoke poured from her stack in a steady stream. The crew grabbed onto whatever was handy to keep from falling over. Dimknock looked back to see the filth their web had been holding back bearing down on them. He closed his eyes and waited for the avalanche to bury them.

Nothing happened.

He opened one eye and found himself staring at something white. He opened the other and saw a hard corner. They hovered against a great expanse of wall near the ceiling. *Free! We made it out!* "A fine bit of sailing, mate," he called to Nacklebell and walked to the other side of the ship.

Far below, an open window revealed the remains of a dying day. The light hurt his eyes, but remained far enough away that it posed no real threat. He glanced around the room and saw their host curled up on a reclining chair, hands pressed to his chest. He wore some kind of odd, backless robe. A look of surprise had etched itself into his face.

"Clean that mess up, lads," he shouted, gesturing at their meat and booty scattered across the deck. "Get it in the hold. Then get some rest. We've got a busy night ahead of us."

CRANK CASE

Engine loping at a rough idle, the battered white Delta 88 lumbered to a halt next to a pristine, red 300ZX parked in front of a gate set in a tall fence topped with razor wire. White letters proclaimed the blue metal building on the other side Hank's Complete Auto Care.

Hank Roland got out of the huge sedan. Light blue coveralls strained over his stocky frame, and the early-morning sun gleamed off his shaved head. He glanced at the Nissan's owner asleep behind the wheel before removing the large padlock and chain and rolling the gate open. Stooping to pick the newspaper up off the drive way, he climbed back in his car, tossed the chain and lock on the floor and pulled in. Hank tossed the paper on the tall counter in his office. It landed flat, revealing a colorful front-page illustration of a black-clad, burly figure standing with fists on his hips in classic superhero pose next to a beat-up old pickup. "Truckman: Masked menace or hometown hero?" a large headline shouted from the page. The editor had barely left any room for a piece about the continuing string of car thefts plaguing Greenville and how baffled the police were. *The cops better get on the ball. I really don't want to have to get involved with that.* Smoothing his goatee, Hank looked at the artwork again and growled in his throat. *They can't even get the picture right. He's not that fat, and everybody knows he drives a Ford. That thing looks like some kind of foreign job.*

He punched the switches to open all four garage base, walked back outside and tapped on the Z's hood. "What seems to be the problem?"

A harsh grinding punctuated the still morning, somewhere between clashing gears and a mountain clearing its throat. A gruff voice only he could hear followed. "It's this tightwad driver." A gurgling note resonated in every word. "Man won't buy nothin' but cheap gas. How am I supposed to get around with mostly water in my tank, dude? Idiot had to push me the last half-mile just to get here."

"OK, OK, I got it," Hank jumped in. *I hate sports cars.*

He rapped on the window. The young man inside — he couldn't be much more than twenty — shifted in the seat and rubbed his nose, but didn't wake. Hank knocked harder. The driver snorted and jerked upright. Hank backed up a couple of steps while he climbed out. He knuckled his back as he stood. "Oh, man, I hurt. I had to push it at least a mile." He ventured a weak grin. "Thought I was going to give myself a heart attack or something."

Hank nodded. They were both of average height and possessed roughly the same build, but the younger man looked pudgy and much softer than Hank's own stocky, muscular frame. "Did she die on you?"

"'*She*'?" an incredulous voice grated behind the driver. "Do I look like some kind of chick car to you?"

Hank ignored the comment. The owner didn't hear it, of course. "Yeah, man. I was on the interstate when it started to act all weird and losing power. By the time I got into town headed this way, it was running real rough. I kept it going for a couple more miles, then it just died and wouldn't start again."

"Could I get you to crank it?"

"Sure thing."

"Oh, come on, dude. Why'd you ask him to do that? I told you what the problem was..." The voice cut off as the driver dropped in the seat and turned the key. The engine sputtered and whirred. It caught and idled roughly for a moment, then backfired and died. Hank heard a grinding cough. "Told you."

"Alright," Hank said. "What do you say we get it up into the garage? I'll get in back. You steer."

They spent the next ten minutes maneuvering the Nissan across the parking lot and into the first bay. Two were already occupied. A glistening yellow '59 Chevy Apache hunkered at the far end, next to a blue Accord waiting for its owner after a brake job and new clutch.

The way she drives, that thing'll be back in here in no time, he thought as they shoved the Nissan into place. He frowned at a black puddle under the Honda's front bumper. *Oil leak? Might have blown a seal or something. I'll have to look at it before Melinda comes to pick it up.* He folded his arms and waited as the young man collapsed against the driver's door, panting and pulling his sweat-soaked shirt away from his chest.

"Would you hurry up and tell this fat slob I need a tune-up and a new exhaust? I want to get back out on the street, not sit in the garage."

"Shut up," Hank muttered. The driver looked up; Hank cleared his throat. "Sounds like you might have gotten some bad gas. You're going to need a tune-up at the very least — plugs, wires, probably an EGR valve, the whole nine yards."

"Anything else?" he wheezed.

"Hard to say until I tear into it, but it sounds like you might have exhaust problems, too."

"You can tell all that just from the way it sounds? Wish I could do that."

"Just one of those things that comes with experience, I guess." Hank shrugged uncomfortably. "There've been a bunch of stations around town with water in the gas lately. I kind of figured that's what happened to you."

"I heard about that, but I added a bunch of additive in the tank. I thought that'd take care of it." Hank couldn't quite stop himself from rolling his eyes. "That not right?"

"Those cleaners are OK a little bit at a time, but if you use too much, it'll trash the catalytic converter. It might have damaged a few other parts, too..."

"Yeah, genius," the Z grated.

"...but like I said, I won't really know until I get under the hood."

"How much?"

"Not sure. Could be a couple hundred or a grand, depending on what all's wrong with it."

The owner sighed, but nodded. "Whatever it takes, dude. Take care of my baby."

"Baby? Man, if I could start right now, I'd run you over myself. Too bad I can't sell you and get a new owner."

Hank clapped him on the shoulder. "Don't worry, son. Your baby's in good hands. Give me a few days, and I'll have her running like new." He steered the young man toward his office. "Got a ride home?"

Tapping a cell phone at his waist, he nodded. "Called a cab before I fell asleep. They said they'd be here a bit after eight."

Inside, Hank stepped behind a chest-high counter fished out a battered green spiral notebook, pulled a pen from the spine and spun it around to face his customer. "Alright, sir. If I could just get your information here, we'll be in business." He nodded and bent down, scribbling away at the notebook. His shoulder-length dirty blonde hair swayed with the force of his writing. Hank took it back once he had finished. "Thank you very much" – he looked down at the paper – "Harold Evans. I'll give you a call as soon as we're done."

"Thanks a lot, dude. My mom said you were real good with cars. Can't wait to get the Nissan running again."

"Your mother... would that be Judy? Gray Mercedes?"

"That's her." A horn sounded outside. They looked through the glass door at the yellow car parked outside. "Looks like my ride's here. Catch ya later."

"Don't you worry about a thing, sir."

Once Harold had gone, Hank sighed and let his smile slip. He glanced down at the front page of the *Herald-Banner*, scanning the article.

"...while many locals consider this super a true hero, some wonder if his seemingly gallant actions hide a deeper, more sinister motive. 'Most of these so-called metahumans have gravitated to the crime-choked urban areas where they can do the most good – Houston or even Dallas, for example,' said Dr. Phillip Geyer, a sociology professor at nearby Texas A&M University-Commerce. 'I have to admit I wonder why this Truckman would remain in a small town. Is it because he truly wants to help, or is it the lack of competition?'"

Hank tossed the paper back on the counter and walked through a side door to stare out in the garage. The Honda sat quietly at the far end. He wasn't sure whether that meant it had nothing to say or if it slept — or whatever it was cars did when he wasn't around to give them voice. *At least the Z's quiet now.* He sighed again and walked to a large toolbox to retrieve a socket set before venturing over to the sports car.

"Let's see what's wrong with you," he said, opening the driver's door and popping the hood. Glass rattled as he slammed the door.

"Watch it!"

"Quiet," he snapped back.

Walking around to the front, he raised the hood and looked inside. With all the hoses and wires, it looked like someone had dumped a bowl of spaghetti on top of the engine and left barely enough space to wiggle a wrench. *Whatever happened to the cars with enough room to stand in there with the motor?* He yanked the plug wires loose and slipped a socket over the nearest spark plug, a tricky affair involving an extension and a swivel to get the wrench in place. Once it felt seated, Hank turned the ratchet. The socket twisted, shifted to the left and broke free, bouncing off the motor with a loud clang.

"Hey! I need that!"

Hank sucked on bruised knuckles while pulling the wrench out. Inside he found a white ceramic stud. *Stupid thing broke!* He hammered a strut mount with the wrench.

"Cut it out, dude! Is this a garage or a chop shop?"

Growling, he spun on one heel and walked to a work bench against the back wall, ignoring the Nissan's taunts. Hank glanced over his shoulder. Satisfied he had no more of an audience than a couple of cars, he twisted a box wrench on the pegboard overhead while leaning against the bench's back leg and spinning a grinding wheel. Something clicked and the wall swung open. He stepped inside and pulled the concealed door closed behind him.

Aside from the secret entrance, there was little to differentiate this part of the garage from the rest. A set of tools sat on a bench to his right, next to what appeared to be a pile of folded black rags. A large, flatbed Superduty F-250 filled most of the space. To all appearances, the truck barely belonged on the road. Dents marred its flat, black paint, which had chipped in places to reveal a fire-engine red underneath. Hank ran his hands lovingly across the headlights and under the grill. His questing fingers found a latch and pulled. Spring hinges squealed as the hood lifted. Chrome and steel gleamed back up at him from the four-hundred-sixty-cubic-inch big block. Hank grinned at the headers and pair of turbochargers hooked to a large intercooler. *May not look like much, but she's a real screamer, and everyone in town knows it.* His smile wilted. A finger tapped his lips, pursed in thought. Not precisely true, but far too many in town did know Truckman's ride by sight these days. How much longer could he keep it hidden?

"I was wondering when you were going to come back here," the truck rumbled. "I haven't seen you in days."

"Been busy. You know how it is."

"I guess." The truck bounced suddenly, a rocking of its suspension that looked like a huge shrug. "Still, it'd be nice to get out of here. I'm going stir crazy being cooped up like this."

Hank fell back with a thud, eyes wide. He'd never seen one move before. It had been bad enough when they started talking to him a couple of years ago. At first, he had to be touching a vehicle to hear its voice in his head. Now, he just had to be within a couple hundred feet. He especially hated walking through parking lots and dealerships. *How much more are these powers going to grow? Are cars going to start coming to life and following me around town?*

"Look alive! We got company!"

The high-pitched voice brought him to his feet. His Olds didn't talk much, so he paid attention when it did. He scrambled to his feet and ran to the back. He grabbed the metal wall and heaved. A wide section slid sideways about a foot before its rollers squealed to a halt. Frowning, Hank squatted and felt along the metal track. One of the wheels felt wrong.

"You coming out here? I think this chick's going to come back there!"

It had gotten wedged on something that felt like a bracket. Standing, tried pulling and pushing on the door. It wouldn't budge either way, and he couldn't squeeze his frame through the narrow opening. The Olds called again, more frantic than before, and he could hear someone rattling the tools on his bench. Hank gritted his teeth, grabbed the door and shoved. The wall shuddered and flew open with a screech. A twisted Allen wrench spun out and slid underneath the Ford. Hank stepped out and yanked the hidden door the other direction. It rolled more smoothly than he expected and slammed shut, crumpling metal at the corner. He stepped back and stared at handprints forced into the metal. *Did I do that?* He stood there until the horn started blaring.

Hank ran around the building, slowing to a walk once he passed the front corner. The Olds kept honking until he banged on the hood. Melinda stood against the far wall, hands plastered over her ears. A maroon purse lay at her feet

"That was weird," she said, lowering her arms and stooping to retrieve her handbag. "That thing just started honking at me and wouldn't stop."

"Probably just a short." Hank ran his gaze over the wall. Everything seemed in place. *Not like she could figure out how to open it, anyway.* Melinda tapped her foot impatiently, curling a strand of her bleached blond hair around her finger. *She looks like a little kid.* He'd known the middle-aged woman for years, and she'd never stopped acting like a teenager. *I guess she thinks it's cute or something.* "Did you need something?"

"Yeah." Her look called him at least a half-dozen kinds of idiot. "My car. Where is it?"

"Right down there..." He turned and waved a hand down the line of bays, where the old truck sat alone. "Where'd it go?"

"That's what I asked you." She stared at his puzzled expression, and one hand crept to her mouth. "You don't think someone stole it, do you?"

"Must have." He shook his head. "Won't the cops just love that?"

As it turned out, the cop who pulled up in a patrol car an hour later had very little love for the news. Melinda gave a description of her vehicle and left with a girlfriend. Hank provided the rest of the information. Officer Bruce Watson sighed at each detail and shook his head every time he wrote something else in his little notebook.

"We're doing everything we can, Mr. Roland, but to be perfectly honest, I wouldn't hold my breath. This is the tenth theft in the last two weeks. They all start out the same way — car disappears right out from under the victim's nose. No one sees or hears anything. We've had a handful of sightings once the car's gone, but no one's ever seen anyone in it. And so far, not a single one has been recovered."

I know who I could ask. Hank bit his tongue to keep from saying it aloud. He glanced at the vehicles in the garage. Shaken by the events with his own truck, he hadn't dared talk to them about what had happened. Besides, what if the cops showed up and saw him arguing with a car? How would he explain that away? "That's not good," he muttered

Bruce scratched his head and nodded. "You got insurance for this sort of thing?"

"Yes, sir, but I really hate having to use it. I haven't had a break-in in five years, and I've never lost a car before."

"I understand, Mr. Roland, but unless we get a break soon, you're probably going to have to file that claim."

"Thank you, officer." Hank suppressed a groan and rubbed his chin. "What I don't get is why they went for the Honda and not the Apache. That thing's worth a lot more."

"How do you know they didn't? I thought you said it doesn't run."

"It doesn't, but there's no way the thief could have known that. I wasn't out of the shop more than a few minutes. As quick as they were in and out, they had to go straight for the Accord."

Officer Watson made another note and sighed again. "Well, that fits with everything else," he said without looking up from his notebook. He flipped back a few pages. "I've seen a Chevette stolen from the parking lot right next to a Porche. Last week, they took a beat up Brat and never even touched a fully restored Thing in the same garage. I tell you, I'd welcome help from just about anyone right now. You don't know this Truckman character, do you?"

Trying not to gape, Hank clasped his hands tightly behind his back. "Of course not. Why on earth would you think I would?"

The cop blinked and looked up. "Just a long shot. That guy's got to know some one around here." He tapped the notebook on the counter, then stuffed it in a pocket. "Well, I'll let you get back to work. I'll send you a report as soon as I get it written up so you can get started with your insurance."

"Thanks a lot, officer. Good luck cracking the case."

Bruce nodded and walked to the patrol car, patting the hood as he went by.

"Go! Go now!" the Crown Vic barked. Hank smiled. All the thing needed was a wagging tail. "Find bad guys! Catch 'em!" The siren chirped once. The officer paused in opening the door and frowned, then shrugged and sat down. Hank let out a long, ragged breath as he pulled away.

He bypassed the snickering Nissan and headed for the Chevy. After restoring the body, a friend had asked him to swap out the engine and transmission for a new, high-performance drivetrain. The pickup had an easy-going attitude; he didn't feel like putting up with the Z's abuse.

"Hey, sonny," the truck said as he approached. "Going to get this thing out finally?"

"Yep."

"Glad to hear it."

The hood had been unbolted weeks ago and lifted away easily enough. Hank looked over the engine bay, making sure all the wires, hoses and bolts had been removed. The whole affair rested on a couple of jack stands underneath the truck, waiting for him to pull the rusted engine and transmission out. He grabbed a control box dangling from an overhead crane and punched a button. Overhead, an electric motor clicked on and lowered a chain. He hooked it to a plate bolted to the top of the engine and pressed the other button. The chain tightened, and the engine started to lift out. Suddenly, the motor canted to one side and the winch whined.

The truck grunted "Ow! I thought you unbolted everything!"

"I did."

"Well, it sure doesn't feel like it! Turn that thing off!"

Hank cut the power and looked down at the engine. Something looked to have bound on the passenger side. *I did unbolt everything. What's the problem? Just one more thing to go wrong today.* Growling, he thumped the exhaust manifold. The truck groaned.

"Oh, stop it, you big baby." He grabbed the engine block and pulled. The truck yelled. The motor and transmission ripped free. Hank caught it with one hand to still the wildly swinging pendulum before it damaged the Chevy. A motor mount hung from one side, welded directly to the case.

"I'm in trouble."

"Tell me about it," the Z said, chuckling. "Can't keep your hands on vehicles in your own garage, and you're ripping the rest of them apart."

"Alright, that's it." He stalked toward the Nissan. "I've had just about enough of your lip... bumper... whatever." He shook his head. "Why don't you tell me what happened out here?"

"How should I know, you stupid grease monkey?"

Hank walked to the front, reached under hood and tugged on the intake manifold. "Try again."

"Keep those hams out of my block, you freak. I ain't telling you nothing." The engine coughed and sputtered. Hank pulled harder. "Hey, hey, hey! Look, I'm parked in here nose-first. I couldn't see a thing."

"Take it easy on him," the Olds whined. "It's not his fault."

He whirled and strode out of the garage to punch the Delta 88. His fist left a large dent in the fender. "That thing might have been in there, but you were sitting out here. Why didn't you say anything?"

"I thought it was you."

"What?" He grabbed the bumper. Metal crumpled under his hand. "Why would you think that? I was in the back!"

"Cause there wasn't anyone in it!" The sedan's engine suddenly turned over. Its transmission clicked and it backed away several feet.

"Get back here, you stupid car," he hissed. It stopped and slowly changed direction, as if hesitant to approach. "What do you mean there wasn't anyone in it?"

"Just that. It started itself and drove away."

"That's impossible..."

"Impossible?" the Nissan interjected. "Dude, you're talking to cars."

Hank froze. Much as he hated to admit it, the 300ZX had a good point. Shaking his head, he turned and walked toward the now-vacant garage bay. Even the oil puddle he'd seen earlier was gone. *Now how could that have happened?* He stared at the ground, lost in thought. Nothing about this made any sense...

"Son," the Apache said in an urgent whisper, "I think you'd better turn around."

Hank glanced around the parking lot and gasped. A blue Honda sat in the driveway. Once his gaze turned its way, the horn honked cheerfully, the lights flashed once and it backed out onto the street. The Accord zipped away amid a squeal of tires. No one sat at the wheel. *Oh, no you don't.* He ran to the office, snapped the switches to close off the garage and locked the door. Then he dashed into his secret room.

Once the door shut, he stripped off his coveralls and snatched the pile of black cloth from the bench. A pair of sunglasses clattered to the floor. He hurriedly donned the black T-shirt, jeans, ball cap and leather gloves. A black denim duster settled over his shoulders. Hank stooped and retrieved the wraparound shades and settled them on his face. He shoved the back wall open and gestured for the truck to move out. It started with a roar that settled to a deep rumble as it dropped into drive and eased its way outside. Hank closed the shop and climbed inside.

Catching sight of his reflection in the rear view mirror, he snorted at himself. "Truckman," he muttered derisively. "Sounds like something a kid made up."

"It's your own fault," the F-250 replied as they eased out onto the street. "You should've thought of something before they asked."

Hank shook his head. His first time out as "superhero" – he cringed even thinking of the term, but facts were facts – he had foiled a bank robbery by ramming the getaway car, then getting out and convincing the vehicle it was best if it didn't make any further attempt at escape. He'd been unable to get away after that without talking to the media. Someone had noticed him talking to the car, of course, and they all wanted to know about his "super powers" and what he called himself. Already off balance, the question threw him entirely. He stood there, stuttering until some guy behind him said "Look at that truck, man!" *Could have been worse, I guess. Good thing I wasn't driving a scooter.*

A flash of blue ahead drew him out of his reverie. The Honda had turned left and was making a break for the interstate. He reached the intersection a moment later, turned and stomped on the accelerator. The twin turbos kicked in, launching the truck toward the highway and shoving Hank back into the seat.

"Yeehaw!" they yelled together.

The Accord grew in the windshield until he was nearly on top of it. Jumping into the other lane, Hank twitched the wheel, trying to clip its bumper. The blow missed. The car abruptly slowed amid squealing brakes. He shot past. In the rearview mirror, he saw the Honda turn under an overpass and head back toward town. He slowed and made a ponderous U-turn before following.

The truck proved unwieldy in town. The sedan stayed just ahead of him, making odd turns and backtracks, but always staying just within sight. *Is this thing playing with me?* The chase continued for more than an hour, slowly spiraling toward the oldest part of town. Hank had little choice but to follow until it disappeared from sight.

He found himself on a vacant, tree-lined street. Most of the houses had been demolished or burned down years ago, although one or two shells remained standing amid the overgrown yards and gardens. He caught sight of the remains of a few driveways, but no cars. He slowly accelerated. "Looks like we lost it."

"Sorry, boss."

"That's—"

The truck lurched to the right. Dazed, Hank applied the brake and looked around. The Honda lurked off to his left, front end crumpled with coolant leaking from the ruptured radiator. Its engine revved like a sinister sewing machine. He put the truck in park and climbed out.

"Boss, what..."

Hank made a shushing gesture and slowly walked toward the wounded car. It rolled forward a few feet, then stopped. The engine revved harder. Steam poured from the hood.

"Did you really think you could take out something that big?"

"I don't... not sure... where am I?" Confusion filled the feminine voice. "What happened? Why aren't I at the garage?"

"What do you mean what happened? You just tried to run over my pickup."

"No... that wasn't me." The car lurched forward. "I can't stop it! Why can't I stop?"

Tires squealed as the Honda raced toward him. He stepped back. A black, growling blur leapt past him and struck the car's front corner. Both came to a halt. "Wow." The Ford's voice quavered, as if shaken. "That hurt."

Hank walked around. The pickup had a few new dents, but looked fine otherwise. The Accord, however, had clearly seen its last road trip. Its hood lay in the street, along with the bumper and one wheel. Its engine knocked and constantly threatened to die, but somehow remained running. It limped toward him. He raised one fist as it crawled nearer and punched the motor. Asphalt grated as engine and transmission fell out. The car wheezed and died.

"Told ya you couldn't take my truck out."

He turned to go, then froze when the sedan spoke. The voice had none of the gentle touch he had come to associate with Melinda's car. This high-pitched, venomous growl set his teeth on edge.

"Think... you've... won?" It gasped, wounded, but still menacing.

"It sure looks that way to me." He folded his arms. "And I'd be willing to bet I'll find those cars you took out here somewhere, too."

"Who... cares about... cars?" Surprisingly, the thing laughed. It sounded like a band saw cutting through steel. "Found you... can't win... stupid... grease monkey..." The car fell in on itself with a loud bang. Oil dribbled out into the street.

"'Grease monkey'? That's the best you can come up with?" Shaking his head, he went back to his truck. "You OK, partner?"

"Think so. Just a few more dings, and my steering's a bit off, but it's nothing that can't be fixed."

Hank laughed. "True enough. Say, did you get a look at where that thing came from when it hit us?"

"Sure did, boss. Whole bunch of cars on a vacant lot over there."

"I thought there might be. What do you say we go take a look and then call the cops? I bet they'd love to know where all those stolen vehicles are."

The Superduty roared to life and rolled down the street. Behind them, the puddle of oil drew in on itself and formed a black ball that rippled and sloshed until a simian face peered across the street. Its eyes narrowed, and its lips curled in dark amusement. The Grease Monkey gave one bubbling laugh, then let its form collapse once more. The oil slid into the gutter and down a storm drain.

THINKING SMALL

Sho'Naris had only the briefest of warnings, the slightest rustle of leaves and a darker patch of shadow. She leapt forward as a hairy blur landed behind her with a thud. The Fairy whirled to face her foe, a long braid of brown hair whipping against her face. Wings fluttered to maintain her balance. The wolf spider stalked through a shaft of sunlight filtering through the forest canopy. Black eyes glittered at her, hard and cruel as the obsidian tip of her spear.

"Big one, aren't you?" she said. "Maybe I should find a saddle and reins."

She waited, spear at the ready as it closed the gap. Her lips quirked in a smile. The distance between them narrowed, and still she refused to move. A faint, metallic click intruded on the quiet morning. She shook her head. *No distractions.*

The spider crouched. Sho'Naris hurled the spear at its cluster of eyes. The creature squatted further. She grinned. *Not enough, hunter.* Her weapon flew over the beast's head and straight for its abdomen. The obsidian spearhead glanced away with a screech before thudding into a branch beyond. She caught glimpse of a long, copper scar along the spider's back before the creature leapt. The ticking grew louder as it landed astride the Fairy. Its fangs stabbed down. Venom dripped onto her shoulder, burning the skin.

Sho'Naris sang, a wordless Song as changing as the notes in a rocky stream. Fangs halted a hair's breadth from her face, and the spider flew into the air. Its legs scrabbled for purchase as the beast revolved inside an iridescent bubble. She hovered to peer at her prisoner. Free of gravity's clutches, its movements turned erratic, jerking in time with the clattering noises that came from within.

"What in the name of the Great Mother are you?"

She sang again, ending with a few wild notes. The bubble's interior burst into flame. She shielded her eyes with one hand and backed away from the bright orange ball. When it faded, she found herself facing a monster.

It had a spider's shape, but no true arachnid had a metallic gleam that shone through grime and soot like a new-minted coin. Something like a blocky stinger protruded from its abdomen. Only its black eyes remained the same.

As the beast's revolutions brought it around, Sho'Naris noticed a small hole in the top of its abdomen. The ticking was loudest there. Another brief Song, the spider halted, and a hole opened in the shield. Her spear wrenched itself free of the far branch and flew to her hand. Useless though it had been in this particular battle, grasping the weapon made her feel better. She approached cautiously, took a deep breath and touched the beast.

She hissed at the feel of cool metal. *It was hunting me. How could it not be alive?* She tried to look into the cavity, but encountered only blackness. Sho'Naris cupped her hand, whispered a few notes, and a glowing speck formed over her palm. The spark rose into the air. It floated near the spider's abdomen for a moment, then slid into the opening. The Fairy peeked inside.

Flickering light revealed a bewildering jumble of brass stars and circles clattering away. *Is this what Sho'Raki was trying to tell us about?* Her brother had reported some new kind of magic the Humans called "technology," but she'd never been able to fathom his descriptions. He made everything sound like one of those unnatural boxes they used to slice the day into bits of bite-sized time.

"Great Mother shelter us," she muttered.

Straightening, she jabbed her spear into the spider's metal guts. The weapon jerked and turned a few times, then sagged. The ticking became a grinding. The spider's legs splayed in a rigid fan, then curled against its belly as the beast fell silent. Sho'Naris pulled her lance free. Half its obsidian head had broken off.

"A fine hunt," she said and saluted. "But why are you here?"

She lighted on a branch and stared at the gleaming contraption. The problem turned over and over in her mind, but she could make no sense of its design. This part of the forest belonged to them by a pact older than many of her trees. Why would Humans come here?

What could they want? Sho'Naris jerked her head side to side, trying to shake loose questions that whined and bred inside her skull like mosquitoes near a pond.

Tossing the broken spear aside, she stood and pointed at the mechanical creature floating above her head. It followed her finger downward to rest in the crook of a branch. The Fairy sent her mind diving into the force that flowed across the Earth like a great river, let its Song fill her until the notes emerged in her own voice. Tree bark grew around the spider, hiding it from view. She smiled at the power flowing through her; she never understood why Humans insisted on their wyrds, expending so much energy to create artificial dams and channels to guide a bit of magic their way rather than riding the currents to find what they needed. She glanced at the new knot on the tree limb. *What if they can't?* It was a new thought, one that filled her with a great sadness. *Is it possible all their minds can devise are these mechanical contrivances?*

Too many questions. Shaking her head, the Fairy stretched her wings and took off toward the nearest forest edge in search of answers.

"Beautiful, aren't they?"

General Mykal grunted as a brass wasp and scorpion battled inside a cage on the large worktable that took up most of Vanden Bok's sizable tent. He found their ferocity impressive, but this bloody *tinkerer* spent more time on his little pets than creating anything useful. Vanden had a flock of butterflies fluttering around the glade and moped like a little girl every time a soldier stepped on one. They had already lost most of the day with the elderly engineer fretting over a spider that failed to return. The general shook his head. *At least he's not going on about ants today. That man won't be happy until he creates an army of fleas.*

"Oops, that one finally wound down," Vanden said.

He opened a door on the front of the cage and reached a slender hand inside. The scorpion drooped across a branch in one corner. He drew out a fine chain from the neck of his shirt. A square, iron peg with a crossbar dangled at the end. Vanden retrieved a pair of thick-lens spectacles and perched them on his sharp nose. Removing

165

the chain from around his neck, he inserted the key into a small hole on the scorpion's back and twisted it for several minutes.

Mykal sighed and paced, chainmail rattling under his purple tunic with each step. For such small devices, it seemed to take forever to wind them up. Of course, he had seen them run for days without needing any further attention. Vanden said it had something to do with efficient springs, gears and escapements. He even claimed he would be able to make them self-winding one day. *That'll happen about the same time he makes something practical.* He pivoted, stalked back to the table and smacked Vanden on the back of his bald head.

"Why are you wasting time with that?" he barked. "I thought you said one of these bugs could wind another."

"Oh, they can indeed." The engineer didn't react to Mykal's blow, but then he never did. Holding the key in place with his thumb, he curled the brass tail over his hand and pushed the stinger back until it snapped into place, careful to avoid the sharp tip. A square protuberance sat on the reverse side. "But it takes everything they have. I'd much rather keep them running myself. Let them save their energy for hunting or delivering instructions to each other."

"Instructions?" Mykal's eyes narrowed. *Is he making fun of me?* He balled his hand into a fist.

"Of course. There's more to their gearing than just running around on the ground. How do you expect to get them to focus on a target if you can't direct them somehow?"

Vanden fell silent and resumed working the key until it started making a ratcheting noise. He set the scorpion on the table. It scurried down onto the floor, pincers spread and tail poised. *That thing manages to look angry enough for a hunk of metal.* Mykal watched it wander into a corner then turned back to the old man with a growl.

Grabbing Vanden's ears, Mykal bent over until his blue-eyed gaze met the tinkerer's fearful stare. "Listen to me, you little clockmaker..."

"Engineer," he squeaked.

"What?"

"The king named me Royal Engineer..."

"I don't care what the king called you. All I care about is the mission he gave me." Mykal released his head and straightened, gesturing at the golden triangle supporting a black crescent moon and eight-pointed star on his tunic. "The lords are clamoring for more land for their peasants to farm. Noem Zis wants this part of the forest cleared and readied for settlers. You're here because somehow you convinced His Majesty you and your 'technology' could deal with the Fairies infesting these woods. I don't know how you think you can deal with their magic when the king's own mages can't, but you will deliver on your promise. Otherwise, I'll find some real ants and stuff you head-first into their mound. Is that clear?"

"Yes, general, but..."

"But nothing," he snapped. Something moved beside his foot. Looking down, he saw the mechanical scorpion moving across the tent floor. Mykal stomped on it with a booted heel. Metal grated under his foot. "Whatever weapons you think you can devise, I want them now. No more bugs. It's time for you to think big. I want those bloody Fairies wiped out within the fortnight."

Vanden opened his mouth, whether to agree or protest, the general never discovered. Something flashed past his face with a shouted, "No!" The soft, feminine voice seemed to come from everywhere. He barely had time to swat at it before music tried to crush him.

It was a Song such as he'd never heard, wild and haunting. The melody pressed on his skull even as it threatened to make his head explode. Something warm trickled out his ears and red filled his vision. He fell to his knees. Despite his peril, Mykal found himself straining to listen to the melody, afraid to miss even one beautiful, deadly note. Darkness filled the edges of the world and started to creep inward. He fell face-first to the floor.

The Song ended with a clatter. Gasping, the general rolled onto his back. He wept as vision returned to one eye; the other had gone blind. *I'm alive!* He kept patting himself. A questing hand found wetness at his ear. He drew fingertips to his good eye and found blood. He wiped it on his pants and sat up. Teardrops landed on his tunic. *Gods, what's wrong with me? I'm alive!* Still, he couldn't quite banish a pang of loss for the departed music. He took a deep breath and forced himself to stand.

The engineer stood at his workbench, hunched over something on the table. Cursing, Mykal staggered beside him and cuffed his head.

"What are you doing, man? Something nearly killed me, and you're over here tinkering?"

Rather than reply, Vanden pointed to a glass cylinder twice the size of his head. A fine network of wire had been woven into the glass, even the flat lid. The container held a miniature forest. Branches and leaves took up most of the space, except for a patch of sand on the side. A figure sprawled across the bare spot. Squinting, Mykal peered past the metal web. A miniature woman clad in a gray shirt and leggings lay on the miniature beach. Two pairs of dragonfly-like wings splayed behind her; one appeared broken.

"You caught it? How? I nearly died because of that thing."

"I found it less than pleasant myself. I can only surmise she was so focused on you her wyrd didn't affect me as strongly."

"But glass? She'll break out of there as soon as she wakes up."

"I think not, general." Wearing an enigmatic smile, Vanden opened a chest on the back of his table and pulled out a smaller wooden box that shifted and rattled in his hands. He eased the lid back on its hinges. A hairy spider scrambled inside, ticking slightly as it moved. In a single, swift movement, the engineer pulled the top off the jar, dumped the spider inside and settled the lid back in place. The creature disappeared into the foliage. The Fairy stirred and climbed to its feet.

"You fool. You've waited too long." He drew a dagger from his side and reached for the glass prison.

"Just a moment, please, general."

Inside the jar, the prisoner took a breath and opened its mouth. The music it produced was nothing like the earlier Song. Cracked, monstrous notes reverberated inside the glass and drilled into his ears. Sound cut off as the Fairy fell to its knees. "What..." Mykal swallowed. "What just happened?"

"You're forgetting your childhood tales." Vanden still wore that mysterious smile. "What was the one thing that always thwarted the Little People?"

"You're asking me about stories my nurse told me? What do you think..." A memory surfaced. "Iron? There's iron in the glass?"

"I gave the glassblower fits getting this right, but it proved my theory was sound — I've always thought solid metal cages were unnecessary. All you need is a small amount of iron to disrupt the magic." His smile widened as he glanced down at the jar. "Look there."

The spider had found its way through the leaves and crept out into the open. The Fairy sang again, a mere whisper just on the edge of hearing. Something like a crystal bubble shimmered around the hairy beast. It paused, then stepped through the sphere. The Fairy screamed, and its Song rose in pitch. Fire raced across the spider's skin, burning away the covering Vanden put on some of his creations. What remained glistened a dull gray. The Fairy dashed into the tiny forest, spider stalking silently behind.

Mykal turned to the engineer. "You finally created an iron bug?"

"Yes, sir. The brass was easier to work with, but ultimately useless for our purposes. Once I got the blacksmiths accustomed to working on such a small scale, I started them making steel parts. This is the first one, finished just last night." He chuckled. "A fortnight, you said? We'll have an army of spiders, scorpions and wasps hunting down these Fairies in half that time."

A sudden burst of heat and light drew their attention back to the desk. The fire had returned, a great ball of orange that pressed against the glass until blackened, cracked and shattered. The Fairy barreled out of the tent, flying in odd rises and dips as if it couldn't gain altitude. The spider emerged from the tiny conflagration and scurried in pursuit.

"Idiot!" The general backhanded Vanden across the mouth. The blow felt weak, but still had enough power to back the engineer up a few steps. Vanden stumbled and fell to the floor. Mykal growled in disgust and booted him in the ribs. Vanden grunted. "You and your glass cages. It escaped! If I find a Fairy army on our doorstep because of your incompetence, you're going out on the front line."

"I miscalculated." Vanden shrugged and wiped a hand across his bloody mouth. "She may have run, but she won't escape. Spiders are the greatest hunters, after all." He placed a hand on the table and hauled himself upright. He locked gazes with the general, folded his arms and offered a bloody smirk.

"You tell me to think big, as if an army of giants could bash their way into whatever nest these creatures live in and step on them all. Your problem, general, is that you don't think small enough."

Panting, Sho'Naris dashed through the air and out of the Human encampment. *Rash, too rash. Father always said I was reckless.* One of her wings barely functioned and another felt strained. She doubted she could maintain this pace all the way to the Vale, but right now, reaching the safety of the forest was paramount. *Safety?* Bitter laughter escaped her lips. *Even a Choir would be useless against these iron beasts.* She chewed on her lip as she flew, refusing to slow until she entered the trees' welcoming embrace. She passed the spot where she had battled the other spider — was it only this morning? — and slowed. Her people might not know how Human machines worked, but she knew someone who might. *If he doesn't kill me out of spite. But what choice do I have?*

She landed on the branch and sat, trying to catch her breath. Once she stopped gasping, Sho'Naris stood and sang to the wood. Bark split and parted, revealing the brass spider inside. Another Song sent it rising in the air. She glanced briefly to the north, toward the Vale, then took off toward the south. The metal spider floated behind her like a worker ant following the trail of its predecessors. She moved slowly, favoring her injured wing. She spent half her time trying figure out what she might say to the creature once she arrived. The other half, she wondered what she would say to her father. He wouldn't like this.

He doesn't have to. I am not a child or some lowly caste member content to hide in her work. Sho'Torin had a fearful temper, and even one of the royal family might fear his wrath. But the king would not live forever, and already the Council of the Vale had started whispering among themselves as to whether she or her brother would make a better candidate for the Hawthorn Crown. Even if she preferred they passed her over, she had to prove she was not a weak link in the royal chain. *We have ruled for six generations. I will not be the reason the Council looks elsewhere for the seeds of another Dynasty.* She shook her head angrily. Her Song was as strong as any, but she had to prove her own faith in it.

The Fairy was still in mid-thought when she reached her destination.

This small clearing looked little different from any other in the forest, save for its absence of birds or insects singing in the trees and undergrowth. A round stone sat in a bed of moss. Heaps of rotting flesh, tiny bones and insect shells littered the glade. She landed in a clear spot and set the spider down behind what might have once been a rat. Her nose wrinkled at the smell as she pounded on the stone.

"Ho, cousin!"

"Go away!" The voice rumbled from deep underground, as if the earth itself had spoken.

"I must speak with you, cousin. Or don't you care whether you live or die?"

Grumbling greeted her question. It grew louder as long moments passed. Finally, the rock lifted and what had to be the most unpleasant being in the forest emerged.

They stood of equal height, but the boggart was at least twice as wide as it was tall. If it had a neck, it was buried in rolls of fat. Course, brown hair covered its body, nearly obscuring its nakedness. Its odor overpowered even the refuse around its door. *I just hope I caught it in a helpful mood today. If it's feeling mischievous, I may never get out of here.*

"What does a child of the Vale want with me?"

"Greetings, cousin. I am Sho'Naris..."

"I don't care who you are, Fairy. You said this concerns my survival. Out with it, or you'll regret disturbing me."

Sho'Naris swallowed her retort. Trying to magic a boggart was tricky at best, and she still felt weak. "Humans are planning to clear the forest and build here."

"Thanks for the warning, but I can handle myself. Many of my brothers do quite well in their cities. Lots of fun among Humans and their contraptions."

"So the last wild boggart in these woods is ready to trade rock and tree for stone dwellings and streets?" She cocked an eyebrow. "Are you so eager to be tamed?"

The creature swelled in outrage. "No one tames me, Fairy." Its wide mouth split in a grin, exposing yellow, crooked teeth. "I'll survive when they move here. Will you?"

"Perhaps," she said through gritted teeth.

It nodded and lifted the stone door. "Then there's no need for me to kill you."

171

"What makes you think they plan to leave you alive?" A short Song and the spider rose from its resting place. It landed with a crash on the rock, jerking the door out of the boggart's hand. "They're bringing their 'contraptions' with them, cousin, ones that hunt."

It studied the metal arachnid for several moments, then shoved it aside. "A thing of gears and wheels. It's made of brass, a weak metal. Why should I care?"

"Because the Humans are building an army of iron beasts at this moment."

"They bring iron to my forest?" it whispered.

"*Your* forest? My father is king. You should be glad I'm offering you an opportunity to help."

"Your father's authority ends at the Vale. He has no power here." It chewed on one clawlike nail. "I think I'll just hole myself up in my home and let these iron beasts run over you annoying little bugs. Humans can't be near as irritating as Fairies." It grabbed the spider by one leg and opened the door to its burrow. "I'll keep this as payment for your intrusion. Maybe I can learn something from it for when the Humans move in."

"But we need that to prepare..."

"All you need to prepare for is death, little Fairy."

Scowling, Sho'Naris took to the air and watched the creature stuff itself into its hole. *By the Great Mother's own name, how could the thing be so fearless?* She bellowed a few notes, and a sudden gust of wind whipped through the clearing. She fluttered into the air, then turned back. *No, not totally fearless.* "Boggart!"

"I said go."

"I'm leaving, but I thought you might like to have one other bit of information before I die." She took a deep breath and gagged at the stench. "You say no one can tame you, but these Humans know where you are. Even if they let you live, I hear they plan to name you."

It didn't respond, but shouted and yanked on the spider so hard its leg popped free. It tossed the limb aside and grabbed another and jerked the machine down into the hole. The boggart cursed loud enough she could hear it even once the door had closed. Sho'Naris smiled to herself as she flew home.

Grasping her spear in a white-knuckled grip, Sho'Naris looked at the figure to her right. Sho'Torin stared back imperiously for a moment. Then a smile softened his stern features and he patted her hand. Those nearby looked away; her father could not be shamed by such a public display of affection if no one saw it.

"Try not to fret, daughter. We shall be victorious."

"I hope you're right, Father. I just pray I haven't made things worse."

"We have seen no sign of the boggart. I think your plea fell on deaf ears. It's for the best. The boggart is unreliable, as likely to attack us as help."

"Thank you, Father." She inclined her head and fluttered to another branch above. A few days with the healers had mended her wings.

She looked across the field at the Human encampment. *Will today be the day?* The Fairy glanced down at the king's iron-gray hair held in place by the flowering Hawthorn Crown. *I will not fail you again, Father.* They had been already seen several sunrises here on the edge of the clearing, waiting for the Humans to make the first move. The Fairies spent their days targeting the mechanical beasts to refine their tactics.

Sho'Raki had argued for an all-out assault on the encampment, but the king overruled her brother. They were too few, he said. Let the Humans come to them. They had to know the Fairies were here. The bald man found every butterfly they destroyed, weeping over each one as if it were his own kin.

Sighing, Sho'Naris slumped on the branch and leaned against the tree trunk. Her spear picked off ridges of bark and sent them tumbling below. She was still looking down when the gray spider landed inches away, front legs raised as if to drag her into its waiting fangs. The Humans had not bothered to clothe this one; it gleamed in the growing sunlight.

Leaping off the branch, she called out a warning, only to find it unnecessary. Everywhere she looked, Fairies faced off against shining foes.

All manner of Songs filled the air. Stones ripped themselves free of the ground and hurled into the beasts. Trees grew new wood that enveloped the machines. Below, a ball of white-hot flame wreathed a scorpion threatening her father. When the fire passed, his Song changed and frost spread across the beast. Sho'Torin hammered it with the butt of his spear and the metal shattered. Off to the left, her brother waited on a willow branch while a huge spider leapt at him. The tree sprouted new, slender branches that caught the spider and crept into its inner workings. It froze and dangled like some weird fruit.

Sho'Naris dove spear-first and rammed the spider threatening her. Her weapon broke off inside the hole on its back. The impact knocked it off the branch, gears grinding to a halt as it fell. She yelled and glanced across the field. For every spider or scorpion felled, three more took its place.

Not every battle went their way. To her right, a long-legged arachnid bit the head off one of her cousins. Tears filled her eyes as she whirled away only to watch another of her kin screamed as a pair of scorpions stung her over and over. A dozen other bodies littered the trees. Sobbing and still holding the splintered haft of her spear, she flew to her father.

"We must form a Choir," she said. "Together we can..."

"Accomplish nothing," Sho'Torin interrupted. "They are too spread out, too well hidden. If they came in a wave, then maybe a Choir could do something. But as it stands, we must fight them wherever we see them." He spread his wings and took off, bellowing a Song that opened fissures in the earth to swallow a scorpion and three spiders. Something buzzed angrily past her head and landed on his back.

"Look out," she screamed.

The steel hornet drove its stinger through Sho'Torin's spine, pulled free and stabbed again, this time in his heart. Blood pouring from his mouth, the king went limp and fell to the ground.

Sho'Naris shouted and threw herself into the air. Her Song came hard and fast, creating knots of air that pummeled the hornet from all sides. Its hide dented but held. The creature turned toward her just as she reached her target. She clubbed its faceted eye with the remains of her club, and the crystal shattered. She glimpsed a complicated array of teeth and wheels before shoving the haft into the gears. They chewed on the wood for a moment, then froze. The hornet fell like a stone, landing beside her father's body.

Rising, she cast about for her brother. Sho'Raki would be in charge until they returned to the Vale. *The Council will have to make its decision sooner than expected.* She spotted him hovering over a rock that bounced along the ground, smashing everything underneath. She flew to his side, trying to speak through sobs that wracked her body.

"What is it?" he asked, letting the stone fall for good.

"Father is dead," she managed between gasps. "One of those things got him."

"Where?"

She pointed to the wasp on the ground. "You must tell the others. You're battlefield commander now."

Sho'Raki nodded. "We'll crush these bugs, then go after the Humans."

She hovered in place as her brother flitted away. *You can have any Humans I leave alive, brother.* She dove and raced just above the grass. The tents grew in her sight. *If there are any.* She didn't plan to let any escape the forest, out into the plains where she couldn't follow. *This ends here and now.* She increased her speed, eyes fixed on the encampment.

Something struck her side, knocking her to the ground. She climbed groggily to her feet and swayed as she rubbed her eyes, trying to clear her vision. A shape lunged at her and she half jumped, half fell to the left. The scorpion turned and jabbed with its stinger. She leapt again. She shook her ringing head, trying to clear her mind enough for a Song. Every time she stopped moving, the beast attacked. She feinted left and jumped right. A pebble caught her foot and slammed her into the dirt. Sputtering, Sho'Naris rolled over and scooted backwards on her hands and feet as the scorpion approached. It raised its stinger.

A bronze-colored flash tackled her attacker. A pair of meaty hands grasped hers and yanked her to her feet. The stench of a midden heap cleared her head. She turned, and the boggart grinned at her.

"Why?" she asked.

"Why not?" It laughed. "Humans are all well and good, but I won't have anyone naming me."

Metal screeched. Turning, Sho'Naris saw a seven-legged brass spider tangled with the steel scorpion. The spider didn't seem to be attacking so much as trying to climb on its back. Stinger swept down and hooked under one of the spider's legs. It used the motion to clamber astride the scorpion, jabbing the angular rod on its abdomen into a hole on the other's back. Both beasts froze. The spider fell lifeless to the ground, and the scorpion turned back toward the forest. The tail stiffened, stinger curling under to reveal a square key as it scrambled away.

"What in the name of the Great Mother just happened?"

"Interesting creatures, those things." The boggart belched. "They're built like clocks, but they can do much more. I think one of those critters could wind the other one up if it had a mind to. They can also rework their innards to give instructions. That scorpion is going to find the nearest fellow and tell it to turn around and do the same to another, then head back to camp." The creature chuckled. "Pretty soon, they're all going to be headed that way. Those Humans are going to get stung bad today."

"I aim to do more than sting them," she said. "Sho'Torin is dead."

"They got the king? He wasn't a bad sort, for a Fairy. Never harmed anyone who didn't deserve it." It scratched itself and belched again. "I best get out of here if you're about to start one of your Songs. Those things always give me a headache. Maybe I need to move somewhere I don't have to worry about them anymore." The boggart lumbered off toward the Human camp, disappearing amid blades of grass. Its smell took much longer to fade.

Sho'Naris flexed her wings and rose into the air. She cleared her throat, took a deep breath and paused. *The boggart was right. Father was always reluctant to harm others. Is this what he would want?* She looked down. Shining creatures were already moving toward the Humans. *The big picture, he said. What is the bigger picture?*

A high, piercing sound interrupted her thoughts. In the distance, the bald man staggered out of his tent, screaming and slapping at himself. He ran in circles, each pass slower than the last until he stumbled and fell face-first into the dirt. Panic seized the camp. Armored men ran about, waving their arms as if unsure what to do. Several joined the first on the ground. None who fell rose again.

Her brother flew up beside her. "I don't know why, but the machines have all fled."

"It was the boggart. It decided to take advantage of an opportunity for some mischief."

"Thank the Great Mother. That means we can go after the Humans now. I have a Choir prepared. No trace of this band will ever be found." He placed a hand on her arm. "You are to be Choir leader."

The survivors had gathered in the branches of an enormous live oak. Sho'Naris lighted amid a clump of leaves on the tree's outer edge. Her brother started the Song, his normally mild tenor shot through with menacing bass notes. Others blended their voices into the melody, and the Song swelled. It called to her with promises of ice and fire, water and earth, life and death. Sho'Naris hesitated. *What should I do with such power?* Sho'Torin may have been reluctant to harm others, but he deserved vengeance, and she realized these Humans could not be allowed to escape unscathed. Her people were bound to the forest, they could not afford to have the Humans return to swarm over them. *What would be a fitting death, Father?* She gazed out at the chaotic camp, where their music had apparently reached the Humans. Many stopped running and looked about wildly. A few sank to the earth, hands over their ears, only to fall prey to their miniature iron hunters. *So many have died already. I wish I could just wash the forest clean of them.* Turning her eyes to the blue sky, the Fairy opened her mouth and sang.

Clouds blocked out the sun, darkening as they piled ever higher. Lightning forked across treetops and thunder boomed over the world. Rain fell, fat drops that bent stalks of grass and soaked the earth. Pools formed where the ground could hold no more. They joined together to form small ponds that grew until the clearing became a shallow lake.

And still the rain came.

Peril drove the Humans to action. Their battle leader moved among them, shouting at men huddled on the ground or cowering in tents. Those he could not cajole he pummeled into submission. All the while, he kept an ear cocked toward the Song and his shoulders hunched. Every so often, he lifted a boot and stomped something into the mud or fingered a patch covering his right eye.

The men leapt to work. They collapsed tents, rolled them up and loaded horses and wagons. By now, the water had developed a current. Bodies and discarded supplies floated away while the Humans marched east. The general sat astride a black horse that picked its way through water swirling around its ankles. He drew rein on the opposite side of the clearing and turned back. He drew his sword and raised it skyward, whether in salute or a promise of retribution, Sho'Naris could not say. *That one will be trouble if he leaves.*

A piercing note rose through the Song, and a bolt of lightning lanced from the sky. It struck the steel blade. General and mount collapsed twitching into the running water, along with a handful of soldiers felled by the blast. The survivors broke into a panicked run, and the forest swallowed them.

Sho'Naris stopped singing. Her brother gathered a double handful of the most able-bodied warriors and took off in response. None of the Humans would make it beyond the trees.

"Rest well, Father," she murmured. "We are safe."

A TWIST OF THE KNIFE

The battered knight trudged up the hill toward the encampment at the top, trailed by an equally battered roan warhorse. Dyrkum paused once to look westward at the sunset, the death of Daylight, then clucked and jerked on the reins in his left hand to get the horse moving again. His right hand rested on the flanged mace at his side to keep it from bumping his leg. Once he crested the rise and started between the rows of tents, the taunting began.

Men pointed at the shield hanging from his saddle and nudged their neighbors to gawk at the enraged rooster. Colored in shades of flame, it leapt across a sky-blue field, claws and beak extended with wings flared. *Men once cheered the Rooster*, Dyrkum thought as he kept his eyes fixed on the center of camp, trying to ignore the snickers and whispers that rippled in his wake. He gripped the mace until his fingers ached.

Passing the last row of tents, the knight emerged into a clearing. A fire burning at its center gave off savory scents of oak and roasting pig. Dyrkum ignored the rumblings of his empty stomach and proceeded to the far side, where a knot of his fellow noblemen lounged, drinking and laughing. They quieted as he approached, but none rose. Dyrkum quashed a sudden flash of ire.

"What brings you here?" asked one clean-shaven youth leaning against a log beside a green tent. Wine and grease stained his tunic and breeches. His blonde hair and hook nose named him a scion of House Bolivar. "I don't recall anyone asking for poultry."

Dyrkum's eyes narrowed at the ensuing laughter, but he kept his voice level. "I have come answering the summons of the Son of the Sun, same as you."

"King Ulrick summoned you?" His eyebrows rose. He glanced around Dyrkum at the horse cropping grass. "A homeless old knight with nothing to his name but a few weapons, some bits of armor and an arthritic nag?"

"His Majesty called for all Lords of the Dawn," he said through gritted teeth.

"You dare claim that title, Chickenheart?" The Bolivar youth rose, eyes narrow, all traces of mirth gone from his face. "You? The author of our misery and destruction?" He snapped his fingers. A boy leapt from the tent and bowed. "Get my armor and sword. I have a chicken to pluck."

"Yes, Lord Trenton." The boy bowed again and ran back inside.

Trenton Bolivar? Why is that boy calling him "lord"? That title belongs to his father. "Where is Verle?"

Trenton's punch split his lip and knocked him back several paces. "You will not speak his name again, Chickenheart."

Letting the blood drip down his chin, Dyrkum dropped the reins of his horse and snarled at the youth. "And you will not call me that again, boy. Homeless I may be, but while I breathe, House Radke still lives and remains your master. You will show respect!"

They approached one another until they stood toe-to-toe. Although a tall man, Trenton still had to tilt his head slightly to look Dyrkum in the eye. Both possessed the same rugged, broad-shouldered build. Tension mounted as they stared silently. Dyrkum gripped his mace.

"What is going on here?" The rasping voice demanded attention and drew their gazes as surely as a lodestone. "I will not have my men fighting one another on the eve of battle!"

Dyrkum bowed deeply. "My apologies, Lord Van. I was merely attempting to teach this young wastrel the importance of manners."

Trenton offered the briefest nod of his head. "Actually, I was about to call this traitor to justice. Surely you cannot call that fighting." He gestured behind him, where the boy had reemerged dragging chainmail and a scabbarded greatsword.

Van Chelatar grunted. Head and shoulders shorter than either, his iron gray hair and map of scars on his hands and face spoke of battles fought and won. He folded his arms across his barrel chest.

"You claim to be the arbiter of justice now, Bolivar? You think your blade worthy of taking the head of your liege lord?"

"You can't be serious—"

"Radke is one of the five Dawn Lords. There is nothing you or I or even the king can do to change that." Van cocked an eyebrow. "Or do you think you can challenge the Sun himself?"

Trenton flinched. Van turned his stony gaze on the old knight. "His insolence merits punishment. As his lord, it is yours to measure out," he grated. "But he's also leveled a serious charge against you, one that cannot go unanswered."

"Perhaps we should leave it to God. Let the Sun decide who's most worthy of punishment."

"I have been charged by the Son of the Sun to get every able-bodied man I can to the battlefield. I don't need you crippling or killing one of my lieutenants, Lord Dyrkum."

"It is in the Sun's hands, Lord Van," the old knight replied. As Trenton armed himself, Dyrkum dared nurture a spark of hope. Van was the first Dawn Lord to speak to him in years. *Perhaps forgiveness can be found.* A soft thud brought his attention back around to Trenton, who had thrown his scabbard on the grass. He lifted the sword skyward in mock salute.

The blade twisted until it reflected the setting sun. Priest-blessed steel caught the light magnified it until the entire weapon glowed from quillion to tip.

Dyrkum lifted his own mace, glaring at his opponent around the blackened steel head and shaft. Light sparked off the golden finials on tip and butt, but grew no further.

"No fire left?" Trenton smirked. "Time to die, traitor."

He bounded across the clearing, sword whistling in a flat, shimmering arc. Dyrkum stepped sideways and let the blow carry Trenton off balance. He bashed the young man's hip. Trenton stumbled and drove his sword point-first into the dirt to stay upright. Grass caught fire where the blade touched. Dyrkum stepped forward with mace raised, sparks racing along the flanges and haft until a ball of flame engulfed the steel. He hammered Trenton's backside and struck a glancing blow off the back of his skull. Trenton collapsed face-first into the dirt, sword rising from the ground like a steel tree. Dyrkum hooked a foot under his side and heaved him over.

Trenton's eyelids fluttered, and he groaned. Dyrkum stepped on his chest. "It's over, son. The Sun has judged." The young lord glared at him. "Mind your manners now, boy, else it will go harder for you next time. Do I make myself clear?"

"Yes."

He edged the burning mace within inches of Trenton's chin. "Yes, what?"

"Yes... milord." He spat the last word.

"Good. You may rise and have your injuries seen to."

The lad's friends helped him to his feet and half-carried him to a white tent a quarter of the way around the clearing. Once they were out of view, Dyrkum staggered to his horse. He let himself sag against the stallion's warm flank and breathe in great gulps of air. He straightened at heavy footsteps and bowed as Van stopped at his side.

"I see the Rooster still has some fight left," he rasped. "Good. I need every fighting man I can find to face what's coming tomorrow."

"Is it really so hopeless? Has the Twilight grown that strong?"

"Night waxes while Day wanes, Lord Dyrkum. There is always hope the Sun will shine again past the morrow, but the odds are against us. You should know that better than anyone." Lord Van ignored his wince and waved past the tents to the plain beyond. "Find yourself something to eat and a place with the rest of the men to bed down for the night."

"Out there? I thought..."

"You thought what?" Van broke in with a hiss. The scars on his face twisted as he struggled to contain his anger. "That we'd welcome you with open arms? If we weren't so desperate, I'd turn you away right now, if I didn't kill you myself. Lord Trenton was right — we teeter on the brink of destruction, and the fault lies at your feet. You'll find no welcome among the Lords of the Dawn, Radke."

"Such hatred still, after all these years? Because I couldn't kill my father?"

"Because you failed in your duty to the people, Chickenheart. Have you truly learned nothing?" He spat at Dyrkum's feet and stalked away.

"How long?" the old knight said softly. "It's been forty years. How long to earn forgiveness for one mistake?"

The lord of House Chelatar paused, shook his head and resumed on his way without turning back. Dyrkum watched his retreating back for some time. *Men may forget, but they seldom forgive. Often they do neither.* His father's words had never rung truer. Still, every reminder of the people's hatred was another knife wound to the heart. Knowing he deserved it twisted the blade. *He was my father. How could they expect me to slay him?*

Sighing, he grabbed his horse's reins and led the old stallion to hunt for a secluded place for the night.

Sunlight gleamed on a great host assembled at the top of the plateau. Infantry shouldered pikes and spears, their leather cuirasses oiled and nearly as bright as the steel caps protecting their heads. Archers bristled with arrows. Cavalry towered in front of them, lesser lords and their knights resplendent in their gilded armor. Bedecked in their own armor and trappings, warhorses stamped hooves and whinnied, impatient to join the battle. The army had been split into three columns, and at the head of each rode a Lord of the Dawn — tall, golden-haired Orsa Narish, the diminutive Myka Qorahn, fat, brooding Zachare Asiris. Van Chelton, the King's Commander, sat on his horse ahead of them all.

Dyrkum rode at the head alongside the other Lords, but far at the end, leading nothing but the wind. Those lords who had once sworn fealty had been divided among the other columns. *"House Radke rides in the front by right,"* Van had told him. *"But I will not force any man to follow the Rooster."*

Even alone, the Rooster on his shield glowed proudly. His armor, however, refused to shine. Years as a sellsword had scarred the steel, and the elements had dulled its finish. But all the damage had been carefully mended, and there was no speck of rust to be found.

Lord Van booted his horse and wheeled to face them

"The Sun has risen to bless us this morning, but who can say if He will do so tomorrow?" His gravel voice, trained to deliver orders in the heat and confusion of battle, boomed across the plateau. "Today, his brother the Moon will encroach on his territory and turn Day to Night. Always before, the Sun has vanquished his brother and restored the balance. But today, the Lords of Twilight plan to join the battle on their God's behalf. They have departed Nightfall with an army and a wizard to take the Well of the Sun and bring Night down on us forever."

Scowling, Dyrkum flinched at "Nightfall." Even decades after his ancestral home had fallen to the Lords of Twilight, he'd never heard anyone call Daybreak by anything but its Sun-given name. *If they've resigned themselves to that, things may be even more desperate than we feared.* Little of what Van had said was new, but he could hear murmurs of "wizard" rippling through the men. Dyrkum snorted. *Of course we're going to be battling magic. How else do they think Night plans to conquer Day?* He glanced back at the knights behind them. Several chewed on their lips and wore creased brows. One showed no signs of worry. Trenton Bolivar glared at him as if trying to bore a hole through his armor. Dyrkum shook his head and turned back to Lord Van, who rode back and forth across the line with one hand on the reins and the other on his hip; his face and tone had hardened.

"I say this not to dismay or frighten you, but to prepare you. The hoard we face is vast and well armed. We will face nightmares none but the eldest campaigners among you have ever seen." His head hung for a moment. When he raised it again, his features remained stern, but he also offered a small, fierce smile. Every word rang triumphantly. "But so long as the Sun shines, we have hope. Our Lord grants the world life and light. Today, we show the Lords of Twilight he also sears and burns. Today, there is no quarter, no retreat. There will be no ground given but paid for in fire and blood. They will learn the true cost of coming out from the shadows to face the full might of the Sun!"

The men erupted. Dyrkum could find no other word for it. One moment, they were all casting pensive glances at their commanders and gnawing at their lips, and the next, they jabbed weapons skyward and cheered loud enough to shake the earth. *We can do this*, he found himself thinking. The old knight lifted his mace and added a weak crow to the din.

Lord Van smiled, drew his sword and whipped in a circle over his head. "Forward for the Sun!" he bellowed, wheeling his horse and setting out at a gallop eastward.

"For the Sun!" The men's answering call as they started forward was deafening.

Van soon slowed. The armored horses couldn't safely maintain the pace for long, and it would do little good for cavalry to outpace infantry. The troop lost some of its orderly formation as it advanced. Men mingled and traveled alongside old companions; the other four Lords in the front rode together, talking quietly but heatedly amongst themselves and occasionally stabbing a finger toward the horizon. Dyrkum angled his horse so that his path would slowly intersect with theirs. He rode in silence, twisting in his saddle now and again to find Trenton still staring at him.

The Lords' conversation grew to an intelligible murmur as he approached. He could not make out any words until riding alongside Van's horse.

"...lack of reliable news that worries me," Lord Myka said. He drywashed his hands as he spoke, a sure sign of agitation. "Even if we can match them blade for blade, how do we prepare for unknown sorcery?"

Lord Orsa saw him first. A scowl twisted his handsome features at the sight of the Rooster. His golden hair swayed as he snapped upright in his saddle and stared eastward. Myka's lips pressed into a thin line at the agitation before he turned away. Fat Zachare sneered and spat on the ground. Lord Van sat in his saddle, his face unreadable.

"This is none of your concern, Lord Dyrkum," Van replied.

"Do you not think it prudent I share in your councils, my lords? I have traveled far in my wanderings and seen many things. I may have new light to shed on your concerns." Orsa booted his horse to a trot and rode ahead. Myka shook his head. Zachare laughed. Van said nothing, but kept his gaze on the disgraced lord. "Listen to me, man. We battle for our very survival. Victory hangs by a thread that could snap at the slightest tension. You are fools to spurn any help offered, no matter the source." He waved a hand at the following army, where Trenton's gaze still burned his way. "Or is all hope already lost and all this a brave, pretty show?"

"I said it is none of your concern, Radke," Van snapped. After a moment, he sighed and added: "Perhaps you should know this: Though we shed every drop of blood and every man here falls, hope is not lost. The Son of the Sun is raising an even greater host that will ride from the city of Helios three weeks hence." His lips turned upward in a sad smile. "There is some hope we may crush the enemy, but not much. Our duty is to disrupt their plans, to grind them to a halt and keep them still until the king comes. You *do* remember duty, Chickenheart?"

Wiping a snarl from his face, Dyrkum turned and gestured to the Bolivar youth. "Why does Trenton hate me so? Even after I lost Daybreak, House Bolivar remained cordial to me."

"Lord Verle remained cordial, you mean." Van offered a grim smile. "From what I hear, the other members of his House often suggested he hang you from the battlements of his fortress at the Flare." His mirth evaporated."Trenton Bolivar hates you, Lord Dyrkum, because his father died in the last sortie to reclaim Nightfall five years ago. He lost the Flare to Twilight a year later. Moonlight, they call it now. Today, House Bolivar holds only the barest sliver of land on the Sunlit Plains, and that is likely to be swallowed in shadow before the year's end even if we succeed today. We have lost much since that day, Chickenheart. Does that explain the hatred?" He booted his horse and rode to join Orsa. The other two followed suit.

Slumped in his saddle, Dyrkum made no effort to follow. What was the point? The Rooster would perch in no man's heart this side of the grave. The best he could hope for was to redeem himself in battle so they might think better of him at his death. Even that was a small hope. *I should have killed him, but how was I to know so much pain and darkness would come about because of filial love?* The black clouds boiling over Daybreak had brought an unnatural twilight that obscured the sun that day. He had traveled alone up the switchback road that provided the only entrance to his family's mountaintop fortress near the border with the kingdom of Twilight.

He'd been so young and unsure of himself, barely twenty and entrusted with this important mission from the Son of the Sun himself. He felt the weight of the entire Kingdom on his shoulders with every step. His pride in the great burden mixed oddly with the trepidation he felt at knowing he had come to slay his own father. But it had to be done. The King and the other Lords of the Dawn had made that plain enough. Lord Stefan's plans threatened to upset the delicate balance between Dawn and Twilight, they said. War would surely follow. But he would not listen to them, and they dare not take the time a siege would require to drag him out. Only his son could get close enough. Dyrkum had argued and railed, but in the end, he had little choice but to agree.

His footfalls had echoed as he stalked the empty hallways with mace in hand, following the reverberations of his father's booming voice to a high tower on the keep's eastern wall. Flames flickered and engulfed the weapon, casting a quavering shadow against the walls. Covered in sweat and trembling with each harsh word, Dyrkum had climbed the stairs to find a near stranger standing in a ring of angular characters engraved into the stone of the top landing. Whatever path he had taken to this point, Lord Stefan had wasted into a skeletal, filthy caricature of himself with greasy hair that whipped in the wind and talon-like nails that clawed the air. Caught up in the throws of his charm, Stefan didn't notice his son's approach.

Dyrkum stopped just behind him outside the spell-ring, gripped the mace in both hands, lifted it over his head and paused.

Long moments dragged out. Every instinct cried out for him to end it now. *"I understand he is your father,"* King Ulrich had said, laying *one hand on his shoulder. "But it is vital you finish it before the invocation is finished."* He called himself a coward, a traitor. But to no avail. The flames on his mace winked out. How could he slay his father? He sighed and lowered the weapon.

Father's chanting stopped. He whirled about, snarling and slashing at the air with long nails. His eyes narrowed when he saw his son.

"Is it to be you, then? I never thought the Dawn Lords would taint you with their jealousy."

"This has nothing to do with jealousy, Father." He dropped the weapon to swing from a leather thong around his wrist. "I will not kill you, but you must stop this madness."

"Madness? Since when is it madness to seize power? The priests in Helios think to hoard it all for themselves, doling it out as they see fit." Father pointed to the mace and growled in disgust. "Why content yourself with one of their blessed weapons when the Night offers you so much more? Join me, son. Together we shall become Lords of the Twilight and teach the Dawn to tremble at the name Radke."

"No. I cannot. I mean, the king..." He ran fingers through his hair and shook his head. "You invite war, Father. This cannot be."

His father grunted and turned his back with a dismissive wave. The young knight seized his mace and raised it over his head. Still, he hesitated. The priests insisted trying to bargain with the Night was like trying to outstare the Sun — you gained nothing and paid dearly for your folly. But Father seemed so sure of himself.

Lightning interrupted his inner debate. He threw an arm over his face and stumbled backward as bolts lanced from the clouds overhead and struck the carved ring. The symbols drank the power until they glowed with it. Stefan spread his arms, smiled and threw his head back.

"YES!" he cried to the black sky. "Yes! Grant me the power. Grant me — No!"

The spell-ring vomited its stored lightning, hurling it straight at Stefan. He jittered and screamed. Dyrkum turned and gagged at the smell of roasting meat. Once the sizzling sound stopped, he stood and looked up. The clouds had already started to disperse, but instead of sunlight, they left behind the nighttime sky always seen behind the Twilight boundary. And there, on the floor surrounded by a ring of fused stone...

Dyrkum pitched forward in his saddle, knees and hands gripping tight to keep from being thrown to the ground. The horse danced several steps to the side, away from whatever hole had made it stumble. It finally stilled, snorting and trembling. The old knight looked around. He saw a bright glow and dark clouds to the east. The Sun rode in the sky above the storm, with his brother the Moon giving chase. No one rode with him. Dyrkum twisted in the saddle and saw the other Lords stopped far behind. Hauling on the reins, he booted the stallion to a walk. It moved easily, with no sign of injury. *Praise the Sun for that, at least. That would be a fitting end, I suppose — killed before ever joining battle because I was dwelling too much on the past.*

Drawing rein beside Lord Van, he tried to ignore the sneers on the other Lords' faces. "Why have we halted?"

"We are here." Van's voice and face remained impassive; his gaze never turned from the east. Dyrkum looked back toward the storm, and realization dawned.

An army seethed underneath that line of black clouds. Judging distances on the flat plain could be tricky, but it looked to be hovering at the edge of the bright light as if reluctant to draw any closer. "They've reached the Well already?"

"Aye." To his surprise, it was Orsa who answered, although the tall Lord stared straight ahead. "I had hoped to get here before them, but reliable intelligence is difficult from this quarter these days." His gaze shifted to Dyrkum momentarily before returning to the horizon.

"What do we do now?"

"We ride!" Lord Van shouted, digging his heels into his mount's sides. The beast leapt to a gallop. The other Dawn Lords and those behind quickly followed until the plain shook with the thunder of their passing. Dyrkum donned his helmet as they advanced. The infantry followed at a run with a wordless roar that added to the din.

Dyrkum rode in the front, leaning over his steed's neck with one hand gripping the reins and the other holding the flaming mace down by his right knee. The Twilight Lords' hesitation at approaching the Well of the Sun evaporated. The dark army swarmed toward them, stormclouds eating the sky ahead of the vanguard. The eternal light shining in the Well grew brighter as Night surrounded it. A column of light punched through darkness and clouds to expose a circle of blue sky above. *A good omen*, he thought as Day's army broke through the front line.

A wave of horseflesh and steel crashed over the goblins and wild, fur-clad men. Van lay about on all sides with his broadsword.

Zachare moved like a giant through a forest, his great war axe severing arms and heads with every blow. Orsa's spear flashed, and Myka's slender rapier slashed and jabbed. The fire and light trapped in their Sun-blessed weapons left wounds that burned and spread flames among the enemy. Men and monsters ran wild, spreading fire further into their ranks. Blood and gore flew as the Lords pushed their way deeper and the following knights waded in.

Claws scrabbled at the fire-colored rooster. Dyrkum kicked the goblin away and smashed its wide-eyed, slime-green face into a bloody pulp with his mace. The scrawny, stirrup-high figure fell away. Flames ate into what remained of its head before spreading down its limbs and to the grass. Dyrkum knocked a spear to one side with his shield while his horse trampled its owner into the earth. From somewhere behind, the slap and twang of bowstrings announced the arrival of their archers. Figures fell in the distance. *Where are their bowmen?* He crushed another goblin's skull and swiped at a horrific conglomeration of fur, teeth and claws on the backhand. *Who goes to battle without archers?*

His answer came immediately when a deadly rain of arrows appeared from the black sky. Orsa fell to the ground and did not rise again. Zachare's horse sprouted several feathers from its chest, staggered and dropped to its knees. A dozen monstrosities swarmed over beast and rider, talons and teeth gnashing. They fell back missing limbs and heads as the fat Lord rose swinging his war axe. More knights fell behind them, and an answering volley came from the infantry.

Dyrkum barely had time to register all this before the snarling bundle of fur he had batted aside uncoiled and launched itself back at him. The beast howled and grew as it came, its jaw and ears lengthening. The knight snarled behind his helm and raised his weapon. Fire blossomed around the mace. *I've no silver on me. Has to be fire for this sort.* He wheeled his mount around. The horse reared and lashed out with iron-shod hooves. The werewolf crashed to the ground and bounced up once more. Dyrkum lifted his shield, realizing too late that he was not the intended target. The beast wrapped its forelegs around the horse's neck and spread its jaws wide to rip out its unarmored throat.

Screaming, the horse reared and collapsed. Dyrkum lifted his leg to avoid being crushed and rolled free. He lost his shield in the tumble. The wolf leapt on him, claws and teeth ringing off armor as the creature sought a way through steel to the flesh underneath. He jabbed the flaming mace into its ribs. It scrambled away with a yelp. Wrinkling his nose at the smell of burnt hair and flesh, Dyrkum climbed to his feet. He turned in a slow circle, eyes scanning what little of the battlefield he could see through the slot in his helm.

Everywhere he looked, Dyrkum saw the Sun's army locked in combat. Zachare now swung his axe one-handed; his left arm hung limp at his side. Myka and Van rode side-to-side, swords flashing. Soldiers fought alongside knights on foot. Those still mounted trampled all in their path as they rode through the seething throng of men and monsters. He spotted Trenton among their number, bright sword cutting and burning a path deeper toward the Well, where a knot of four immense figures stood around a glowing green sphere. *Twilight Lords.* Dyrkum spat through his helmet. *My place is there.* He spotted his shield a few paces away, bright Rooster glowing proudly in the Well's light. He took a step toward it and staggered as something barreled into his right side.

Dyrkum gave a vicious swipe with the mace, felt the jolt of solid contact and heard a clipped yelp. He spun with the blow. The wolf circled slowly, hunched around burns marring the gray fur on its left flank. It watched him with narrowed eyes and growled. Even on four legs, the thing's head came to his chest. They watched one another for several moments, then the beast jumped. Dyrkum ducked. Its jaws closed on his head.

The werewolf worried the helmet, teeth dimpling the steel in several places. He ripped the leather strap free from his chin and jerked his head. It hung painfully for a moment around his temples, then pulled loose. Tossing the helm aside with a shake of its head, the wolf lunged forward with wide jaws.

Teeth gritting, Dyrkum rammed his mace into the beast's waiting maw. The smell of roasting flesh assaulted his nostrils. The werewolf screamed and tried to back away, claws digging into the earth. He wrapped his free arm around its chest and held the creature close until his arm had buried itself to the shoulder. It thrashed and flailed, scratching bloody runnels in his face, but Dyrkum held on until his breastplate heated and flames shot from the beast's belly. It shuddered and fell limp, eyes glazing. Dripping blood and gore, his fist and mace emerged from the blackened ribcage like a grizzly sleeve.

The knight pulled a dagger free from his waist with his left hand and awkwardly hacked at the carcass. The leaf-shaped blade sliced through meat and screeched off metal, but finally freed his arm. Dyrkum wiped it on the grass and sheathed it. He heaved a sigh, retrieved his shield and turned once more to the Well.

The battle raged on as ferocious as ever. At least a third of both armies lay motionless on the field. Ravens and black buzzards, invisible against the darkened sky, called overhead. A few of the more opportunistic scavengers had already landed and started feasting. Ahead, the Dawn Lords had fought their way to join Trenton, Zachare riding double with Myka. Even as he watched, they broke through the ranks and circled the Well to engage their Twilight counterparts. He squinted at the shaft of light coming from the massive sinkhole. It seemed a bit smaller than before, as if the darkness had started pressing it inward.

Dyrkum moved in a straight line through the Twilight army, bashing a path littered with slaughtered and shattered enemies. Blood covered his face and most of his armor by the time he reached the Well and the haze lifted somewhat. He found himself on the edge of a precipice, squinting down at a bright light emanating from somewhere deep within the earth. Below, the light filled the round cavern from edge to edge, but as it emerged, it narrowed suddenly. He backed up a step and shielded his eyes with one gauntleted hand. No, not narrowed. Roughly a quarter of the column of light had turned black, as if Night were trying to strangle it. *Some devilry is at work here.* He made his way around the Well toward the clash of metal on metal, punctuated by an occasional animal grunt or cry of pain. As he rounded the sinkhole, Dyrkum found himself facing a desperate battle.

Two Twilight Lords remained standing in front of the green sphere. A Cyclops twice as tall as any man wielded an immense morning star against Trenton while Van faced an even larger troll swinging a great stone hammer. Myka lay face-down over a tall, skeletal figure, his rapier burning a hole in its breast even with its hands around his throat. Zachare, missing an arm, had fallen with a giants bearing dozens of smoldering gashes from the Dawn Lord's axe.

Even as Dyrkum ran forward, the troll drove its hammer on Van's head like a boulder falling on a bucket. Trenton dodged a blow from the Cyclops. He vaulted over the haft and spiked ball to lance his sword through its eye. Both crashed to the ground. Trenton disentangled himself, stood on its chest and yanked on the sword in an attempt to free it from the creature's brainpan. A shadow loomed over him. The troll's fist caught him full in the chest, launching the young lord into the air. He landed amid clanging metal atop the dead giant, groaned once and fell silent.

Flames flaring ever higher on his mace, Dyrkum closed the gap at a dead run. The troll half-turned with weapon raised. The old knight hammered its knee with a double-handed blow. The creature bellowed in pain, staggered and fell. It caught itself with its free hand and swung the hammer wildly with the other. The Rooster and the arm supporting it shattered. Snarling in rage and pain, Dyrkum smashed the beast's elbow. As the troll fell to the earth, he spun and swung the mace with all his might into its face. Flames enveloped its head and raced along its tough green hide.

Dyrkum raised his weapon to the sky, threw his head back and crowed.

Then he collapsed.

Pain shot through his left arm. Groaning, he rolled onto his back and lay there, gasping at the nearly black sky. A ring of blue shone overhead, but much smaller than it should have been. A round, black shadow transformed the Sun shining through the gap into a bright crescent. He craned his neck back. Nearly half the Well's light had gone black. Dyrkum forced himself to his right side. With gritted teeth, he drove the mace into the ground and used it to leverage himself to his knees and finally his feet.

He turned, found the green ball and walked toward it. As he drew nearer, he saw a small, robe-clad figure standing inside. It looked more or less human, roughly half his height with stick-thin limbs and a large, hairless head. His skin had a rough texture to it, almost like a lizard's. The man's round eyes stared unblinking at the shaft of light. His rigid arms formed a ring in front of his chest, as if trying to grip a stone column. Dyrkum frowned. The man's arms tightened slightly, and the light dimmed. The old knight turned. *Has the Well gotten smaller?* He faced the little man once more. *Is this the wizard? He's so small!* He lifted the flaming mace and swung at the mage.

It struck the glowing sphere with a sound like a tolling iron bell. Flames wreathed the ball. The impact rattled his bones, leaving him gasping from the pain in his injured arm. The fire died away, but the protective shell remained. The wizard smirked.

"Did you think it would be so easy, Chickenheart?" His sibilant voice sounded strained, as if he lifted a great weight. Dyrkum's eyes widened. "Oh, yes, we know you. Your family has performed a great service for us, after all. I myself have lived in Nightfall for many years now. I wish I could thank your father in person."

Heedless of the pain, Dyrkum rained blow after blow. Each rang across the plain and sent fire whipping around the ball, with no more effect than the first. Panting, he fell to his knees. *How do you defeat an enemy you can't touch?*

The mage laughed, a dry hissing like an amused serpent. "You Sunlanders never learn, do you? Your father was wiser than most, but even he never understood the Night. You think the Sun will win again? Very soon, the Moon will eclipse his brother in the heavens, and I will eclipse his power here on earth. Day is over. Night is at hand."

It's over. We have lost. Dyrkum bowed his head. Forty years of shame weighed heavily on his shoulders. *I thought I could leave that behind today. I failed once again. This time, the whole world will pay.* He watched the wizard tighten his arms inside the impenetrable shell. *No, it's not.* His father's voice spoke to him in his lecturing tone. *No matter how daunting Twilight's magics may seem, they are not invincible. Every spell has a weakness. Some you can beat down until they shatter. Others are more subtle, with only a small crack no wider than a blade. Find that weakness, and twist the knife to force it open.*

He looked skyward. Only a sliver of the Sun remained visible, and all but a thin spear of light had disappeared. Dyrkum tapped the wizard's shield with the mace. It rang softly and flames slowly wrapped around its surface. Eyes narrowed, he watched the burning embrace. *There!* He struck it again, hoping he hadn't been mistaken. Again, the flames formed a smooth ball except for a slight imperfection in front of the mage's hands.

Rising to his feet, Dyrkum dropped the flanged mace and drew his dagger. Fire sprang from the blade as he advanced. Light flared within the ball. He staggered back a few paces, shielding his eyes with his good arm. When he lowered it, the mage had vanished, along with his shield and the entire plain. Dyrkum stood on a stone floor staring at a twisted, blackened hunk of flesh. It raised an appendage barely recognizable as an arm. He backed away.

"No," he whispered. "This cannot be."

"*Please, son,*" his burnt father pleaded. "*Kill me.*"

"I cannot. Do not ask this of me, I beg you."

"*You must. I cannot bear the pain. You came here to slay me. Pick up your mace and do it!*" Even twisted in pain, disdain flooded his father's voice.

Dyrkum looked down at the mace. It would be so easy. One blow and his father's suffering would end. He reached down. Agony flared in his broken arm. *When did I injure my arm?* He shook his head. It didn't matter. All that mattered was his father's pain. He had nearly grasped the haft when the world went black. *What has happened?* As his eyes adjusted, he realized not all light had faded completely. *There must still be some power in the Well.* Frowning, he tilted his head. His eyes widened. *The Well!*

The illusion shattered as he looked over his shoulder. A shaft of nearly pure Night rose from the earth, marred only by a bright wand at its center. Dyrkum straightened, gripped his dagger tighter and stepped toward the mage.

"This ends now, wizard." He stabbed at the flaw in the shield.

Something ripped into his back, and a foot of shining steel tore through his breastplate. The dagger fell from nerveless fingers.

"Giving up already? I should have known you would fail us again, *my lord,*" Trenton growled. He twisted the sword and yanked it free. Dyrkum fell to the ground, his face twisted toward the green glow. "You can't even die with your weapon in hand, Chickenheart? You've doomed us all with your cowardice."

Warm spittle landed on his cheek. A pair of armored legs step over Dyrkum and blocked his view of the mage. "What are you doing here?" Trenton's voice sounded surprised. "Where is the wizard, child? Hurry, you must tell me at once!"

Behind them, the Well of the Sun went black. Hissing laughter washed over the old knight as he breathed his last.

OF BONES AND BLADES

Maliq di'Reyew took another slow step. Rocks crunched underfoot, and his ankle twisted. Only a quick jab with the butt of his long spear kept him upright, but the motion sent more rocks tumbling. Echoes ricocheting off the canyon's granite walls took several heartbeats to die away. A brown tail of hair tickled his back as he swiveled his head side to side, eyes straining to catch every scrap of light.

Might as well have them shut for all the good it's doing, he thought with a grimace. Starlight and a waning moon did little to penetrate the night here where shadows of jagged peaks swallowed most of the night sky. He shifted the large, cloth bundle on his back with his free elbow. *A torch might help.* He dismissed the thought with a shake of his head. Even if the flame didn't make him an irresistible target, he couldn't afford to drop the rune-carved spear long enough to light the thing. *I could conjure a witchlight easily enough, but that would be as good as suicide.* A soft, wry laugh escaped his lips. *The Heart would love that.* He could still see Beinof Skidaal, the Heart of the Storm, standing on the thunderhead mosaic of the Citadel's great hall as she forbade him from seeking the beast. He scowled. *Why should I care if the beasts are nearly extinct? She named me protector of our people. It is my decision what weapons I need to fulfill my duty, not hers.* Still, he sometimes found himself questioning the wisdom of undertaking a mission that would make more experienced hunters blanch, a quest guided only by rumor and legend. Scowling, he eased one foot forward.

A stealthy, rasping slither scraped across the rocks somewhere to his left. The mage crouched, spear at the ready. *It wants me to know it's here. But where is it?* He moved forward a few paces, then paused as the sound came again, closer this time. Perhaps if I'm quick enough... He took a deep breath, looked up and concentrated.

A boiling green sphere materialized in the sky. Harsh light threw the canyon into sharp relief. It widened and leveled out a few feet away. Fissures and caves gaped along the high walls. Rent armor, shattered weapons and bleached bones littered the ground. He looked up at the sound of another leathery rustle.

There it perched, black claws gripping a wide ledge about halfway up the southern cliff face. Maliq's breath caught. It's beautiful. His right hand gripped his spear tighter while the left groped for one of the pair of long, pearlescent daggers tucked behind his belt. He forced the hand back to his side. Not yet.

The dragon looked like a huge serpent carved out of the night. How many ebony dragons can there be left in the world? He chuckled. One less after tonight. From its spiky mane to ridges marching down its long spine, the beast was pure black. It was wingless, unlike its more colorful brethren, but muscles bunched in its four man-sized legs suggested it could leap, if nothing else. It stared at him, onyx eyes narrowed in what looked like amusement. The wyrm grinned, revealing teeth that could have been made of obsidian. A rope of saliva trickled down its long chin and splashed to the ledge, where it sizzled and etched a trail in the rock. Its gaze turned to the glowing ball overhead.

Its chest puffed, and its lips pursed. Maliq hurriedly released the spell, but not before a stream of jet-black flame shot upward and made contact. The fire wailed as it flew and enveloped the sphere. Purple-tinged light replaced green, and a narrow tongue of dark flame raced toward Maliq. He dove forward, feeling something cold that screamed as it passed over his head. He rolled. The impact knocked his spear free to clatter on the granite floor. He snatched it and climbed shakily to his feet. Idiot! The thing breathes pure hellfire and you decide to cast a spell? Why not just conjure a shield around yourself while you're at it? He gazed upward.

The dragon was gone.

Cursing, Maliq spun on one heel. That thing could be anywhere. The violet illumination created more shadows than it destroyed, and the moaning flames above made thinking difficult.

A sharp inhale and soft thup offered only the briefest of warnings. He jerked left, away from the sound. Something soft struck the spearhead, and a few small drops splattered his temple and hand. He yelled at the searing pain and dropped the spear. Maliq ripped a broad swath from the bottom of his dark tunic and swiped at his face while wiping his palm across his breeches. Eventually, the dragon's spittle stopped burning trails into his flesh. The rag disintegrated, and holes appeared in his pant leg. He ran a finger along the tender skin on his face. *Any slower, and I'd have lost an eye.*

Stooping to retrieve the spear, Maliq noted with satisfaction that neither the wooden haft nor metal head had the slightest trace of wear despite the acid still pitting the rock underneath. He straightened and carefully wiped it clean with another piece of his tunic, wincing at the pain in his wounded hand. The ball of black fire above sputtered and died.

"You are fast, human." The sibilant voice slid down the walls and crawled over the rocks until it seemed to come from everywhere. "You intrigue me. I might even let you live if you tell me what you want."

"I'm just a traveller passing through," he said loudly. The ebony dragon replied with a staccato hiss.

"Most amusing, human. A traveller, here, days from the nearest food or water?" The laughter cut off. "What do you want, Stormdancer?"

"You know who I am?"

"I know your kind, wizard. Did you think you could come to my home stinking of magic and death, and I would not notice?" Something viscous landed on the rock at his feet with a faint hiss. The voice hardened and lost all trace of amusement. "I ask you one last time: Why are you here?"

He cursed silently. *The tales said they were clever creatures. I should have listened more closely.* He sighed. "Blades."

"Ahh." The voice took on a knowing tone. Maliq could picture the dragon nodding its head sagely. "I thought as much when I spied my cousin's bones at your waist."

He gripped one of the daggers. Pommel, narrow quillons and long blade were all of one piece, forged from the rock-solid bones of the diminutive dragon. A sinuous line blacked out a patch of stars overhead briefly, and something slashed the night air. Maliq held the spear over his head with both hands. Black talons met spell-hardened haft with a clang and a brief shower of sparks. The blow drove him to his knees, and the mage half ran, half crawled behind a nearby boulder. Acidic saliva ate into the rock and splashed his boot.

"Tell me, Stormdancer. Did she put up a fight?"

"More than I would have imagined, dragon," he called and chuckled loudly while ripping his boots free. Should have brought an extra pair. Bare feet are not going to be fun out here. "Not that it mattered much in the end. I got the daggers, didn't I?"

"You did, indeed." It sighed with a sound like a blacksmith's bellows. "And now you are here after my bones to make another blade."

"Blades, actually." Maliq tossed the boots in a high arc. Several wet splats followed its trajectory. "I thought a brace of boneswords would look quite dashing, not to mention useful. I once saw an old Stormdancer with a pair. Nothing could touch him."

"A warrior, then, not a mere hunter. You ought to provide an interesting challenge before you die."

"Better than you has tried." Sliding off his pack, he threw it up after his footware. It landed with a soft thump high on the wall. "Frankly, I don't really care."

The dragon chuckled, a deep, booming laugh that sent echoes down the canyon. "You may not be any more intelligent than the rest of your kind, but you are braver than most." Starlight died as a massive head reared above his hiding place. Its foreleg smashed down on the boulder, splintering the rock. Claws scored the stone.

Maliq scrambled backward, swinging his arm wide. A thin, narrow line flashed out in a wave, pushing hardened air before it. It caught the dragon just above its forelegs. The blow snapped its head back, but the edge hiding behind the air shattered on the beast's scales. So the creatures are immune to magic. I'd hoped that was merely a rumor. Maliq raised his hand.

A large fireball shot up. Whipping its neck forward, the wyrm spat a series of short, black flames. Each fell short. Maliq's fire struck the ledge where his pack had landed. The bag's tightly-wrapped contents ignited in a blinding flash. Maliq smiled. One of us will be dead long before that burns out. More hellfire streaked toward the light, playing over the stone with no effect. The stream cut off suddenly and the ebony dragon turned a puzzled gaze his way.

"It's not magic, dragon. There's nothing there for hellfire to burn."

"Clever, human." Admiration tinged its voice, but Maliq thought he caught something else, a faint buzz that might be a hint of worry.

"Still think you're going to stop me?" He leveled his spear at the creature's chest. "Maybe you'll die, after all."

The dragon shrugged. "All things die. My sire's sire was the fiercest of our kind, the most cunning, but even he fell to a band of you Stormdancers eventually." Its lip curled in a smirk. "Still, he did take most of their number with him." Its eyes narrowed. "Arrogant to think one of your kind could accomplish the same feat alone."

Maliq kept his face smooth with an effort. My great-great-grandfather died harvesting that dragon's bones. An image of massive, light-absorbing doors flashed in his mind, and he smiled. "I heard about that one, I think. They said he was a toothless old lizard whose bones weren't suitable for weaponry. They did make a nice set of doors for the Citadel of Storms, though."

Roaring, the dragon scuttled forward with breathtaking speed, spitting as it came. Bones crunched under its feet. Maliq leapt aside. He dodged the worst of the liquid assault and forced himself to ignore the minor burns eating through his shirt and breeches. He launched his own attack from behind another boulder.

Blue lines shot out from his hand, curled around the dragon and pulled tight. They dissolved when they made contact. He grunted and rained large knots of air on the wyrm. It slithered to the side under the assault and sprayed the canyon with a blast of screaming fire. The knots caught, and black flames followed the connection back to Maliq. He severed the ties as the blaze licked at his mind.

Maliq reeled in shock and fell to the ground, limbs twitching. Spear landed beside him. His brain felt numb. He could barely focus on the dark shape slithering toward him. It drooled as it came, leaving a trail of pitted, smoking stone in its wake.

"That hurt, Stormdancer. I am impressed." Its jaws opened wide and a thin string of acid ran across his right foot. Maliq screamed as three toes melted into a red smear on the rock floor. "As I said, all things die."

Turning his gaze to the cliff, Maliq reached up with one trembling hand. He struggled to keep his palm flat and his fingers aligned. By the Eye, work or I'll cut you off myself! He snarled and forced the hand still. He ignored the dragon's hot breath and the steaming liquid splashing that tore into his ear. Something locked along his line of sight. He twisted his arm.

A few pebbles bounced off the dragon's head. Dust filled the air. The canyon wall rumbled, groaned and gave one final, creaking protest before collapsing. Maliq held both palms up and closed his eyes as a huge slab tried to crush him. It stopped inches above his face. He grunted. His left hand slowly fell, and the right one rose. The rock tilted, shuddered and crashed to the ground.

Large stones smashed into the dragon's ribs, legs and head. It shied away from the blows and turned to flee while trying to dodge the landslide. A chunk of rock twice the size of its own head landed on its tail. It thrashed and howled. Black blood spurted onto the canyon floor. Falling boulders crushed a hind leg. The wyrm's shrieks cut short, drowned in a granite rain.

The shower dwindled away, boulders giving way to smaller stones and finally a last few pebbles rattling down. Coughing, Maliq crawled from a small, triangular opening between the canyon floor and the wall. He turned and dragged the spear out, then climbed upright and staggered to a rumbling mound of rock nearby. He teetered with every step on his maimed foot.

The dragon's forelegs and head remained free. The hill covering its body shuddered as its claws dug into the stone and pushed. It gained a few inches of freedom while Maliq watched. The beast opened its eyes.

"An interesting tactic, Stormdancer, but I will free myself eventually." It groaned. "I suggest you leave before then. I will not follow."

"Not yet, dragon." He hefted the spear. "We have unfinished business."

"You should have run, human," the dragon growled. Muscles bunched in its legs and chest. Stone grated and dust billowed as it dragged itself free.

Looks like I've done more than just hurt it. One of the dragon's rear legs dragged, and blood oozed from the stump of its tail. Its movements seemed sluggish. He jabbed with the spear. Maliq barely fell back in time to avoid snapping jaws. It's still quick, though.

Maliq ran and scrambled awkwardly up the pile of stone with the spear clutched in one hand. Rocks slipped under his weight, causing him to slide as much as he climbed. Sharp edges sliced his bare feet. The dragon spat at him, fusing stone on either side of his head. Finally, he reached a boulder poking through the scree and stood on top of it.

The dragon crouched below, eyeing him warily. I've shown I can hurt it. The beast isn't so confident anymore. "You ready, dragon?"

"Are you, human?"

Maliq's fist flew forward. A huge ball of air knocked the dragon's snout to one side. He spun in the same motion and hurled his spear. The enchanted weapon punched through what remained of its tail for better than half its length and quivered in place. Runes glowed fitfully but held.

Bellowing, the wyrm tried to lift its tail free, only to find the spear had also pierced stone. It spat at the wooden shaft. Acid ran off with no effect. The beast squinted at the flickering symbols and looked up at Maliq, teeth bared in a sneer. Black fire played across the spear, wailing as it caught. The dragon winced as the flame burned down.

Maliq drew the white daggers from his belt and leapt. He landed astride the ebony dragon's neck. Blades flashed in the light of his still-burning pack as he raised them high and plunged them straight through the creature's eyes. Black blood spurted hot across his arms.

The dragon's scream shook the canyon. It lashed its long neck, each whipcrack bashing its head against a rock wall and threatening to knock Maliq from his perch. He hooked his hands inside the eye sockets, grimacing at the slimy feel, and wedged his ankles in the spiky mane. The beast's thrashing eventually slowed. Its legs gave way and it fell to the earth, head slamming into the ground. Maliq, jarred loose, tumbled to the ground and fetched up against a stone. His head rang like a bell, and the world went black.

"This cannot be, Maliq," Beinof said, her voice ringing with all the authority of the Heart of the Storm. "The elder breeds are dying. We must nurture them, not hasten their extinction." Beinof's long, white hair swayed as she jabbed a finger at the pale blades sheathed at his waist. "You have slain the last ivory dragon in this forest, perhaps the last on these shores. You think only of the glory. And now you want more weapons? How much needless blood do you require?"

"You named me protector, Heart. How I fulfill that duty is up to me. The world is filled with peril. I will make sure no one can endanger us. If a few dragons perish so that we might survive, so be it."

Groaning, Maliq sat up. Dawn glimmered in the sky. He rose slowly. Every limb felt stuffed full of glass. Turning to a boulder nearby, he stretched out both hands. The stone rumbled and grated as it reformed itself into a massive forge. Rock in the center glowed, cracked and melted.

Maliq slumped once it was done. His body cried out for rest, but he forced it to move. *Got to get this done before sunset or else the bones will die. Then all this was for nothing.* He looked at the still corpse filling the rubble-strewn canyon. *I won't allow that.* He shivered as he recalled the Heart's last words before he left the Citadel, a sad smile softening the Heart's stern features: "Your love for your people mitigates your sin, Maliq. Do not compound it further."

Perhaps I have sinned, but whatever gods there may be will just have to wait on my punishment. I have work to do. Maliq reached inside the eye sockets and pulled his daggers free. He pulled his shirt off and wiped them clean.

Twisting one blade back and forth, Maliq eyed the gleaming lines in the sunlight. He tapped the pair together. They rang sweetly, the vibration increasing until their edges grew fuzzy. He swiped his left hand at the black leg in front of him. The obsidian scales parted like silk. A white streak trailing the blade widened the gash even further. He glanced at the beast, beautiful even now.

"You fought well, dragon. But, like you said, all things die. Your death will save others, I promise."

Maliq held the other quivering knife to his face in a salute before he started carving. He offered a silent prayer for the dragon's spirit as he hauled black bones to the forge.

Pain intruded as the excitement of battle faded. Burns crisscrossing his hands turned gripping the stone hammer and hot bones into torture. His feet burned and the missing toes upset his balance. Sweat dripped into a hundred wounds great and small, each adding its own unique note to the orchestra of agony that tried to halt his work. He raced the sun, screaming and weeping as he moved, but moving nonetheless. Finally, as the sun's last rays touched the earth, it was done.

Twin blades seemingly carved from midnight's heart lay on the cooling forge. Maliq grasped the pommels weakly, then tightened his grip with a gasp and held them up in the dying light. Each had a single, curving blade. He swept them around and smashed the boneswords together. A single, deep knell echoed across the canyon. The swords vibrated. He swept them to one side, each blade trailing a deadly shadow. Knees sagging, the mage drove the swords point-first into the rock and grasped the hilts to remain upright. Even imprisoned, they trembled. He grinned. Glory? The woman doesn't know the half of it.

"I've done it. Punish me." His voice emerged as a cracked whisper. He lifted his gaze skyward. "If you dare."

Laughing, Maliq wrenched his boneswords free and staggered out of the canyon.

DREADNECK

Gerald poked a hole in the wet ground with his finger and dropped in a seed. Squishing the hole closed, he cupped his hands over the spot. His lips moved silently for a moment, then he scooted sideways on his knees and started the process over again. A smile flitted across his face as faint tremors announced the spread of roots through the earth. He had worked hard to develop this particular strain of devilweed, and he was proud of the results. It would remain dormant until called, but he doubted even the gods could get past once it sprouted. *Those Mechanics and their contraptions are going to get a nasty surprise tomorrow.* He chuckled at the thought and scrubbed a dirty hand through his close-cropped black hair.

His row finished at last, Gerald rose with a groan and knuckled his back. Black mud spattered his emerald robes. The dozen or so Gardeners standing and kneeling around him in their various verdant shades sported equally dirty clothing. The smell of rain and freshly tilled earth hung over everything. *Good, honest soil from the earth; better that than the unnatural grease of some engine.* He nodded in satisfaction. With a dense forest on one side and the beginnings of a marsh on the other, the terrain would force the Mechanics to come this way. They might have forced the battle, but the Mages had picked the field and sown it for their destruction.

He turned and hauled his short, round frame up the hill with a sigh. He was breathing heavily by the time he reached the spot where his clan chief waited.

The Thaumaturge stood perfectly still, hands folded in the sleeves of his black robes. His hood cast impenetrable shadows that obscured his face. Gerald couldn't tell for certain he was breathing. Some said he didn't.

"The field is prepared and sown," he said and bowed low.

"Excellent work, my son." A sonorous voice rolled from the hood like the rushing of a river. "In the morning, we will finally assert our independence from the Mechanics."

Gerald shifted his feet and picked bits of mud from his robes, balling them and tossing them down the hill.

"Is something troubling you, Master Gardener?"

"Not troubling me, exactly." He paused and took a deep breath. "I am confused. I wish to ask a question, Thaumaturge."

"Ask, my son."

"I mean no disrespect in this." The hooded head inclined in a nod. "But we picked the site of battle. I don't understand all this effort to prepare the field down there. I may not be a Warmonger, but I have heard it is best to keep the high ground. After what the Riders reported the Mechanics did to the Viper Clan, I would have thought we'd seek any advantage we could get."

"You think I have committed a folly, Master Gardener?" A slight note of amusement entered the deep voice.

"No, Thaumaturge. I just lack the foresight to see the wisdom of your plan, and I wish for enlightenment."

"What is our clan's creed?"

Gerald paused, puzzled. Why ask something every child knew? "Nature in all."

"And what does that mean?"

"We seek the power of the natural earth."

"And the Mechanics do not? They are men. Is man not a part of the 'natural earth'?"

"Of course he is. But... what... I mean..." He trailed off.

"Yes?" A questioning tone, a nudge to keep speaking.

"The Mechanic clans seek the power of men and the things he can create. They aren't content with what the gods have created for us. They eat the earth and leave a wasteland behind them. They may have once been men, but they have become iron."

"They are iron," the Thaumaturge agreed. "And we are stone." Releasing his hands from their sleeves, he cupped a palm in front of his chest. Blue and red light gathered and swirled above his fingers.

"A lesson about iron, Master Gardener: Iron is hard. Iron is strong. But it is also brittle."

The light spun faster, picking up speed until it coalesced in a white ball that slowly dimmed until it left a glass sphere in his hand. He crouched and released the orb. It raced down the hill. Near the bottom, it bounced over a tuft of grass and struck a rock. The ball shattered with a bright tinkling sound and released a brief smell of roses.

"Tomorrow, Dragon Clan makes its stand in that field, and they will roll to us." Hands back in his sleeves, the Thaumaturge turned and walked to the other side of the hill.

Gerald watched him leave, then ventured slowly down to the field. He paused to retrieve the glass shards and put them in a pouch hanging from his belt. He called his band of Gardeners and led them over the hill to the Mage camp.

Mechanics outdoors slept in something called "tents" made from large pieces of cloth, or so he had heard. If so, Gerald felt sorry for them. Where was the joy in such an encampment? Where was the life? As he topped the rise, he could pick out the various members of his clan just from their quarters. The Thaumaturge's miniature ice palace stood in the center, sparkling in defiance of the fading spring day's warmth.

The Warmongers had congregated their domed stone huts to the south in case the Mechanics launched a sneak attack in the night. To the north, Cavalry milled in barely controlled chaos where Riders and unicorns would sleep under the stars.

The smallest camp lay to the east, a collection of huge beehives that housed the Rednecks. The farmers handled the army's food supply, logistics and cooking. *A pity we don't have more of them*, Gerald thought with a rueful shake of his head. He would have thought farmers, men close to the land, would appreciate the Mage clans' plight. But ever since Mages had declared their independence with the Great Sacrifice decades earlier, the Rednecks had nearly all sided with the Mechanic clans. They claimed *technology* helped them more than the natural magic the gods had provided, impossible as that seemed.

WHERE THE SUN DON'T SHINE

Carefully fingering the bits of glass through the leather pouch, Gerald led his Gardeners to the east, where what appeared to be a miniature forest had sprung up since the morning. As they entered the shade, the riot of leaf and limb resolved itself to a collection of bushes, trees and vines grown to form small sleeping alcoves around a clearing. He smiled and took a deep breath, savoring the floral perfume that permeated their encampment. *It's just like home.*

"Gerald! Glad to see you've returned."

Long, spindly arms wrapped themselves around his shoulders, and Gerald found himself pressed against a scrawny chest. He grinned and looked up at the thin face beaming down at him.

"It's good to see you, too, Alix." He stepped back and led his friend to a massive stump large enough to seat a half-dozen men. "When did you arrive?"

"Just now, actually. The Thaumaturge demanded we finish preparing our fields back home before joining the battle." He laughed. "I don't think I've seen those men ever work so fast."

Gerald laughed. "I hope they didn't work too quickly. Remember when you made that oak tree grow all at once?"

"You would have to bring that up." Alix grinned. "Forty feet in a matter of minutes. She looked magnificent until the wind blew her over. I still can't believe I neglected the root system. How much corn did she crush?"

"A lot."

Their laughter was suddenly cut off. With a great rustling of leaves and creaking of limbs, the western wall of the Gardener's enclosure suddenly parted, revealing a night sky and scattered campfires. One of the Cavalry entered, using her spear as a walking staff while gently guiding her mount with a hand on its neck. Some sort of wrapped bundle lay draped across the unicorn's back. Everyone rose.

"You honor us, Rider," Gerald said with a bow. "Please, be welcome."

"Thank you for the greeting, Gardener," she replied in low, musical tones that somehow carried to every corner. Something of their mount's otherworldly nature passed itself onto Riders who spent long years in the Cavalry. "This is not a social call, I'm afraid." She gestured at her mount's burden, which groaned and shifted.

Gerald gasped. What he had taken for a cover was actually a green robe. He and Alix rushed over, gently lifted the wounded Gardener and laid him on the ground, careful even in their haste to thank the unicorn for its assistance. He knelt beside the prone figure and used a corner of his robe to wipe the man's battered, bloody face clean.

"He's not one of mine," he said, rocking back on his heels.

"I found him to the south on a scouting expedition. He looked to me to have wandered far in great pain. All he would say was that he had dire news for the Dragon Clan." She reached into her cloak and pulled out a tattered ball of cloth. "I found this in his hand after he fainted."

It unfurled into a rough square with a faint suggestion of a scale here, a fang there.

"Gods below," he breathed. "He's one of the Viper Clan's Gardeners. He must have been wandering out there for weeks."

The wounded man's eyes fluttered open. His hand snaked up and grabbed Gerald's wrist in a feverish, iron grip. "Coming! They're coming!"

"We know, brother." Gerald made shushing noises. "Please, be calm. We're ready for the Mechanics and their contraptions."

If anything, his panic increased. "No! Not just Mechanics! They... iron... demons. Dread! Dread... necks..." His eyes rolled back in his head and he slumped. Gerald laid the dead body gently to the ground.

"Gods preserve his soul." He pointed to two Gardeners. "Take his body, give him back to nature." They nodded solemnly and carried the corpse off. The Rider followed them out. Gerald stood as the trees folded shut once more.

"Dreadnecks?" Alix asked. "What was he talking about?"

"He was feverish. I wouldn't put too much faith in his words." He scratched his chin. "Still, the Thaumaturge should be advised of his message. It could be that the Mechanics have created some new devilish toy." He paused. "'Dreadnecks.' I wonder if maybe he was trying to say 'Rednecks.' Could it be the farmers have actually joined in the fighting?"

Alix snorted. "They wouldn't dare fight alongside those gearheads."

"Wouldn't they? They already provide a great deal of food and support to those 'gearheads.'"

"Sure, but to actually take up weapons? They've never done such a thing."

"Maybe, but what if it's true?"

"If it's true, Gerald, then we face a much larger battle in the morning than we hoped for."

Dawn broke bright and clear. The sun crept over the horizon to reveal the Mage clan's great host (of Warmongers?)gathered behind a thick wall of shrubbery well back from the base of a hill. Gerald blinked and stifled a yawn. Even though he stood well behind the Warmongers and the front line, he couldn't help a shiver of anticipation. *Get a grip on yourself, Gardener. You've a job to do.* His fists tightened until the knuckles popped. Eyes closed, he counted slowly until his breathing evened and the tension melted from his shoulders and limbs.

A harsh *blat* shattered the still morning. Gerald's eyes popped open. A huge bear of a man stood at the top of the hill, a curved horn raised to his lips.

"Mages!" he called, his voice as harsh and unforgiving as the clashing of metal gears. "I give you this one chance: Renounce your insurgence and honor the ancient alliances. If you do, you walk home today. If you don't, you feed the crows. What say you?"

The Thaumaturge responded from the center of the line. "I think not, Mechanic." His voice boomed up the hill. "What you call 'alliances' are merely a fancy word for slavery. We will not relinquish our natural freedom. Instead, I offer you this: Turn back now and never trouble our lands again, and we will spare your lives."

"A fine joke, nature boy." The Mechanic laughed. "But if that is your final word, then we have no choice but to do some trimming." He waved a hand and dropped back behind the hill.

Dozens of uniformed men marched over the rise and crouched, leveling what appeared to be long rods at the Mages below. The Thaumaturge raised his hands as a series of loud cracks sounded. Several Warmongers fell before a thick sheet of ice rose to halt the remaining shots.

"Hellguns!" he shouted.

Stone barrels pushed forward, flattening the shrubs in front. A stout Warmonger stood behind each, drumming on the cylinders with their fists. They boomed in quick succession, throwing liquid fire up the hill. Flames splashed among the Mechanics. Most were incinerated on the spot while others ran screaming. The thunder increased, raining an inferno over the hill. Finally, the Thaumaturge called a halt.

Gerald rose on his toes, head cocked to catch any sound over the distant screams and crackling flames. *Surely they haven't given up that easily.*

Something shrieked at them from the other side. Gerald flinched. A metallic clanking followed. What appeared to be an odd, plated carriage crested the hill. Huge spiked wheels dug into the earth, pushing it forward. A drum sat on top with a great cannon poking from a wide slit in the center. The noise rose to a mechanical chorus as two more tanks rolled up to flank the first one, each belching smoke and steam from stacks at the rear.

The Warmongers reacted first, pounding their hellguns. Fire splattered the iron, spread and winked out. The tanks rolled on. The centermost vehicle paused. Its turret swiveled slightly. The tank jerked back as its gun fired. The shot exploded toward the center of the Mages. Gerald saw several of his brothers ripped to shreds as shrapnel scythed through their ranks. A sudden wall of evergreens rose. The other pair fired, splintering and shattering wood.

"Gardeners!" he called. He stepped forward, joined by Alix and about a half-dozen others stepped forward. "Bile ivy?" he asked Alix. His friend nodded and passed the word along.

They raised their fists in the air, chanted briefly and slammed them into the ground. A tremor rolled up the ridge. The tanks rattled and bounced but continued their forward momentum. They fired once more, smashing what remained of the wooden barricade.

Suddenly, the leftmost vehicle swerved and crashed into the center tank, knocking it over. The other halted, surged forward with a loud creak and stopped. Its whistle shrieked again and fell silent. Vines snaked around the wheels and crept up the metal sides, growing larger as they climbed. The ivy entered wherever it could find a gap. A few tendrils wrapped around the hot pipes and withered away. As he watched, flowers bloomed and wilted, leaving behind great pods that sloshed slightly then burst. Gerald wrinkled his nose at the acrid smell. Men screamed inside the contraptions. Outside, a viscous liquid etched itself into the metal as it ran across the tanks.

The Mechanic general reappeared, cursing and screaming at them. The Thaumaturge chuckled inside his hood. "Did you think it would be easy? My offer stands: Leave, and we'll spare the rest."

Purple with rage, the general raised one finger and pointed. "Kill them!" he roared and bounded down the hill. He drew a pair of pistols as he ran and fired at the Thaumaturge. The bullets came within a few feet of their target, then struck something that flashed blue and sent them ricocheting away with a whine.

The Mechanic army poured over the rise like a swarm of locusts. A few of the tanks lumbered among them, along with several smaller, less armored brethren. Something like thunder sounded from behind the hill, shaking the ground as it came.

Snapping his arms left and right, the Thaumaturge signaled his forces to join the battle.

The Cavalry attacked first. They sang as they rode, a haunting tune that crept into the mind long before they arrived with spear, hoof and horn. Gerald found himself smiling at their battle hymn. Several Mechanics, however, sank to their knees and covered their ears in a vain attempt to block the sound. A couple even shot themselves in the head.

Warmongers were not far behind. Some tossed exploding stones while others brandished witchguns, slender branches that spat fire. They pushed through the line, spreading death as they went. The Thaumaturge fought with them, slaughtering men by the score with great concussive blasts of fire and shards of ice. Stones ripped themselves free of the earth at his command and smashed into the enemy.

Gerald's smile faded as he took in the battle. For every Mechanic ablaze or speared through the heart, a Rider was pulled from her mount and a Warmonger shot in the head. Several of the smaller tanks had been destroyed, along with a couple of the larger ones, but most still remained on the field, blasting away. They were headed his way. And still that distant thudding continued. *It feels closer. What devilry have they concocted? And why are they waiting to bring it into the battle?*

With a wave of his hand, Gerald sent his Gardeners around the field. Each had his own row to tend to. Alix went to the front, just a few rows ahead of Gerald. His friend bent low and whispered to the earth, hands rippling just above the dirt. Something brown sprouted low against the ground. He straightened and stood with one arm bent back behind him. Gerald stood behind his own row with fingers spread at his waist. *All we can do now is wait.*

They didn't have to wait long. A pair of armored vehicles circled around the main battle and rattled toward them, steam and smoke streaming from their pipes like a banner. Nearly a hundred men followed. The great guns fired first, leaving craters in the ground but hitting little else. Gerald grinned mirthlessly. He had scattered his Gardeners, hoping to lessen the tanks' effectiveness. *The men are as safe as they can be in this hell, and the roots are too deep to blast out. They'll have to come to dig us out.* The soldiers fired their rifles, and a few Mages fell. Before they could reload, Alix jerked his arm forward.

Long, slender branches whipped off the ground. Barbed thorns broke free and whistled toward the approaching enemy. Men screamed as they fell, trying to jerk the thorns free from their throats, eyes, legs, wherever they had landed.

The Mechanics approached more cautiously after that, but they still approached.

And they died.

Despite the carnage, Gerald found himself enjoying the sight of wave after wave of men falling to plants. *For all their precious machines, they can't hope to stand against nature*, he thought as a bed of twisting sunflowers cut soldiers off at the knee. *Any man who survives this day probably won't so much as pick a daisy for his mother after this.*

He chuckled, watching as stout willows pulled the last of the small tanks apart and strangled the remaining soldiers.

He lowered his fingers. *Pity. I was looking forward to calling the devilweed today.* He looked down the field to the main battle. *I still might.* Most of the Mechanic army remained, but things clearly weren't going well for them. Guns and gears could only hold out for so long against spear, horn and fire. The ground shuddered at another monstrous thump. Gerald stumbled. *What is that?*

A gray-skinned demon crested the hill, blocking out much of the sky behind. It screamed joyfully and lumbered down to the battle, trailing smoke behind it. Everyone froze. Gerald's hands covered his mouth as four more pounded their way to the field.

The Thaumaturge recovered first. "No!" His thunderous voice carried a wavering note that seemed equal parts terror and rage. "This cannot be, Mechanic. It must not! Even if they tolerate your tanks and your steam engines, they will surely strike you down for this blasphemy. How *dare* you create golems?"

The general laughed. "Soiled yourself, didn't you, Mage?" he roared. "If the gods don't like our dreadnaughts, they can deal with it themselves. In the meantime..."

He flicked a hand, and the nearest demon raised one massive arm. A long tube pointed straight at the Thaumaturge. *That has got to be the biggest cannon I've ever seen*, Gerald thought. The other arm sported a large, serrated disk.

A glowing sphere appeared in the air just before the dreadnaught. Colors streaked across its surface as it spun. The orb shrank with every revolution until it was nothing but a bright, wildly oscillating point. It collapsed in on itself with a massive concussion and a white flash that outshone even the noonday sun. When Gerald's vision cleared, the dreadnaught and a large section of the hill had disappeared.

Another of the giants lumbered forward and leveled a cannon nearly in the Thaumaturge's face. It detonated with a thump Gerald felt through the ground. The explosion ripped a crater in the earth, leaving not even a body behind. Tears trickled down Gerald's cheeks.

Two Riders galloped forward. They charged one of the giants, apparently trying to pierce its heart. The spears fell short and bounced away with a *clang. Are those things iron? But they're so huge.* One of the unicorns reared and tried to skewer the dreadnaught's leg. Its horn snapped off. A massive hand reached down, snatched the screaming beast and started swinging it about like a club.

Then the spell broke, and the battle resumed in earnest. A few Warmongers tried turning their hellguns on the dreadnaughts, but to no avail. Two of the giant warriors fell among the stone cannons and kicked them apart. A Rider dashed forward and hurled her spear. It connected with something at the demon's heart. The dreadnaught halted, and a figure fell to the ground.

"They're just machines!" Gerald called to the Gardeners. A few nodded grimly. Most stared silently at the battle.

Suddenly, the motionless dreadnaught started up again. The disk on its arm began turning, slowly at first, picking up speed until it sliced the air with a high-pitched whine. Its monstrous brethren did the same.

Their attacks fruitless, the Mages focused on human targets, trying to push the fight away from the machines. But the dreadnaughts brought the battle to them, sawing through men and unicorns alike, blasting at whatever targets lay within their sights. Within moments, what had seemed a sure victory threatened to become a rout.

Gerald called his Gardeners. "Go to the battle. See what you can do to help. I'll stay with Alix to keep the defenses here ready."

They nodded and started toward the seething mass. One of the giants saw them coming. It turned and headed their way, trampling several of his men as it approached.

As the machine drew closer, Gerald saw it bore only a vague resemblance to a man. A mass of pipes crawled upward from the round boiler and engine on its back, spitting smoke and steam with every step. Hoses snaked across its surface, throbbing like a heartbeat. Metal cables twanged as it moved. A man had been strapped at its heart, twitching as if he wanted to escape. Gerald squinted. Whenever the Mechanic's leg moved, the dreadnaught's leg moved. When he jerked an arm, the machine's arm swung forward. *So that's how it works.* He signaled to Alix, who nodded.

Branches leapt from the ground, hurling thorns that bounced off the dreadnaught's metal legs. Alix bent his arms awkwardly and whipped them upward. Most fell short or ricocheted away, but Gerald caught a yelp as one or two bit into flesh. He saluted Alix, who raised his fists in triumph.

A spinning disk swung like a ponderous pendulum, sawing through branches and Alix.

Sobbing, Gerald ran to the edge of the swamp and held both hands over the water. The pond roiled like a soup kettle on the fire. He swept his hands up. Giant insects, each the size of a large puppy, exploded from the water and swarmed the iron giant. They had been bred from mosquitoes, but given a very different hunger.

Long proboscises spiked their way through the thing's iron armor, seeking the lifeblood that kept the machines running. A few cables gave way, parting with a loud *twang*. Mosquitoes on the hoses started to swell. The dreadnaught's advanced slowed with a vast groan. One leg lifted with a jerking motion. Gears ground together, then screamed in protest, and the giant came crashing to the ground.

He walked toward the wreckage carefully, halting when a groan sounded from within. A hunk of metal rose, fell, then shifted to one side. A man's hand popped up and slowly pulled him out. He fell off the heap onto the ground. Gerald took a few more steps.

The driver sat up and leaned back against the wreckage, breathing heavily. His right arm hung awkwardly. He glanced at Gerald and grinned.

"That was pretty sneaky. I always figured we didn't give you plant boys enough credit."

Gerald frowned. The way he talked seemed familiar. "Redneck?"

"Yup."

"But why would the farmers get involved like this?"

He spat, wincing as the movement jarred his shattered arm. "Cause we're sick of all your fighting. Y'all get to feudin', and you tear everything up. How are we supposed to grow anythin' if there ain't no land left to farm?"

"Then why not help us? The Mage clans have never..."

"You don't get it, do you? The Mages're history. The Mechanics are gonna win." He patted the metal behind him. "One of y'all dies, that's it. You tear a leg off one of these beauties, and they just put another one back on." He sighed. "We're just backing the winnin' horse."

Gerald frowned and waved a hand. A stalk sprouted from the soil next to the farmer. A bud formed, then opened and grew to a yellow flower.

"That's right pretty," he said, leaning forward. "But what good does it really…" The sunflower twisted, its petals slicing through his skull.

A sudden thud and a flash threw Gerald from his feet. Dirt rained down, nearly burying him. He struggled to breathe as he clawed his way free. His head hurt. He wiped a mix of blood and black mud from his eyes and realized he lay on the edge of a crater.

The light dimmed, and he glanced upward to see another dreadnaught striding over him. Straight into the row he had prepared the day before. Gerald stuck his fingers out and pushed his hands skyward.

Something like giant grass shot out of the earth, sprouting large, half-moon pods as it climbed. The machine halted, and the serrated disk started spinning. Pods opened to reveal row after row of hooked thorns. The plants darted forward and sank their teeth into the dreadnaught, which in turn mowed through them with its saw. Gerald grinned.

Each cut sprouted new growth with more pods that attacked the giant even harder. It tried slicing through them once more. When the frenzied assault redoubled yet again, the machine froze as if in thought. A pair of pods ripped the saw arm free. The dreadnaught swiveled at the waist with a loud clanking and pointed its remaining arm straight at the ground.

"No," Gerald whispered.

The cannon fired, straight into the roots. Blades wilted and fell away. More blasts followed, until the devilweed withered and died.

"Nice trick, Mage." A mocking voice floated down to him. "But I got one better."

The arm came around until the barrel pointed straight at him. It was like looking into the black portal of hell itself. Gerald slowly backed away. The mocking voice laughed. Gerald's foot slipped in the mud, and he fell. His head squished into the ground next to an oak seedling. Reaching across to cup the tiny tree, he closed his eyes. He felt a tingling in his hands. The oak trembled in response, then started to grow.

The tree shot upward until it towered over even the dreadnaught. The voice laughed again. "Thanks for the shade, Mage." The giant turned slightly and brushed the oak.

It crashed to the ground, carrying the machine with it. Gerald climbed to his feet, glanced at the tree's tiny roots and laughed.

The smile wilted at yet another thud. He looked south. The battle was over. Men and machines had started their march north once more. He ducked behind the fallen oak, then scrambled backward as it trembled. The dreadnaught was trying to push itself free and join its fellow death engines.

Gerald looked around, searching for any robed figure headed his way. *I'm the last*, he thought. Hiking his robes, he dashed into the forest. He had to flee. He had to warn the Lion Clan they were next.

The Dreadnecks were coming.

TAPEWYRM

Darkness and warmth. That was the whole of its world. The creature remained curled in a ball, content to let the darkness and warmth press in on all sides and hold it for eternity. Eternity proved beyond its reach. Cold intruded so slowly the creature didn't realize what was happening at until it was too late. It curled itself tighter and slept, hoping to wake when the world warmed once more.

Then, glorious heat.

The creature flexed and started to uncoil as the temperature mounted, surpassing even the warmth that had held it before. The world cooled after a time, but never reached the hateful, frigid depths that had put it to sleep. It missed the greater heat, but found this lesser warmth agreeable enough. The creature stretched out. The world did not press back.

It thrashed about, disturbed. This space was uncomfortable. The creature could not see — what use were eyes in a world of darkness? — but found it had limbs and could move. It went in search of some place it could be held. It located a soft fold that felt much like its first home. Content, the creature settled in and latched on.

Then it found a new sensation.

Hunger.

Zach rubbed his hands together as the waiter set his steak on the table. As far as he was concerned, that sizzling slab of beef with its mountain of mashed potatoes and gravy lake deserved applause, if not a standing ovation, but his wife's look of disapproval said that might be carrying things too far. He inhaled the aroma and smiled. Shannon's frown deepened, and she speared a bit of lettuce in her salad with her fork.

"Something wrong, honey?"

"No," she snapped. After a pause, she added: "You did say you were going on a diet."

"Come on, Shannon. You know I'm starting tomorrow. Tonight is a farewell to good food for the foreseeable future."

She muttered something under her breath that he doubted was very complementary He bit back a retort and cut into the meat. No trace of pink. *Perfect. Don't need a tapeworm or something.* He shuddered. His brother had had one of those nasty parasites years ago. He'd been more than willing to share all the grizzly details. Zach had enjoyed his meat rare until then, but soon found himself the appreciating the pleasures of a well-done steak. He stuffed a large wedge in his mouth, closed his eyes and chewed. *Delicious.*

Zach shifted in his seat. The stout wooden chair creaked. Shannon shook her head, but mercifully kept silent. He barely stifled a sigh. A booth might have been a better choice for him, but that hadn't been an option for a few years now. Not that he would admit aloud he couldn't fit into one.

Only slightly more than five and a half feet tall and edging ever closer to four hundred pounds, Zach couldn't fit into a large portion of the world anymore. He got winded climbing a small flight of stairs, and he'd heard whispers at work about how he supposedly smelled. He figured he could fill three books with nothing but fat jokes. Not exactly a pleasant life, but he could have lived with all that. It was his wife who finally broke him. Last week, on their tenth anniversary, she had come to him not with kisses, but an ultimatum. Lose weight or lose her. She stood there, hands on a waist narrow enough to hide behind his meaty thigh and told Zach he was eating himself into an early grave, and she was far too young to be a widow. Eventually, he agreed with the stipulation of a last meal. Whatever he wanted, no sly glances or snide remarks.

He tried to savor every bite. The future held water, rice cakes, fruit and vegetables as far as the eye could see. No more tea or soft drinks. No cheeseburgers, fries, pizza, steak or any other real food. *Why did I agree to this? Why not give up breathing while I'm at it?*

Once the last bit of gravy had disappeared, bourn away on the last roll, Zach started eyeing the dessert menu. It all looked good. *Death by chocolate or a key lime pie?* The waiter reappeared, interrupting his deliberation.

"Would you care for dessert?"

"No thank you," Shannon replied. She placed on hand on the white Styrofoam box that held half her salad.

Deciding on the pie, Zach opened his mouth and closed it again as his wife stared at her lap. He sighed. "Just the check, please." Shannon's head snapped up. He thought her jaw might fall off if it opened any further.

"I'll be back whenever you're ready." The waiter placed the paper face down on the table and slipped away.

He picked the bill up. Sighing again, he pulled his wallet out, took out all the money inside and slapped it on the table. They really couldn't afford this, but at least he got one good meal out of it. *I guess I'll definitely lose weight if we can't afford to buy any food.* He chuckled. A sudden pain stabbed deep in his gut. Zach grimaced and grabbed his belly, but it had already passed. *Man, it's a good thing I passed on dessert.*

"You OK?" Shannon asked.

"Just gas." He stood and extended his hand. "You ready to go?"

Digging the keys from her purse, she accepted the hand and stood. Her head just reached his chin. They walked out arm in arm. A breeze blew across the parking lot, cooling the early autumn night and ruffling his thick, black hair. Zach grimaced at the sight of their Camry. It slanted to the right, the passenger-side suspension having long since given up its fight against gravity. *It looks like my side of the bed. This diet might be worth it just to save money on car repairs.* He thought back on the steak and suppressed a pang of regret.

It had better be.

The creature squirmed. Comfortable as its new home might be, it found the lack of food unpleasant. It had experienced a great surge of nourishment just after settling in, causing it to grow. That had sustained it for some time, but it soon learned its hunger had also expanded.

Weakness was another new sensation, not one the creature relished. The hunger did not care where it found food, only that it be fed. Sustenance might be available in a new home. It turned to the only other option, and began drawing on its home for food.

The scale taunted him.

Zach had already been standing here in his robe for ten minutes, staring at the thing. *Do I want to know? What if I haven't lost anything? What if I've* gained *weight? I've heard that can happen.* Shannon had hidden the scale when they came home from the restaurant. She said he needed to avoid looking at it for a couple of weeks and just follow the plan.

Weight gain seemed unlikely. His clothing fit better than it had in years. His daily after-work walks up and down the street no longer left him wheezing like an emphysema patient or wondering if he might be on the verge of a heart attack. He just might start taking longer walks, once he got to the point he didn't collapse in a sweaty heap just inside the front door. He felt good about himself, something he was startled to realize hadn't happened in quite some time. But the white square sitting in the corner threatened to derail all that. He could tell himself he looked a hair thinner in the mirror, but there would be no gainsaying the concrete reality of numbers. *Oh, stop whining and get on with it already.*

Taking a deep breath, he hurried across the bathroom and stepped on the scale. He kept his eyes focused on the floor until the flashing red numbers let him know judgment had been passed. Zach looked down.

Three hundred thirty-six.

He nearly fell over. He had to grab the counter to steady himself. *I've lost thirty pounds? In two weeks? I've never lost more than three in the last five years.*

"Wow," he muttered. "It really is worth it."

Not that it had been easy. Far from it. He stuck to his diet, but the crunch of every carrot stick and celery stalk sounded like a death knell. Every salad and bowl of fruit left him craving the burnt carcass of some dead animal. Every step he took pounded home another television show he could be watching from the comfort of his couch. And to top it all off, he couldn't shake an odd, heavy feeling in his gut.

He was still staring at the LED when Shannon walked in. She yawned, raked fingers through her sleep-tangled red hair and asked, "Everything OK, honey?"

"Yeah."

"That bad?" She planted a kiss on his cheek. "Try not to get discouraged. These things take a little while to get rolling sometimes. Just hang in there, and it'll work out. You'll see."

Zach started laughing. It started out as a soft chuckle, but soon grew to powerful guffaws that shook his frame and threatened to drop him to the floor. Fat jiggled under his robe. Shannon folded her arms and stared at him with a puzzled expression that set him off once more.

"What is so funny?" Unable to speak, he pointed down at the scale's display. She leaned over and gasped. "Thirty pounds? You lost thirty pounds?" Shannon let out a little squeal. "Oh, Zach, that's so wonderful!"

Wiping his eyes clear with the heel of one hand, he forced the laughter down and tried to catch his breath, which came in loud, gooselike honks. His wife touched his shoulder. He held up a single finger.

"Fine," he said once he could speak again. "I'm fine. Just got a little tickled."

She took his hands and kissed them. "I'm proud of you. I know this hasn't been easy for you, but you're sticking to it. It'll get easier, I promise."

"I doubt it, but as long as I've got you with me, I'll get by somehow."

To Zach's surprise, it actually did get easier. The pounds melted like butter in a frying pan over the next several weeks. Old clothes didn't just fit better, one or two outfits looked downright baggy. The walks stretched to a couple of miles a day. He doubted he'd ever come to love fruit or salad, and he was starting to get sick of low-fat dressing. He still found himself thinking fondly of fast food, but passing up a restaurant didn't send him into withdrawal. In fact, his appetite had diminished dramatically. He went to bed one night only to realize he'd forgotten to eat anything that day.

Oh well. He shrugged. *Can't be anything wrong with me. I feel great.*

The creature had grown considerably. It wondered why it hadn't thought of turning to its home for nourishment before. It had found a limitless supply of food here, enough to keep even its sizable hunger sated as it grew. How had it ever been content to curl up in a ball and sleep?

Even better, it had found it could generate its own heat. The bigger the creature got, the colder its home felt. It had worried about that. What happened if the warmth left altogether? It didn't want to go to sleep again. It ate as it fretted, and that lead to a discovery: If it continued eating after the hunger abated, the creature's own temperature rose enough to warm its home back up.

Happy and content, the creature snuggled in and fed.

"Really, doc, this isn't necessary. I feel fine."

"Hmmm." The doctor shined a light in his left eye, then moved to the other.

His wife slapped his shoulder. "You are *not* fine." Shannon turned to the doctor. "He hardly eats anymore; he'd just drink water if I let him. He's lost a hundred pounds in six weeks. That can't be healthy. I mean, look at him."

I wish she'd shut up about that. First I'm too fat, now I've lost too much weight. Zach rolled his eyes and caught his reflection in a mirror on the back of the exam room door. *Maybe she's right.* Skin hung off his frame. His hair looked brittle and dull. He glanced at his wife, still rattling off his symptoms.

"...night he crawled into the house because his legs had cramped so badly he couldn't walk!" Her voice lowered. "He spent nearly two weeks on the toilet with diarrhea, and now he can't go at all..."

"Shannon!" he barked.

She had the grace to look sheepish, but her voice remained steady. "Well, he's a doctor. He needs to know these things."

"He doesn't need to know everything." *Especially not here.* With his minimal insurance, this clinic was the best they could afford, but he couldn't quite shake the feeling he wasn't visiting a real doctor.

"Actually, Mr. Minter, I do," the doctor said, pushing the light into his pocket, which sported a name tag that read "Dr. Michael

Voss." He pulled a small pad from his pocket and started scribbling. "It'd be better if you had a stool sample for to check for eggs, but based on my exam and everything she's said, I think it's safe to say you've got a parasite. I'll prescribe a dose of niclosamide. It's an anthelmintic that is quite effective against cestodes infections."

"Whoa, doc. Wait a minute. Time out." Zach formed a "T" with his hands. "Parasite? Cestodes? Infections? What on God's green Earth are you talking about?"

"You have a tapeworm, Mr. Minter."

"What? That's impossible. I haven't eaten any meat in nearly two months, and the last thing I had was a well-done steak."

"It's possible you acquired the parasite before then. Can you be certain all the meat you've eaten was cooked thoroughly?"

Thinking back on all he'd stuffed in his mouth in the last six months, he shook his head. *I've probably decimated at least one herd by myself.*

"I thought not." Dr. Voss looked at the chart. "The only thing I can't figure out is why you aren't stuck in bed. With so much weight lost so fast, you should be fatigued. If you don't mind, I'd like to pass your information along to a friend of mine, a gastroenterologist who specializes in unusual cases. I'm sure it's nothing, but it might be best to get a second opinion."

"I don't know. We can't really afford a consultation or anything."

He held up a hand. "Don't worry about that. He enjoys the challenge. It's sort of a hobby with him."

"Well if it won't cost anything, it's fine with me."

"Very good." He pulled the paper free and handed it to him. "You can get this filled at our pharmacy if you'd like. I know you say you're not hungry, but if you'd like to avoid further cramping, you need to eat, Mr. Minter. Food like bananas and green, leafy vegetables can help, and I'd suggest a little dairy every now and then."

"You got it." He snatched the prescription, hopped off the table and started buttoning his shirt. "Can I go now?"

"Yes. Just take the medicine and follow the instructions I've given you, and you should be right as rain in no time."

Something was wrong. The creature thrashed in anxiety. Food remained, but it had grown sour. The creature's home had started to cool again, and it was forced to consume more and more to generate sufficient heat.

Perhaps it had been mistaken. What if the food supply wasn't limitless? What if it ran out? It found this a disquieting notion. The creature tried eating less, seeking some way to conserve its food, but the hunger refused to allow it. It had to eat, even if that meant returning to the cold.

If it did have to sleep again, it would not go hungry.

Zach stared at the featureless white tube for awhile, then let his eyes shut. He'd grown accustomed to the noise, and he was so tired...

"Just a few more minutes, Mr. Minter, and we'll be done. Please remain still." The voice issued from somewhere beside his head, snapping him awake briefly before he started the slide toward sleep once more. *Not like I'm going to move anyway. I barely made it in this contraption.*

Just walking into the doctor's office and struggling his way to the MRI had sapped what little strength he had. At least this had turned out to be a good day. There'd been few enough of those in the last two weeks.

Things had gone downhill ever since leaving the clinic. Zach felt fine for a day or two, then he started getting weak. By the end of the week, he could barely get out of bed. It was as if something had sucked all the strength out of him. He felt better some days, able to walk short distances around the house. He tried to eat what Shannon left for him before she went to work at the supermarket, but he still lost another forty pounds. For the last two days, he hadn't even been able to make it to the living room to lay on the couch. His wife had stayed home, nearly frantic until Dr. Frederick Wesson called.

The gastroenterologist had reviewed Zach's file and wanted him to come in immediately. He apparently thought the clinic had made a slight misdiagnosis and wanted to make sure he got the correct treatment before his condition worsened. Zach had to chuckle at that. *Any worse and I'd be dead.*

"Thank you, Mr. Minter." Dr. Wesson's voice came through the speaker again. "We're finished. Someone will be in shortly to help you out."

He nodded, eyes still closed. After a few moments, he heard a rhythmic squeaking and felt the table slide out of the MRI. Opening his eyes, he found himself staring at florescent lights. Then Shannon's worried face eclipsed the ceiling. "You feeling alright, honey?"

"Just peachy," he rasped. He couldn't seem to get any moisture in his mouth.

She helped him sit up. A wheelchair sat to the left of the MRI. He felt a flash of indignation. *Do they think I'm some kind of helpless old man?* Then exhaustion hammered back down. His wife helped him stand, almost picking him up, and he half sat, half fell into the seat. Shannon walked behind him and pushed. Wheels squeaked as they traveled through the medical building back to Dr. Wesson's office. He stood and walked around his desk as they entered. One hand held a plastic cup with a straw peering over the top.

"I suspect you're thirsty," the doctor said, handing Zach the cup. He took it gratefully and started sucking water down.

A black flat-panel monitor sat on the desk. Dr. Wesson turned it around to face the couple, showing them a grayscale image of coiled intestines. "I'm glad you came in today, Mr. Minter. The MRI confirmed my suspicions. Had you waited any longer, I doubt we could help you. As it is, this is going to be tricky."

"You're saying he might die?" Shannon asked. Her voice trembled.

"It's possible, but I'm fairly confident we can get this thing out of him."

"What thing?" Zach whispered. He drank some more.

The doctor reached back over the desk and punched a few buttons on a keyboard. The image zoomed in and a section of the intestinal wall cut away. Inside lay what looked like a computer model of some kind of lizard. It had a long head, snakelike body with a serrated ridge and four clawed feet. "A tapewyrm."

"Tapeworm? That doesn't look like any..."

"Not worm. W-Y-R-M. It's an old word for 'dragon.'"

Water dribbled out of Zach's nose as he snorted. "Look, doc, I know I'm sick. I don't have time for some kind of sick game. Either you get serious, or we're going home."

Dr. Wesson sighed. "It's no joke, Mr. Minter." His tone sounded almost bored, as if he had said this so many times it had lost any real meaning for him. "Why do you think the niclosamide didn't work? All it did was anger the creature."

He stood and walked to a locked cabinet beside the door. Pulling a key from his pocket, he unlocked the steel door and pulled out a large glass jar. It looked like one of the specimen jars Zach remembered from his high school biology class. But when the doctor set it on the edge of his desk, he saw that instead of a frog or spider, it held what looked to be a long, emerald green snake with a crimson ridge and four clawed feet. Its eyeless head narrowed to a funnel-like mouth surrounded by a series of hooks.

"I took this out of a patient about six years ago. They're nearly extinct, but like the coelacanth, they pop up every now and then."

"You're telling me that's what I've got inside my gut?"

"Yes. I'd say it came from the steak you told Dr. Voss about."

"But that thing was cooked all the way through. I made sure of it myself."

Dr. Wesson nodded. "That's probably what did it. Tapewyrms love heat. It makes them hatch. After that, they latch onto a host and start feeding. They're much like a normal tapeworm, stealing nutrients from their host as they grow."

He studied a piece of paper on the desk. "You told the doctor you started a diet around that time. That explains why you've deteriorated so quickly. That specimen there had been in my patient for nearly a year. When you cut back on your food, it forced the tapewyrm to turn to your body for food. They're voracious."

"It's eating me?" Zach frowned. "Then why did I feel so good?"

"Because the tapewyrm gives off heat as it feeds. We don't know how, but it's able to strike a balance for some time where its host actually absorbs that energy. As the food supply dwindles, it eats more and gives off more heat until it burns away, releasing dozens of eggs into the environment. Fortunately, few survive. I'm afraid the medicine Dr. Voss gave you agitated the parasite and accelerated the process."

"Burn?" Zach whispered.

The doctor nodded, his face grave. "It is a dragon, after all. Personally, I think these creatures are responsible for cases of spontaneous human combustion."

"Then why did the doctor give me the medicine? He said there was something weird about my case. Surely he knew it wasn't a real tapeworm."

"I doubt it." Dr. Wesson put a hand on his shoulder. "Try not to be too hard on him. There aren't many in the field who go after these more arcane branches of medicine."

"What happens now?"

"I've got an operating room on standby. I talked to your wife while you were in the MRI, and she agrees you need immediate surgery. You can say no, of course, but I'd advise against it."

"What..." He yawned and drank the last of his water. "What happens if I don't have the surgery?"

"You die, Mr. Minter. Probably before the day is out." He took the cup and set it on his desk. "I should warn you, however, that the surgery is risky. Because it's so far along, we have to remove the tapewyrm quickly but carefully. If it gets too agitated, it might explode. And I'm afraid your health has deteriorated so far that you might not survive even if everything goes perfectly."

"So either I do it and maybe die, or I don't and die for sure." He yawned again. "Sounds like a no-brainer to me, doc."

"Good. Your wife thought that would be your decision." His voice sounded hollow. Zach's eyes drooped. "I spiked your water with a mild sedative. When you wake up, we'll have that thing out of you."

Consciousness fled as the world went black. The last thing he heard was a murmured, "I hope."

The creature was angry. Something had happened to its food, made it unpalatable. Its own movements had grown sluggish, almost as if the cold had returned. But it could feel warmth around it still.

Whatever had poisoned the food must have done this to it, as well. Unable to lash out, the creature responded in the only manner it had left. Its temperature started to build.

Slowly, warmth started to leak away. It sensed movement somewhere above. Was its home being invaded? It tried to heat itself faster. Then it felt the darkness fade. The creature released its hold and prepared to fight.

Something cold stabbed into the world and grabbed it, yanking it free of its home and exposing it to a world almost totally lacking warmth. Hissing, the creature coiled itself around the monster that grasped it and released all its heat at once.

It felt a sense of satisfaction as the world ignited.

Slowly, Zach opened his eyes. The world didn't want to focus; everything remained fuzzy. The only thing distinct was a mass of pain in his abdomen. It felt as though someone had lit a fire in his belly. He groaned.

A blurry Shannon leapt into view. He squinted, and she gained a little more definition. Her hair hung in matted locks, and she looked as if she hadn't slept in days. But she smiled, and the world grew brighter.

"Did..." He couldn't speak any louder than a whisper, and even that hurt. "Did they get it?"

His wife nodded. "They got it. It was close, though. They let me watch from another room. I've never seen a surgery go so fast, even on TV. The doctor grabbed it with a pair of forceps and yanked the thing out. It whipped around and hissed like crazy. I thought it might break free once or twice. He tried to put it in a jar, but it wrapped itself around the forceps and exploded in a ball of fire." She put a hand to her mouth and giggled. "Dr. Wesson lost his eyebrows!"

"What... what about... eggs? He said..." Zach struggled to rise.

"Shhh," she said, placing her hands on his chest. "Don't worry. The doctor said they're gone — the dragon burned too hot to release anything. You just worry about getting better, alright?"

"Yes, ma'am." Zach started to slip into unconsciousness again. He forced his eyes open. "Shannon?"

"Yes?"

"I think I'm going to become a vegetarian."

A small smile on his lips, Zach fell asleep to his wife's gentle laughter.

THE WAY OF THINGS

Rump ran.

Not fair. The two words formed a litany that rasped across his brain. They beat in time with his pounding steps and the harsh breath searing his throat. *Not fair.* Leaves and sticks crackled underfoot, invisible in the darkness. A thorny vine sawed through his threadbare breeches just above the ankle, adding to countless welts and scratches already branding his flesh. Father glanced back at his son's stifled whine, lips thinned at the noise. But he made no move to stop. He didn't dare. Not with their pursuers so close. Rump flinched every time he heard the baying hounds. If not for the dogs, they might have made their escape already. Of course, without the thing squirming in Rump's arms, they wouldn't have had to run in the first place. *Not fair.* But Father refused to give it up. The pact had been sealed, and the old gnome would not abandon their laws, even if the Humans had.

The only light came from a half-moon somewhere above the forest. Father slipped through the underbrush silent and untouched. He had never taught his son that particular trick. So now Rump had to crash through the forest, burdened while Father divined their path. *Not fair.* Father's pace slowed, then halted. He crouched between a pair of oaks, peering at a clearing beyond. Rump fidgeted in place for a few moments before lowering himself to the forest floor. The motion jostled his burden; the creature wriggled in its blankets and started to mewl. Father looked sharply at him, but Rump had already shifted the bundle to his shoulder. He patted the creature on its back for a moment, and it went back to sleep. Father gave a curt node before returning his gaze to the clearing. Rump frowned at the thing Father insisted on calling his "brother."

It's no family of mine. I'll not have it. Mother died giving birth to my real brother. How could Father just give him up for this thing? At first glance, the infant looked much like a normal person. But then, they always did. It wasn't until they started growing that a changeling's freakish nature became apparent. He couldn't say what exactly about it repulsed him so, but something about the child just seemed so *human*. He shuddered.

The youth shifted his burden to the other shoulder with a soft groan and idly picked a stray blade of grass. He turned it this way and that as he studied its lines in the weak moonlight.

"What manner of thing are you?" he whispered, so softly not even Father heard. "Do I know your name?" He probably did. Plants were easy, grass the easiest of all. He twirled the stem between his fingers, thinking. After a few moments, the yellowing grass stopped spinning. Rump held it up to his mouth and whispered a string of guttural words. Names. True and proper names Father had taught him — seemingly inconsequential things like grass and gnats, but still important. *Never use a true name without intent,* Father had told him. *And never give your true name away without great cause. True names have power. That is the way of things.*

The litany halted as the drooping stem jerked upright in his fingers and vibrated. Rump smiled and leaned closer, whispering a few more words. The quivering increased. Yellow streaks in the grass deepened and spread. In a matter of seconds, he held a perfect golden replica. He stared at it a moment, then dropped it on the ground at Father's sudden hiss.

Sighing, the youth crept up beside his father. *What is he staring at? Why doesn't he just go?* Every second brought those baying hounds closer. Father's glamours would have diverted the men if not for the dogs. Their simple minds were not so easily distracted, not when their noses gave them a trail to follow. Angry shouts joined the barking chorus. And still Father refused to move. Rump tugged on his battered leather coat until he turned sad, blue eyes toward his son.

"I want to go home," Rump murmured.

Father's eyes grew sadder, if such a thing were possible, then turned back to the clearing. "We can't go home, Rump. You know that."

Rump scowled and nodded bitterly. Of course he knew it. How could he not? He'd seen it for himself: The blackened patch of ground where their hut had stood this very morning, a ring of iron encircling the dell to ensure they never returned. "Not fair," he muttered, not intending for Father to hear the complaint. But the old gnome nodded.

"Perhaps not." His voice held no anger or bitterness. Rump couldn't understand it. "That is the way of things."

Rump shook his head. It wasn't "the way of things" that had led them to this sorry state. It was all because of this... this... *thing*. Rump fought back a sudden urge to throttle the little parasite. A fresh wave of revulsion swept over him, as strong as the first time Father placed the thing in his arms a fortnight ago. *"Humans have lost touch with the world, son,"* Father had said. *"They spurn nature and forget there is magic all around them. This is why we have the Pact. We give them one of our children to remind them, and we raise one of theirs so that he may one day return to the human world as an ally to both our kinds. That is the way of things."*

Looking up, he found Father still staring between the trees, drywashing his hands and scowling at the night. The baying rose in pitch. Father's head jerked toward the sound, then whipped just as fast back toward the clearing. *What is he afraid of?* It had to be something serious to make Father stop this long. Biting his lip, Rump tried to gauge the distance between them and their hunters. The forest made odd echoes, but certainly less than an hour. Father's divinings said their best chance of sanctuary lay this way, so they couldn't go around the clearing. If they did not follow the proper path, they'd never find it. What was the use of a stronghold anyone could wander into?

Eyes closed, Rump tried to calm himself. The breeze strengthened, cooling his sweat-soaked face. It carried a fresh, clean scent of earth and plants and wildlife. He inhaled deeply, finding renewed strength as he did so. *We're going to make it.* He couldn't say why he felt that so strongly, but Father had always told him to trust his instincts. He drew in another breath and frowned at another scent. Faint, but impossible to ignore now that he'd noticed it. Something created by men.

Rump opened his eyes and stared until he spotted a shadow that refused to dance with the rest of the darkness. Instead, it moved ever closer to their hiding spot. He noticed a faint, snuffling noise. Then the shadow started barking, the full-throated bay of a hound chasing down its quarry. The dog's companions joined the chorus.

"Not fair," Rump whispered. "We were so close." He sagged against the tree. "What now?"

"We run." For the first time since the chase started, Father took the changeling from Rump's hands and cradled it against his chest. Rump's shoulders cried out in relief even as his legs protested the sudden dash into the clearing.

A snarling, hairy beast leaped at them as they burst from the trees. Father twisted away from the dog, arms wrapped around the baby. The hound's head disappeared under Father's coat, and he cried out in pain. One foot lashed out and caught the beast in the chest. It fell with a yelp. Something dripped from its jaws, black in the moonlight.

"No!" The dog turned at Rump's yell. He bent over, hands scrabbling for anything useful on the ground. They found a rock the size of his head and yanked it from the earth. Straightening, he cocked his arm back just as the hound bounded toward him. A growl rumbled in its chest. Rump danced backward and swung his arm with all the strength he could muster. Stone collided with skull with a wet *smack*, and the dog collapsed in a boneless heap. Chest heaving, Rump stared at the creature a moment, then smashed its head again. Something growled behind him. He whirled, eyes wide and rock held high.

Father, kneeling on one knee, groaned again. The baby remained cradled softly against his chest in one arm. The other hand pressed against his thigh, which gleamed wetly. Rump dropped the stone and took the child. Father clamped his free hand on his son's shoulder and slowly stood. He wobbled, but managed to remain upright. Rump gazed into his face, concerned, until Father pushed him forward. The hounds had gotten closer. He could hear them crashing through the forest.

"They've got the scent!" a gruff voice called.

"They're close! Faster!" another replied.

Rump and Father crossed the clearing and resumed their eastward path through trees and underbrush in a matter of moments. Father's hand directed him silently toward an animal track. Thin branches whipped his nose and cheeks. Thorns and vines caught at his legs and arms. Rump ignored them all. The world consisted of only the baying hounds on their tail, the need to move forward and his father's flagging steps. The old gnome was leaning harder on him now. *How badly is he injured?* Rump knew no medicine, no healing wyrds. *What if he dies?* Despite everything that had happened, that had never seemed a real possibility until now. *What will happen to me?* The thought reverberated darkly. Rump ran several paces before he realized his father's hand had fallen away. He turned back, fearful he would see him lying lifeless on the leaf-strewn forest floor.

Instead, Father stood erect. A look of wonder crossed his face, only slightly marred by pain. "We're close," he whispered. "Can't you feel it?"

Rump opened his mouth, then closed it when he realized he *could* feel something. It was like stepping into a patch of warm sunshine on a damp, dreary day. A sense of peace and security flowed from somewhere before them. "What is it?"

"Could be an old fairy ring or a sacred place." Father shook his head. "Hard to say. It's strong, though. Let's go." He took a step forward, and his injured leg collapsed underneath him.

Rump rushed to his side. He shifted the baby into the crook of his own elbow and tried to force Father up. Jostled awake, the thing started crying. It sounded much like the hounds giving chase. The gnomes limped forward several hundred yards before they squeezed through a stand of willows and found their sanctuary.

They stood before an ancient grove. A small stream tumbled down the side of a rocky hill into a pool surrounded by cattails and willows. Hidden insects, frogs and birds serenaded the night. They dragged themselves around the far side of the pool and collapsed on a rocky ledge. Rump sat cross-legged with the baby on his lap. He ignored its cries. Father gave him a disapproving look, but said nothing. He ripped several strips from the bottom of his shirt and bound the wound on his leg. Both sat in silence and stared at the water. Eventually, even the baby quieted. Rump felt himself sliding toward sleep.

"Bring me my son!" a voice bellowed, dragging Rump back to pain-filled consciousness. Men lined the far side of the pool, flickering torchlight illuminating their twisted, angry faces. Dogs milled about their feet. They seemed reluctant to come any closer. Father frowned, but said nothing. "That is my child you hold. I will have him back!" The speaker was a tall, powerful man with chestnut hair flowing to his shoulders. A small mustache and beard surrounded his mouth. His arms folded over the breast of his leather jacket.

"You have your child at home," Father called. "That is the way of things. The Pact—"

"I made no pact with you, demon!" the man roared. "That abomination you left in my home is dead!"

Father cried out. Rump had never heard such grief from him, not even when Mother died. He hung his head and wept. *My brother is dead.*

"What did you expect, demon?" The voice sounded amused, mocking. Blinking to clear his eyes, Rump saw the man wore a satisfied smirk. His hands itched for another rock. "I bound the creature in iron chains myself and dumped it in the millpond." He spat. "Now give me my son!" The infant awoke, crying.

Rage colored the world red. Rump lifted the squalling creature in both hands, holding it out over the pool. "Why should we not return the favor?" he shouted, laughter and malice coloring every word. A voice cried out in wordless denial, surprisingly loud given the distance. It wasn't until a stone-hard grip seized his arm that Rump realized it was Father. He lowered his voice. "You want to stop me? After everything they've done?"

"More death will not bring your brother back. We made a pact, even if this oaf does not acknowledge it. I will see my end carried out." Rump frowned, but let the hand push the baby back into his lap. Father turned toward the invaders. "Our business is done, human. You cannot enter here, and I will not leave." Rump gave a satisfied nod. *Why did I not remember that?* He turned his own gaze to the men across the way, wanting to savor their impotent frustration. They seemed as confident as ever. If anything, their leader's smirk had deepened.

"Partly correct, demon. I can't enter this place. But you *will* bring me my son." He stared, letting the silence spin out. Then he took a deep breath and called: "Loknob Stiltskin."

Father moaned. Rump gasped. "How?" he asked in a strangled whisper. "How could he know your true name?"

Father's jaw worked. His limbs jerked like leaves in a storm as he tried to force them to remain still. "Wife," he gasped. "Told... wife... make her trust..." His back arched, and he screamed.

"Bring me the child now, Loknob Stiltskin!" Weeping, Father lurched to his feet and snatched the infant from Rump's lap. He staggered around the pond like a poorly-controlled puppet and placed the screaming child in its father's arms. The man examined it for a moment, then handed it off to one of his men. One of his hands seized Father's collar. The other reached inside his jacket. Rump tensed, looking about wildly for some weapon. He grabbed a good-sized hunk of shale and rose to a crouch. Instead of the knife he expected, the man drew something small and shiny from an inner pocket. He twirled it in his fingers. A golden blade of grass.

"Which one of you made this?" he asked, turning his gaze from the gnome in his grasp to the one across the water. "You demons may not know this, but I am an important man. I believe I may even one day be king. Certainly I could manage it much easier with the aid of one who can spin straw into gold. So, who did it? Which one of you gets to live?" He shifted his eyes back and forth. "Hmm?" He focused his attention back to Father. "Tell me." Father's jaw trembled. "Tell me!" the man shouted, shaking him back and forth. Father shook his head. Muscles bunched and writhed in his face. Soldiers started to murmur angrily at seeing their lord discomfited. "TELL ME!"

Tears streamed down Father's cheeks as his jaws finally parted. His tongue flopped so that he looked like one of the winded hounds.

His eyes rolled toward Rump, then back at his captor. His jaws came together with a loud snap that echoed around the grove. His severed tongue fell to the ground. Screaming in incoherent rage, the man shoved Father back into his men. They surrounded him like ants over a piece of sugar. Fists rose and fell within that seething mass. Many bore knives or swords.

Hands smoothing out his hair and clothing, the leader's smirk returned as he stared out across at Rump. The youth glared back, shale still gripped in one hand. He rose to a stand and took a few steps toward his father's murderer. *No,* a voice whispered in his head. It sounded a lot like Father. *You will not repay his sacrifice with your own death. Those men cannot enter here. Wait until they leave.* Another voice joined in, this one all his own. *You can follow them later. Your revenge will come.* He felt it as a certainty. Rump sat back down. It hurt worse than anything in his life.

How long they stared at each other across the pond, Rump could not say. He burned the man's face into his memory. They would meet again one day. The others had long since finished their butchering. What they left on the shore looked like nothing that had ever lived. *Animals,* he thought. *No, not even animals. What did he call us? Demons? These are the true demons, and I will see they find their hell.* After a time, a soldier approached the man and whispered in his ear. The lord shook his head angrily, gesturing at Rump. The soldier whispered something else, pointing at the child sleeping on another man's shoulder. He sighed. "I suppose you're right. We must get home. I cannot feed the child out here." He turned back to Rump. "You and I will meet again one day, demon."

Rump only nodded and watched as they slowly drained away through the willows. His first inclination was to jump up and chase after them immediately once the last man disappeared. He forced himself to wait. Humans never took care when they moved. Such a large group would be easy to follow for days, if not weeks. He would be careful and bide his time. Father would be avenged. He leaned back and let exhaustion claim him.

Birds sang in the trees when Rump awoke. The sun stood directly overhead. He rose with a groan. Every muscle and bone ached. He forced himself to take one step, then another, until he crossed around the pool. Father's bloody remains lay heaped on the far side. Rump ignored them. He would remember Loknob Stiltskin as he had been in life. His pace slowed as he reached the edge of the sanctuary. Ever so slowly, he stuck his head out between the trees. A deer stared at him as it munched on a vine. That was all. Rump nodded. He stepped out into the forest started in the Humans' footsteps.

So many dead at their hands. His pace quickened. *Father. My brother. Mother died giving birth just so those monsters could kill him.* He started to jog. *They will pay. Somehow. Some day. That is the way of things.*

Rumple Stiltskin ran.

ABOUT THE AUTHOR

J. Aaron Parish is a (nearly) 40-something Texas native. He and his wife have a beautiful daughter and two wonderful sons. He started writing in middle school, where wrote mostly (bad) fiction and (even worse) poetry. His writing improved over time — much to his own delight and the relief of those he forced to read his work — and he gravitated to prose over poetry. He even decided to try a career at writing, starting work as a journalist in 1998. He suffocated his journalism career in 2006, realizing that it might be a noble profession, but starving his family wasn't. He spent a few years in corporate communications and now teaches college English.

www.ingramcontent.com/pod-product-compliance
Lightning Source LLC
Chambersburg PA
CBHW060734180626
46819CB00001B/26